ARBORIA PARK

ARBORIA PARK

PARK

A NOVEL

KATE TYLER WALL

SHE WRITES PRESS

Published 2017
Printed in the United States of America
Print ISBN: 978-1-63152-167-6
E-ISBN: 978-1-63152-168-3
Library of Congress Control Number: 2016955159

For information, address:
She Writes Press
1563 Solano Ave #546
Berkeley, CA 94707

Cover design © Julie Metz, Ltd./metzdesign.com
Interior design by Tabitha Lahr

She Writes Press is a division of SparkPoint Studio, LLC.

"FUCKMYLIFE666"
Written by Laura Jane Grace
Copyright © 2014 Total Treble Music (BMI) administered by Songs In The House Of Hassle (BMI).
Reprinted with permission.

"Open Letter to a Landlord"
Words and Music by Vernon Reid and Tracie Morris
Copyright © 1988 Songs Music Publishing, LLC o/b/o Dare To Dream Music. Administered by Songs Of SMP and Tracie Morris Publishing Designee. All Rights Reserved. Used by Permission. Reprinted by Permission of Hal Leonard Corporation.

For my late father, Eugene Tyler: I'm writing for the two of us.

And Long Live the Queen, the late June Hollins: I'm dancing for the two of us.

"All things made to be destroyed, all moments meant to pass."

—Against Me!

"This is my neighborhood, this is where I come from."

—Living Colour

1—STACY, 1960

....

The moment I learned about the power of place and the world beyond home, I was crouching on the cement curb in front of our house on Arbor Circle. My older brother Matt and his friend Bobby and I were playing a favorite game—Diamonds in the Dirt—which consisted of sifting around in the gritty, sandy residue on the edge of the street looking for tiny bits of broken glass. It drove our mother nuts. I'd brought my favorite "diamond" to my first kindergarten show-and-tell just a couple of weeks before, and when Mom found out, we'd been told our pastime was unacceptable.

Matt had found a loophole, however. Instead of broken glass ("It's a miracle you kids haven't bled to death!" was Mom's objection), we were finding pebbles and throwing them down a small round opening in the manhole cover near the foot of our driveway. I wasn't allowed in the street (part of the reason the gutter games held such fascination), so I was scrounging rocks for the boys to drop. They were trying to hear a "splash," believing that a river of raw sewage coursed under our feet.

We heard a car engine rounding the Circle, and the boys jumped out of the way. Normally Circle kids played in the street with a freedom envied by our neighbors on Elm, a main thoroughfare. Hardly anyone drove on our street except our parents and the garbage truck. And nobody ever drove very fast. Yet this car (a black Volkswagen Beetle) whooshed by so quickly the boys barely got out of the road in time. Its windows were open to the warm September afternoon, and the radio was playing Bobby Rydell's "Wild One." It left a cloud of exhaust in our faces—and yet it all seemed to happen in slow motion. I remember the face of the boy driving: his sunglasses, his grin. I remember, too, how the girl in the passenger seat was sort of shrieking, trying to pull a silk scarf over her sprayed-up blond hair.

The car's brakes squealed as it rounded the corner to Elm, blowing past the stop sign. I was too stunned even to punch Matt in the arm the way we always did when we saw a "punch buggy."

"Matthew John and Anastasia Louise, get out of that street!" our mother yelled from the front porch. She was always hovering, always on patrol to catch us up to no good. "Either come inside or go in the backyard *right now*. You're lucky those racers didn't run you over."

"Can I go to Bobby's?" Matt asked, deftly deflecting her tirade.

"Be back for dinner and *stay out of the street*," Mom replied before going back in the house.

The boys headed around the Circle. Not ready to go inside, I went to the backyard swing set, my favorite place to ponder things.

Our house was on the exterior side of the Circle, the address with the second-most cachet in our subdivision, Arboria Park. Even at age five I was aware of this because of its importance to my mother. The front of the house overlooked the few homes on the Circle, as well as Elm. In the back, meanwhile, parts of three streets were visible, with long rows of nearly identical ranches marching up the block. Despite the development's name, there weren't many mature trees, so nothing broke up the monotony. "Like army barracks," my dad said, winking at us one evening as we sat outside on the back stoop.

"What's army barracks?" Matt asked, but before Dad could answer Mom yelled out the window, "Tom! Don't tell them things like that!"

She was always spying on everybody, even Dad.

I did my own spying on the houses, too, though—seeing who was doing what. My world had only recently expanded from our yard, after all. I now rode the school bus to kindergarten every morning and back home at noon. Before that my paths had been predictable and well-trodden. I went to the Arbor Shopping Center with Mom to buy groceries at A&P, or rode in the back of the station wagon to church on Sundays. Sometimes we visited relatives out of town or went to the beach or for a "Sunday drive" out to Amish country to look at horses and cows. But that was it. At five, I was just beginning to see beyond these rows of houses.

I settled on the swing and pumped my legs lazily, thinking about what I'd just witnessed. Somehow, seeing that car speeding around the Circle felt just like riding the bus for the first time, or going to the state fair with the Franchesinis from down the block. It was a glimpse of a world beyond my limits and even my imagination. Nobody—not Dad, not Mr. Franchesini, and not Mr. Brooks—ever drove a car that fast. And now there were "racers" on our street. Were they like the racecars Dad and my brothers watched on TV sometimes? The VW bug didn't look like those, and on TV there were no girls riding shotgun. And another thought: If the VW had been racing, where were the other cars it was racing against?

Just the day before, Mom had been out front talking to Mrs. Brooks from next door. I stood nearby, hoping to get Mom's attention, because I could hear the bell of the "Popsicle man" in the distance. As I strained my ears to determine if the Popsicle truck was heading up Elm toward us or away toward Mimosa, I heard Mrs. Brooks say something about "those racers." That got my attention.

"Every weekend," she said, drawing on her cigarette. "At the shopping center. Around the parking lot, and some of them take off down Beech to get to Cobbs Road. It's disgraceful."

"They'll kill themselves or someone else," Mom agreed. She could bring death or dismemberment into any conversation. "Someone should do something about it."

"They're setting a terrible example for the teenagers. Danny asked me yesterday if he could race when he gets his license. You bet I gave him the devil!"

I must have made a noise, because Mom finally noticed me. "Stacy, please go inside. Mrs. Brooks and I are talking. Go on." She gently pushed me away.

So now I'd actually seen one of *those racers*. I wondered if they won prizes, or if it was like my older sister Mary Catherine's favorite movie, *Rebel Without a Cause*. I was too young to see it, but she'd described it in endless detail in our room after we'd gone to bed.

Mary was nine years older than me, and in her freshman year of high school. A teenager. Teenagers had it all. They bought 45 records and went to dances and to the Soda Spot up on the Avenue, like in an Archie comic book. The girls, like Edna Sparks and Cindy Vanderwende who walked around our neighborhood tossing their ponytails and leaning on cars to talk to boys, got to wear lipstick and penny loafers, too. Being a teenager seemed like the coolest thing in the world, even better than being a grownup and having your own house and dishes to play with. Mom and her friends never seemed to enjoy that as much as I thought they should, but teenagers always looked like they were having fun. And Mary was on the cusp of it all. She could go to the Soda Spot with her girlfriends until somebody's dad picked them up, and to the movies on weekend nights. And I knew how much she was looking forward to the fall dance at school.

I worked a little harder now, trying to gain altitude, enjoying the sound of the air rushing past me as I picked up speed.

Mary had given me her pencil case after the zipper broke and she got a new one. It had a cartoonish picture on it of a girl with a blond ponytail lying on her stomach, her feet crossed behind her head, writing in a notebook and talking on the telephone at the same time. *That* was what I wanted my life to be like.

Yet these racers weren't teens, according to Mrs. Brooks—and yet they weren't grownups, either, at least not the kind I knew. So there must be a different kind.

Either way, one puzzle piece had fallen into place that afternoon: a connection between Arboria Park and *real life*. And I found that exciting. It meant that not everybody in these houses was the same.

I looked out at our neighbors' houses as I swung higher and higher. Until now, I had assumed that the people I didn't know in the houses around ours were just like the ones I did know. Lots of families like us, many of them Catholic. Fathers who worked at the Air Force base or the Fine Foods plant. Moms like mine, who gossiped over fences and yelled at kids. But now I wasn't so sure. There could be *racers*, or who knows what else, in some of these houses.

I heard Dad's car drive up and the door slam. Through the open kitchen window, his voice mingled with Mom's, accompanied by the clattering of pots and pans. I heard "gutter again" and "talk to them." Then the back door opened, and Dad sat down on the stoop, holding a can of Budweiser.

I ran over and threw myself into him. He hugged me close and said, "Hey, sweetheart. How was school?"

Dad was slender and had a sandy crew cut. He worked at the phone company and usually wore a short-sleeved dress shirt and a tie, and his shirt pocket always contained a pencil and a folding ruler and sometimes bits of wire. Today he had on his company jacket, with his name on the pocket.

I nuzzled up against him. He always smelled of tobacco smoke and aftershave, which I found comforting. "It's not school, it's kindergarten," I said. "We made paintings, but I forgot mine."

"You can bring it home tomorrow." He examined the small garden patch next to the cement steps. "Last of the tomatoes here. Fall's a-coming, even if it doesn't feel like it yet."

The front door slammed so loud it made the back one rattle.

"Tommy! Wash your hands and go find your brother and sister," Mom called out. "We're eating in fifteen minutes."

"They're coming," Tommy hollered back. He was eleven and could roam the entire neighborhood as much as he wanted. Matt was eight and could cross the street. Suddenly I was aware of everybody else's freedom and my lack of it.

The door opened again and I heard my sister's voice. "Mom! Linda Jean just got one of those sweaters from Sears, a red one, and she says they're on sale . . ."

"Set the table, Mary Catherine. We'll see when you get your allowance this weekend."

There were more sounds of plates and silverware and Tommy talking about a football game and Matt coming in and being told to wash his hands. My dad sipped his beer and leaned over to pick a tomato.

"Daddy, are the *racers* going to be on our street now?"

My dad knew everything. He'd be able to explain it all.

"Tom!" Mom yelled out the window. "You're supposed to tell her and Matthew to stay out of the street."

Dad looked up at the window and then back down at me and smiled. "Stay out of the street, sweetheart. There are a lot of new people in this neighborhood who don't know how to behave. Stay in the yard, where it's safe."

"Okay," I agreed, because he said so, but I was waiting impatiently for the day I didn't have to be safe. The day I could cross the street and walk down Elm, even go all the way to the shopping center to watch people race cars if I wanted. It seemed so far away. And until that afternoon, it had never seemed so important.

2—1963

By the time I was eight, my wanderlust was growing in tandem with my knowledge of local geography. I had a bicycle to ride around the neighborhood, and after a few attempts to limit me to the Circle and one block of Elm my parents gave up and expanded my territory. Being the youngest had some perks. The others had been allowed to wander around and nobody had died (not even Matt, the family "daredevil"), so I got the benefit of the doubt. Still, I was limited to our side of Elm, the west side. No farther than Mimosa going south, and *never* busy Cobbs Road to the north.

There were ways around all this, of course. After all, why was Oak any more dangerous than Elm? How was one end of Mimosa different than the other? I made occasional forays around to find out. And once I became friends with Julie Gardner, my parents had to bend the rules a little more.

Julie lived on Elm between Mimosa and Birch. My parents liked her and her parents, and our mothers quickly tired of shuttling us back and forth, so we got permission to walk or ride *straight* to each other's houses, no meandering. And of course Julie's parents had their own rules for where she could go at her end of the neighborhood, so I got to see a fair swath of the development regularly.

My parents had moved to Arboria Park when Mom was expecting Matt. Before that they lived in a little rental house out in the country—because of a "housing shortage" after the war, Dad told us. I couldn't really understand that, since some of the soldiers got killed during the war; there should have been more houses, not less. But anyway, Arboria Park got built in 1951, and like a lot of other people, my parents jumped at the chance to get a brand-new house.

The Park was in an "unincorporated" area outside of town, with Cobbs Road as the dividing line. Cobbs Road started (or ended, depending on how you looked at it) at "the Avenue," which went north straight through town and south into the Arbor Shopping Center, which fronted on the dual highway. Most of the houses in Arboria Park were like ours: three-bedroom, boxy ranches. Details, like the size and shape of the windows, differed from street to street. Some houses (like ours) had porches; some had carports instead. Some had basements, some didn't.

Julie's house was like ours, except backwards. (You walked to the left to go to the bedrooms in her house, and in ours you walked to the right.) She had one brother and her own room to play in.

One fall Saturday, Julie and I were jumping rope on Donna Santorelli's driveway—she lived on Birch—when her brother, Joey, and his friend Kenny rode up to the house on their bikes. Joey was in sixth grade, like Matt.

"We drank all the Kool-Aid already," Donna taunted him. "Ha-ha."

"Shut up," he said.

It sounded just like our house.

The boys parked their bikes and headed for the backyard. Donna followed, obviously intent on annoying Joey some more. Julie and I trailed her.

"We're going to the creek," Joey announced. "You're not sup-posed to go."

"But I *want* to," Donna whined.

Joey shrugged. "Suit yourself."

We followed him through the yard, which wasn't fenced, into another one on Willow. Willow started and ended on Birch, sort of a flattened half circle. Everybody called it the Crescent. The houses there were three-bedroom "split levels," with dens. The ones on the south side backed up against some trees and a small creek.

Mom sometimes wished aloud that we lived in the Cres-cent. I could see why it would be nice (you could go upstairs to bed, like people on TV). Mom was friends with a lady who lived there, Mrs. Newsome. Mom would say, "She has a *beau-ti-ful home*," lingering on each syllable. She talked like that about some of her friends who lived in town, too. As we crossed the street, I glanced down at Mrs. Newsome's. I hoped she wouldn't look out her window, recognize me, and call Mom.

The boys went through someone's backyard and down to the edge of the creek. It wasn't very deep. They crossed over it on some rocks.

"Stay over there," Joey called to Donna. "We're going in the woods near Old Lady Ramsey's farm."

The trees on the other side of the creek weren't that thick. You could sort of see into a field. But to the right, they began to form a thicker grove. We watched the boys disappear into those trees.

"I want to see what's there." Julie stepped over on one of the rocks, then hopped to another one. "It's easy. See?"

Donna and I followed. I missed one of the rocks and stepped in the water. It was cold. Donna fell and got her butt wet.

We could hear the boys up ahead. There was no real trail, but kids had made a rough path. The leaves were just turning colors, and the woods had an earthy scent.

"I heard people come down here to kiss," Julie said.

"Who wants to kiss a boy anyway?" Donna said, making a face.

I knew I didn't.

We caught up to the boys, who had rolled up their jeans and were splashing around, daring each other to stay in the cold water. Julie and Donna threw rocks in the water and pestered the boys some more, but I was intent on seeing where the creek went.

"Hey, shrimp, better not go down there," Kenny yelled to me as I walked away. "That's some serious woods."

The girls had my back. They scampered after me, and Donna told the boys, "We're *exploring*."

"Go ahead, get lost," Joey said. "Don't come crying to me."

With that challenge, we forged ahead. After a while, the path petered out, and we were facing away from the creek. All I could see were trees, and we couldn't hear the boys.

"We're not *lost*," Donna said. "We just go back the way we came."

So we turned around, but soon I had the feeling we weren't where we were supposed to be. Shouldn't we be back down near the creek again? We weren't.

"Over here." Julie had gone up ahead. "Here's the path. See?"

It did seem to be a path—but it wasn't the same one. We seemed to be heading even further away from the creek.

Eventually, we stepped out of the woods into a field. Seeing the house on the far side of the field, Donna gasped. "That's Old Lady Ramsey's. If we go past her house where those trees are, there's the creek. But we have to be careful, 'cause Old Lady Ramsey's a *witch*."

"There's no such thing," Julie scoffed.

We dashed across the field to get to the trees along the creek. But I had to stop and look at the house as we went by. It needed paint, and two back porch rails were broken.

The door opened, and a woman came out. She didn't look like a witch.

"You kids get out of here, or I'll call the police and have you hauled away," she shouted at us, shaking her fist.

Maybe not a witch, but she clearly meant business; she grabbed a shovel propped next to the door and waved it at us.

We ran straight into the shallow creek and splashed across; there were no rocks. Sneakers squishing, we raced back to Birch Street.

"We saw the witch!" Donna danced around. "And she didn't get us!"

Joey and Kenny weren't back yet.

"Maybe she got *them*," Donna said, worried.

"They went the other way." I pointed the opposite direction.

"She could fly on her broom and get them," Donna said.

"She didn't have a broom," Julie said. "Just a shovel. You can't ride a shovel."

"Says you." Donna ran into her house and slammed the door. Julie and I rolled our eyes at each other and headed back to her house.

Julie's mom was in a tizzy. "*Where* have you been? Stacy, you were supposed to be home twenty minutes ago, and your mother has been calling. Mrs. Santorelli thought you-all had come back here. You know better than to wander off like that." She looked down at our soggy Keds. "You were in the creek, weren't you? You know you're not supposed to be down there." She went to the phone. "Stacy, I'm calling your mother to tell her I'm driving you home."

I knew I'd be lucky if I was ever allowed off the Circle again. Still, it would make a fine story to tell Matt later.

••••••••••••••••••••••••

Dad took me out on the back stoop and gave me the what-for when I got home. I was grounded, and Matt wasn't even impressed when I told him. He said he and Tommy had been in the woods before and they'd never seen any old lady, witch or not.

My wings clipped, I sulked around for the rest of the week. Julie was being punished too, so we only saw each other on the bus and at school.

The following Saturday, I sat glumly on the porch step. Mary and Tommy were at the high school football game. Matt had gone off somewhere, no doubt doing something far worse than what I'd done. Mom was out shopping, and Dad was working in the backyard. I wasn't hanging around him because I knew he was still mad at me.

Dad came around the side of the house and put his rake in the shed at the top of the driveway. "I'm finished now. What are you doing for the rest of the day, sweetheart?"

"NOTHING." I stared out at the street. "I can't go anywhere, and Julie can't come here."

"Well, let's do something together, then," Dad said. "Want to ride to the hardware store?"

I shrugged. At least it was away from the house, but it sure wasn't interesting.

"I have a better idea." Dad sat down on the step next to me. "How about you wait here while I clean up, and then we'll take a walk."

I was puzzled. "Where?"

"Here, in the neighborhood. I know you want to explore, so let's do that." He got up and opened the front door. "Let me wash my hands, and we'll go."

I felt a prickle of anticipation. The only times we went for a walk were at a state park or over at the lake, maybe to gather autumn leaves to press or look at the ducks or something. Once Matt snuck home a dead fish he found washed up at the lake.

Dad came out of the house and locked the door. "Where to?"

"*Everywhere.* Every street."

Dad laughed. "That may be too tall an order, but let's see where we end up."

We walked up Elm, past some four-bedroom, L-shaped

ranches clustered on the north end of the street. The families in these houses tended to have six or seven kids; the Vanderwendes had twelve. That seemed like a lot even for a four-bedroom house, but Stevie Vanderwende, who was in my class at school, said some of his brothers lived in the basement, and anyway they were so spread out that somebody usually got drafted in the Army or something just as each new baby came along. I once heard Dad say, "Well, looks like Butch and Peggy Vanderwende got Dutch Elm disease again," and Mom hushed him up. Tommy told us later that meant they were expecting another baby.

We passed their house; Pete Vanderwende was raking leaves, and his sister Carol was chasing screaming brat Kippy up the driveway.

We turned left on Maple. "They built this section first," Dad said. "When we first looked at it, the Circle was just a muddy field. We felt very lucky to get one of these houses. It's a pretty street. Someday, when all the trees grow in some more, this will be a beautiful neighborhood."

As we turned onto Cedar, I glanced at the two dead-end "courts" that jutted out on the west side into a big farm field that stretched between Cobbs Road and the creek. On Pine Court and Spruce Court, the houses were tall, skinny two-bedroom duplexes. They were all painted in the same Easter-egg colors: pink, yellow, sky blue, mint green. Even at age eight, I was aware that these houses were somewhat less desirable. Most were rentals, with people coming and going. Everyone referred to them collectively as "the Pines."

"Why are the houses in the Pines different?" I asked Dad as we passed Spruce.

"They wanted all sorts of houses here. Originally they were going to put another court at the end of Cedar, where that vacant lot is, and build some apartment houses in the field. But when they surveyed, there were some funny boundary lines going back to the 1700s. The Ramseys wanted to hold on to a certain amount of acreage, so they didn't sell that strip after all. They were still raising a lot of potatoes then."

"The Ramseys? Like Old Lady Ramsey?"

Dad chuckled. "She's not so old. Only in her fifties. All of this land, all of Arboria Park, used to be part of their farm. Land on both sides of the creek, all the way up to the Oakley place. Arboria Park used to be an apple orchard."

"Why didn't they call it Orchard Park then?"

"They were going to call it something like that, but that development out by the base, Orchard Acres, got there first. Don't know who came up with Arboria. It's kind of silly since they cut down trees to build it."

We were close to the end of Cedar, where you could see the trees stretching along the creek. I strained to see were we had been the previous week. How far had we walked? I ached to know.

"We can't walk over there." Dad had read my mind. "That's private property. You can see where it meets the Oakley farm, beyond that thick patch of trees where you girls got lost. Mrs. Ramsey rents most of her property out to be farmed. Mainly corn and soybeans now. There used to be a cider mill on the property, and they raised some crops and some chickens, but mostly apples and cherries. The bottom fell out of that during the Depression. They eked out a living, but they were what is called land poor. The land was worth a fortune, but they were barely making it. So Mr. Ramsey sold the orchard for development. He died about ten years ago. From what I hear, Mrs. Ramsey never got over it—him selling the orchard, or his death. That's why she stays on there, letting other people farm her land. She makes enough to get by, but she could be a millionaire if she ever sold it all."

"Why doesn't she, then?"

"Some things are worth more than money, sweetheart. This is her home. She loves the land."

I looked down the line of trees again. "Dad, where does the creek go?"

"Past Oakley's place, then it crosses Foster Road to the mill-pond. You know, where we see all the geese when we drive to the farm stand for strawberries or corn?"

I had never made the connection. "What about the other way?"

"Behind the Crescent, under the main highway by the Shell station, and out to the lake. All creeks like that lead to larger bodies of water, like rivers or lakes. Maybe tomorrow we'll ride in the car and look both ends over."

We passed the last house on Birch, across from the end of the Arbor Shopping Center, where we had run back across the creek from Mrs. Ramsey's. I could see the main highway, cars whizzing by, as we walked down a strip of land behind the Shell station.

"Look through there." Dad pointed down the creek. "Across the creek, just above the water, look carefully and you'll see part of a stone foundation. That was the Ramsey cider mill. It was still open when we first looked at the development. Your mother and I went over and got fresh cider when they were processing the last of their apples and some from other orchards. Then they closed up shop and the place fell apart. Some teenage boys were over there smoking cigarettes around the time you were born and burned it down by accident. That's why Mrs. Ramsey doesn't want anyone on her property."

I squinted until I saw the stone wall. We must have run right past it.

Dad touched my shoulder. "Okay, that's enough for today. We'll look at other streets another time."

We turned up Beech and cut over to Elm on Mimosa. Dad lit a cigarette. "If you want to see something or know where things go, just ask. If I don't know, we'll find out together. When you're a little older, you can go farther, but always be careful about other people's property. I know the boys have gone down there sometimes. Most of the kids in the development have. But it's not really fair to the people who own the farms. That's their home and their living."

I was still processing all he had told me. "Right here, where we're walking, this was an apple orchard?"

"Yes, and where our house is too. This was all farm country, but some of the farmers knew they could make more money selling the land. And the builders knew young families like ours needed houses."

"How many houses are here?" I'd tried to count them but lost track.

"About five hundred, I think."

"I love houses," I said. "They're interesting. I want to draw every house here, but Mary draws better than me."

"Maybe you can work for an architect someday."

"What do they do?"

"They design houses and other buildings."

"If I can learn to draw as good as Mary, maybe I could be one."

"Well, it's usually men who do that, sweetheart. Girls can be teachers, like Mary wants to be, or nurses, or they can work in an office."

I thought that was dumb but I didn't want to argue with Dad, since we'd had such a nice walk.

As we approached the Circle, I asked, "When will I be allowed to go to Julie's again?"

"Soon. We'll talk to her parents so you both get parole at the same time."

"What's parole?"

"When they let the prisoner out, but he has to promise to behave, and they watch him to make sure he does."

Mom had come home, and Matt and a bunch of his friends were getting snacks and drinks. I went out back and got on the swing. I looked up and down the yards, but they seemed different now. I tried to picture rows of apple trees, and a younger Mrs. Ramsey, wearing a big straw hat maybe, walking up and down picking apples. And later, a big, muddy field, just a few houses on Cobbs and Maple, the rest of the neighborhood empty and waiting. All of it just a few years before I was born. An architect had designed these houses, a builder had built them, and they had named all the streets after trees. But there was no Apple Street. And no apple trees for Mrs. Ramsey.

3—1964

....

Mary was getting married. In June she had marched up to the
auditorium stage to get her high school diploma—fifth in her
class, winner of the art award. Our parents were proud and
happy. Now, the weekend she should have been leaving for the
state university, she'd be marching down the aisle in church to
become Mrs. Donald Kozicki. And nobody was very proud or
happy at all.

Mary had "put the cart before the horse," Dad had explained
in one of several euphemisms used in front of me. I was nine, but
I wasn't stupid. For the past few weeks, I'd listened to the arguments in the living room after I was sent to bed, and heard Mary
crying herself to sleep. The rest of us kids were told that she was
getting married, the wedding would be very soon, and we were
not to talk about it with the neighbors or anybody. I still played
with my bride paper dolls and wedding coloring book sometimes
and was fascinated by the whole thing. I knew I was too old to be
a flower girl and too young to be a junior bridesmaid (they gen-
erally wore "tea length" dresses instead of long ones, according to
the coloring book), but I had hoped I'd at least get a new dress,
maybe get to wear flowers in my hair like the real bridesmaids.

Only this wedding wouldn't be like that at all. Mary's best friend, Linda Jean Chaskovich, couldn't be her maid of honor, Mom had carefully explained, because it would put Linda and her parents in an "awkward" position. Nor were we inviting all the relatives or the neighbors or my parents' church friends, or having a big reception somewhere. It wouldn't be "proper," my parents agreed, "under the circumstances."

Mary didn't even get to wear a long white dress and veil. The dress she would wear hung on the back of our bedroom door. She and Mom called it "ivory," but it looked yellow to me. It was made of satin and had puffed sleeves and a full skirt, but it wasn't floor length or even tea length, and it didn't have lace or seed pearls or a train. It was just a marked-down leftover prom dress relegated to the clearance rack. And no veil, either, just a matching pillbox hat with a little bit of netting in front.

The dress Mary had worn to the senior prom, a blue taffeta with straps, was already out of our shared closet, along with the sea-green chiffon one from when she'd been in the Homecoming Court back in the fall. The homecoming dance had been one of her first dates with Don Kozicki, a "nice boy" from a "good" Catholic family who lived on Oak Street. Everybody had been delighted when they started going out. Now they would be moving into one of the rental houses on Spruce Court—downward mobility in the eyes of both families. Some of Mary's dresses were already hanging in the closet at the house.

It also bothered me that Mary wasn't getting many presents. The Spruce house was sparsely furnished with castoffs from our basement or the Kozickis', along with some things Dad had let Mary pick out at the farmers' auction. According to the one bridal magazine Mary had purchased and then flung under her bed, she should be receiving china and silver and crystal, along with a new toaster and towels and stainless steel cookware. But like a white gown, bridesmaids, and bragging to the neighbors, gifts fell under the category of "not appropriate under the circumstances."

I found it grotesquely unfair. I knew where babies came from, having heard plenty of weird tales at recess, but I was still a little fuzzy about how they got there in the first place. It involved getting married and sleeping together, but the mechanics were vague and some of my classmates' theories were abstract and unbelievable. How had Mary had a chance to "sleep" with Don Kozicki? And as long as the outcome was the same (getting married and having a baby), why was everyone acting like it was so tragic? Wasn't that what you were supposed to do when you grew up?

I considered all of this as I sat on my bed the Friday before the wedding, pretending to organize my school supplies for the start of fourth grade the following week. But I was really watching Mary as she pulled things out of our shared dresser and folded them into a suitcase. She wasn't paying any attention to the dress hanging on the door, whereas I could barely keep my eyes off it. After all, it was a *wedding dress*, for heaven's sake, even if it wasn't a fancy one.

Mary pulled a picture off the wall, a colorful garden scene she had painted and won a prize for at a school exhibit. She placed it in a box along with her high school yearbook. Then she turned to the picture of the Beatles she had cut out of *Life* magazine and hung next to the closet. "You can keep the boys," she said.

"You mean you're not going to listen to the Beatles anymore?" I hadn't realized getting married meant so many changes.

"Of course I will, silly. All my records are over at the house already. I just thought you'd like to keep it."

"Thank you," I said. I thought John was cute. Mary preferred Paul.

She took some of her remaining clothes out of the closet. I looked at the wedding dress again and wrote my name on my new notebook and pencil case. I wondered what it would be like to change your last name. Even in third grade, some of my school friends had started writing their first names along with the last names of boys they liked. I kind of liked Gerald Buttenweiser, but no way I'd want that name next to mine.

"Hey." Mary yanked something from the closet. "Forgot about this one." It was the ruffly pink dress she'd worn to the junior prom the previous year. "It's not appropriate for a married woman, too girlish. You can keep it and play dress-up, or save it to wear to a dance someday when you're old enough." She held it up against her body. "I went with Roger Prentice. I can't believe that was only last year."

The pink dress was a real score. I was about to thank Mary and ask if I could try it on when she shoved it back in the closet and then sat down on her bed, holding her stomach. I hoped she didn't feel sick again, like she did sometimes.

"Do you want some ginger ale?" I asked.

She stared straight ahead, not making any sounds at all, but a tear rolled down her cheek. "No, thanks, Stacy. I don't need any." She buried her face in her hands. "It's all just crazy. June 1963 I wore that dress to the prom. June 1964 I got pregnant with a baby. Next June"—she lifted her face again—"next June, Linda and I and some of the other girls were going to get jobs and share a place at the beach for the summer. Work as waitresses, or at the snow-cone place, or sell tickets at Funland." She rubbed her stomach. "Linda and Janet and everyone will be in college and having fun. I wanted to go to college so much, and be an art teacher, and live in my own apartment and have a car before I got married."

Now it made sense why Mary was so unenthused about her wedding. I had thought it was because of Mom and Dad acting so put out and nobody giving her nice things or congratulating her. I hadn't thought about what she was giving up.

"At least you get your own house, and your own stuff," I said, trying to comfort her. "Now you're a grown-up and can do whatever you want. You can buy things. Maybe you can still go to college after the baby gets bigger. And, well"—I felt my face turning red—"you get to be in love."

"In love." Mary wasn't crying now. "I don't know. I mean, in some ways I barely know Don. It seems weird to go from that to living in the same house."

"Maybe you should just go out with him some more and then you can marry him later." I felt out of my depth.

"Stacy, it doesn't work that way. I made a mistake, and now my choices are getting married or a home for unwed mothers far away. No college, no options, not even getting to decide if Don is really the one. He's really cute and nice, but there's a big difference between going steady senior year and, well, a lifetime commitment. And I just turned eighteen." She sighed. "Look, this is all a little complicated, and you won't understand until you're older."

I hated that phrase. Everybody in the family used it to keep me from finding out about anything. It was also a dismissal.

"Maybe I'll explain it all to you someday, but right now I just want to be left alone, okay?" Mary went over to the closet again. "You'll have this whole room to yourself soon."

I walked out of the room, head down, wishing I was older so Mary would talk to me like I mattered. Tommy confronted me in the hallway, holding the toilet plunger like a sword and proclaiming, "Speak out, I charge you by that sense of conscientiousness to which we have never yet appealed in vain!" All he could think about was trying out for *The Pirates of Penzance* when school started.

"Move, stupid," I said.

He waved the plunger at the bathroom door like he was dueling. "Don't bother Mom. She and Mrs. Brooks are making food for tomorrow."

I'd already figured out it was best if I stayed out of Mom's way. She got nervous about big goings-on.

Tommy lunged at the bathroom door, jabbing the plunger over the doorknob. As he pulled it back, the handle came off the rubber part and he fell backwards onto the floor. I laughed, and he grabbed my leg and pulled me down to the floor with him. I shrieked.

Mom yelled from the kitchen, "What are you kids doing?"

I wriggled out of Tommy's grasp. "Nothing!"

"Well, go outside unless you're helping."

That was my cue to escape. "I'm going to ride my bike!"

"Be careful," she called back.

This was gold. She was too preoccupied to hand down a list of restrictions. I made for the door.

Tommy sang after me, "And it is, it is a glorious thing, to be a Pirate King!"

It should be a glorious thing to be a bride, I thought as I pulled my bike out of the shed. Mary shouldn't be in her room crying. She and Mom should be getting their hair done, or unwrapping gifts being delivered to the door. Mary should have had a bridal shower and given me all the ribbons from the presents, and Tommy should be shining his shoes and collecting tin cans to tie to Don's car instead of sword-fighting in the hallway.

Nothing seemed right. I pedaled down Elm to see if Julie was home, but she wasn't.

I cut over to Oak to check out how the Kozickis were preparing for the wedding. Maybe they were mad at Don like Mom and Dad were at Mary. Don was really nice, or at least polite. He never snarled, "Get out of here, squirt," at me the way Roger Prentice had. He drove a two-toned black-and-white '56 Pontiac and looked kind of like Ricky Nelson.

Neither the Pontiac nor the Kozickis' Chevy was in the driveway. The air smelled like chocolate, drifting over from the Fine Foods plant. I headed away to look at Mary's new house again.

Mom and Mary and I had just been over the day before to drop off more things, including an ugly set of red-striped glasses that Mr. Brooks had gotten free for being Fill-Up of the Month at the Avenue Esso. Even furnished with cast-off junk, the house was still pretty cool to me. Mary would have lots of time to fix it up after she got married. She'd have to leave her summer job at Fisher's Department Store before she started showing. They didn't allow any pregnant ladies to work there, married or not.

Her place was one of the pink houses at the end of the court. She didn't like the color. I thought about how everyone on our street talked about the Pines like it was a weird, foreign place, even though it was just a couple of blocks away. As I turned onto Spruce, I saw a man fixing a car in front of the blue houses, and some little kids playing in the street. That seemed normal enough.

As I rode past the man, though, I noticed he seemed dirty, and not just because he was fixing a car. He had greasy hair and wore a stained undershirt, and as he muttered a swear word and kicked the bumper of the old car, I saw a tattoo of a naked lady on his arm.

The kids looked dirty too, and not just play-in-a-mud-puddle dirty. Kids from the Pines rode on my school bus. I'd never really thought about it, but Coby Jolley, who was always hitting other little kids, was from there, and so was Penny Bodine, who was only going into sixth grade but already carried cigarettes in her purse.

A spindly pregnant woman came out on the stoop of the one of the green houses and called to the children, "Get in here before I tan your hides!" She grinned over at me, and I noticed she had a missing front tooth.

So these were Mary's new neighbors. I couldn't picture her running over to see the lady in the green house for bottle-feeding advice. And Don liked to work on cars but he never beat on the fenders with a wrench while spewing a bunch of curses I'd never heard of. I knew instinctively not to ask Mom and Dad what they meant. Maybe Tommy would know.

I circled back out and took off down Cedar as fast as I could, just to feel the chocolaty air rushing past me. Well, newlyweds sometimes started out without much, didn't they? Mary's bridal magazine had an article about how to fix up a tiny apartment so it looked bigger. Mom and Dad had lived in a two-room apartment until Mary was born, they had told us. At least this was a two-bedroom house, and Don would work and make some money and soon they'd move somewhere better, like my parents had.

I turned at Birch and went back up Oak again. Of course, Mary and Don weren't like my parents in one important way. I'd done the math in my head: Mary had been born a little more than a year after my parents' wedding. Mary's baby would be born only six months after hers. A crucial three months on each side of the equation, three months that made the difference between receiving exquisitely wrapped crystal goblets from well-wishers or accepting clownish gas-station tumblers from someone who felt sorry for you. And Mom and Dad had gotten engaged during the war and waited until he came home and landed a good job before they got married. Whereas Don had to give up his plans for college and work a civilian job at the air base his father pulled some strings to get him. And after the baby was born, he might join the Air Force himself, and then he and Mary would have to move wherever he got sent. Maybe he'd even have to fly to Vietnam and be in the war. It was all backwards.

Still no sign of the Kozickis. Their next-door neighbor came out of his house, carrying a toolbox. He smiled at me. "Hello there, young lady. Nice day for a ride."

I said "Hi," and pedaled on. You weren't really supposed to talk to strangers, even though this one looked like my dad. I glanced back. A girl younger than me came out of the house with a jump rope. I heard the man say, "Be careful, sugar. Daddy's fixing the car, and you don't want to get grease on your dress."

I headed away. It was all just too much to figure out at once.

....

The next morning was chaos. We all had to be up early and get dressed so Mary could have the bathroom to take a bubble bath. The rest of us had to take our baths the night before and get ready for bed early, even though I had strenuously objected because I was first and it was still light out. I lay awake, listening to all the bustling around. Mary came to bed early for her, and I listened to see if she was crying again, but she wasn't.

In the morning she set her hair on rollers and disappeared into the bathroom. Tommy, Matt, and I sat uncomfortably in the living room since we couldn't go outside lest we get dirty. The boys wore ties and jackets like it was Sunday. Just to emphasize how un-wedding-like this wedding was, I didn't even have a new dress—Mom had told me to wear the one I'd been wearing to church all summer—and I didn't get a corsage like Mom, either. Even she didn't have a new dress, and Mom wore a new dress for every special occasion. She planned to wear her lavender Easter suit. It was pretty, but it wasn't special.

Mom came out of her bedroom, her eyes moist like she'd been crying. She glanced at us as we sat on the couch, glued to the Saturday morning cartoons, not even teasing or shoving each other like we usually did. Then she went into Mary's room.

Mary exited the bathroom in her robe, and I slid off the couch. No way would I miss seeing her put on her wedding dress.

I sat on my bed and watched them take the rollers out of Mary's light brown hair, fluff it up, and spray it all over with lacquer. Usually she wore it straight down, pulled off her face with a hairband. She put on powder and lipstick and some black stuff on her eyelashes, and then Mom reached for the dress.

"Hold your breath," Mom said, as she zipped Mary into it. "We got this let out as much as we could, but you must be taking on weight since the last fitting."

"I don't see how," Mary said with a sigh. "I never want to eat." That was only partially true. She felt sick in the morning, sometimes, but she was always hungry by dinner time and often ate an extra bowl of ice cream later in the evening when we were watching TV.

"You're eating for two, like they say." Mom stood back and surveyed her. "You look very nice. That full skirt hides a multitude of sins."

Mary flinched and looked like she was going to cry again. She went back to the mirror and fussed with her hair some more.

"Let's get this hat on," Mom said, and then there was more fussing with a hatpin and adjusting the netting just right. "There."

I drew in my breath. It was like prom night again. Mary looked so beautiful.

"Your flowers are in the refrigerator with my corsage," Mom told her. "Stacy, get off that bed and smooth the bedspread. We have people coming over later."

"They won't be in here," I said, but did as I was told. I followed them to the kitchen and slipped out the back door while they went to the refrigerator. I wasn't going to get dirty, but I had a mission—flowers of my own. The petunias wouldn't work; maybe the zinnias? I picked a bunch.

"Anastasia Louise Halloran, get in here!" Mom was at the back door. "We have to leave. And don't even *think* you're bringing those flowers to church."

It was so unfair. I defiantly stuck the zinnias in a glass of water on the kitchen counter. If people were coming over it would be nice to have some flowers out, wouldn't it? But I kept one hidden in my hand, and in the car I twisted it around the handle of my black patent-leather purse. Mary had a tiny nosegay of yellow and white daisies.

We rode in relative silence to the church. As we got out of the car, I heard Mom say to Mary, "God help you if you do anything embarrassing in church. I know you don't want to do this, but don't make it even more humiliating."

I turned and stared. Mom was fussing with Mary's hat again.

"Stacy!" Dad called me. "Go inside with your brothers, please."

Dad hadn't said much the past few days. Now he just looked tired.

Tommy led Matt and me in and we sat down. The only other people in the church were Don's sister and brother, and what looked like an aunt and uncle.

I heard a noise at the back of the church. Linda Jean Chaskovich and Janet Hardy and Buster McDonald and a bunch of Mary and Don's other friends from school were giggling as they came into the church, but they suddenly hushed and looked serious, almost scared. After a brief whispered discussion about where to sit, some of them ended up behind us, the others behind the Kozickis.

Mom and Mrs. Kozicki walked in together, both tight-lipped. For the first time I noticed there wasn't even any organ music. The pews didn't have ribbons. There were flowers on the altar, but they were the ones from last Sunday, looking wilted.

Father Flynn and an altar boy stepped out of the sacristy, and then Don and his father. Don looked like Tommy did when he was dragged to Sears to buy school clothes.

Matt nudged me. "There's Brian," he whispered, gesturing toward the altar boy. "Betcha I can make him laugh." He stuck out his tongue and crossed his eyes. Brian snorted.

Mom turned to Matt and hissed, "God help you when we get home, Matthew."

Father Flynn nodded toward the back of the church, and Dad and Mary walked up the aisle. Maybe it was the stained-glass windows, or the stupid yellow dress, but Mary looked yellow too, and sort of blank. Weren't brides supposed to glow?

When they reached the altar she started to let go of Dad's arm, then clutched on to it tighter. Dad whispered something to her and gave her a kiss, and she nodded.

She stepped up and looked at Don. And just like that, they smiled at each other, and then she did sort of glow, and Don looked like Ricky Nelson again. For the first time I felt good about this wedding. Maybe it would be okay.

Father Flynn frowned through the whole service. Tommy whispered to Matt, loud enough for me to hear, "You couldn't pull a needle out of Father's ass right now."

One of Mary's friends behind us snickered, and Tommy realized he'd been too loud. Mom didn't even bother to get mad, just looked like she was going to cry.

Father rushed through some parts of the mass and skipped others, except for a sermon where he used the word "responsibility" seventeen times, according to Matt, who kept score.

Father Flynn had been mean to Mary before the wedding. She and Don had to go to "counseling" with him, and she said he didn't even care that she'd gone to confession and everything.

Finally, they got to the vows. I moved to the edge of my seat. But Father rushed through those, too, and I could barely hear either Mary or Don say "I do." And then they didn't even do Holy Communion. It was over, just like that.

Nobody threw rice or took pictures, except for Linda Jean, who had her camera. She hugged Mary and they both cried, and then Janet hugged both of them. Mom called out, "Mary, we don't have time for this. We have to get back to the house."

Mary let go of her friends and stared after them wistfully as they headed for Buster's car. They were invited to the house to have something to eat, but they couldn't stay long.

Back home, Mrs. Brooks had set out the canapés she and Mom had prepared the day before, along with a delivery deli platter from Strommer's. Mrs. Brooks stayed as moral support for Mom. Mom had driven her to get her son Danny after he got caught stealing cigarettes from the drugstore, so I figured she did it because she owed her one.

The Kozicki family sat stiffly at our dining room table, eating but not smiling. Mary's friends took their food into the living room and sat on the floor. Mary and Don looked torn about where to eat. Except Mary wasn't eating.

My brothers piled as much food as they could on their plates and went out on the back stoop. Like they both knew it was better for all concerned if they stayed out of sight. Don's brother slipped out after them. I hovered by the food, nibbling at the stuff I liked and ignoring what I didn't, like the stinky cheese and the pickles.

Then Mrs. Brooks brought out the cake from Rosario's Bakery.

It wasn't tall and tiered, like in my coloring book. Just a sheet cake. But it was white and decorated with curlicues and sugar flowers, and it had two silver foil wedding bells on top, tied with a white ribbon.

Mary and Don cut the cake and handed out pieces to everyone. A lot would be left over.

Mom cut out a square around the bells. "We'll save this piece in the freezer, for Mary and Don to have on their anniversary next year," she said with fake cheerfulness. I thought that was romantic, but Mary and Don didn't seem too excited. Their friends finished their cake, said awkward good-byes, and practically ran out the door.

Dad and Mr. Kozicki were making small talk about politics and LBJ. Mom and Mrs. Kozicki didn't say very much. It was weird because they used to chitchat a lot when they saw each other.

"I think I'll go change," Mary said to Mom. "We have to be leaving soon."

At least Mary and Don were getting a honeymoon, kind of. The Kozickis were paying for them to stay at the beach for a couple of days.

Mom forced a smile, but Mrs. Kozicki—well, I guess she was the *old* Mrs. Kozicki now —gave Mary this real nasty look. And I realized that the Kozickis hadn't been very nice to Mary all day. It wasn't enough that Mom and Dad blamed her and not Don; his parents did too. Why did grownups have to be so mean?

Mom and Mary excused themselves and left the room. Dad and Mr. Kozicki went out back to look at Dad's tomatoes, and Mrs. Brooks started cleaning up the kitchen. I didn't want to be alone with Mrs. Kozicki and her dumb daughter Karen, so I went out to the front porch.

Don was standing there, smoking a cigarette. I guessed he just wanted to get away too, because he could've smoked inside. His parents, and Dad, had been doing it all afternoon.

Don used to wear his hair all slicked back, but now he was growing it out to look like the Beatles. I wondered if he knew about Mary's crush on Paul McCartney. He had loosened his tie and looked like he was ready to run away.

"I think it stinks that you guys didn't get a bigger wedding and more presents," I said.

He flicked some ashes off the porch. "That's how it goes."

"And everybody's been mean to Mary. Even your mom. And now Mary can't go to college."

He turned to me, and I realized I'd gone too far. "Well, kid, I'm giving up college too. And it's more important for me. I was going to study engineering, get a good job someday. What was she going to do, meet somebody in college and get married anyway?"

"That doesn't mean everybody has to blame her. She feels bad." I couldn't believe I had to defend my sister to her own husband.

"Yeah, I know." Don sat down on the step. "I feel bad too. Who knows, maybe we would have kept going together through college, and then after we graduated and got jobs we could have that big wedding and live someplace swell. Instead we're moving to a crappy house with crappy stuff and having a baby. Well, that's the breaks, kid. The screwing you get for . . ." He stopped and threw his cigarette butt on the driveway. "Come on, kid, go see where your sister is."

I went back in the house. Everyone was in the living room now, and Mary was coming out of her room—well, my room now. She didn't even have a new dress to go away in, just one of her summer dresses Mom had let out, but I didn't care about that so much because all I could think was, why wouldn't you want to wear your wedding dress all day?

Don came in behind me, and everybody started making good-bye noises. Tommy clapped his hands. "Attention, everyone."

He signaled to Matt, who was standing by the record player. Matt put the needle down on Tommy's Beatles album and played "I Want to Hold Your Hand."

"First dance for the happy couple," Tommy said, like he was hosting a TV show.

Don and Mary looked at each other from opposite ends of the living room. And then they met in the middle and Don twirled her around and they danced. And they looked like what they should have been—a happy teenage couple, having a good time.

Everyone applauded and looked happy too, except maybe Mom and Mrs. Kozicki. Matt let the record play on to "I Saw Her Standing There," and Mary and Don did the twist. Don's brother and sister were twisting too, and me and Tommy.

So they left on a happy note, and Mary said she had left her flowers in my room for me. Maybe the stupid Kozickis would go home and we could have more cake.

Instead, Mrs. Kozicki was shaking her head. "So sad," she said. "They're so young. Well, she'll be facing the consequences of her behavior now."

Mom looked like she'd been hit, and for the first time in days, I kind of felt sorry for her. Dad had a look on his face I'd never seen before.

"Stop being so mean." I went right up to Don's mom. "It's his fault too. Mary didn't even get a real wedding and *you guys*"—I looked at Mom—"tried to ruin the one she had."

"Stacy, that's enough," Dad said. "Go to your room, *now*."

"Okay." I turned and tried to look as tall as I could. "I'll go, but *God help* the *fucking bastard* who tries to make me go to bed again when it's light out."

I could see the admiration in my brothers' eyes as I marched out of the room. I knew I was in real trouble now and that I'd probably never get another crumb of that wedding cake, but I didn't care. The curse words I'd learned on Spruce Court had gotten attention, and maybe now *everybody* would think about the consequences of their behavior.

4—1967

························

I got off the school bus a couple of stops early so I could walk over to Mary's. I liked to see Autumn, who had just turned two. Mom and Dad hadn't been pleased with the name Mary and Don had chosen for their baby. "She can't be baptized in the church with that name!" Mom objected. "Can you use her middle name?" (It was Marie.)

Mary and Don had laughed. They didn't have her baptized. They didn't have much use for the church after Father Flynn.

Autumn was cute and sweet, with dark hair and eyes like Don. She walked on schedule and talked early. I helped Mary and Mom with her, and recently they'd even let me watch her alone in the yard.

I trudged over to Spruce. The Pines had changed in the two and half years since Mary and Don moved in. Some of the trashy people were gone. New people had arrived, ones my dad called beatniks. Tommy said they were actually hippies. To Mary, they were her friends.

Autumn was playing with her blocks on the floor, Mary was ironing, and *Secret Storm* was on TV. I was glad, because another reason I liked to go after to Mary's after school was to catch things like *Dark Shadows* and *Edge of Night*—shows that Mom didn't want me to watch. I put my schoolbooks and jacket on a chair and sat down with Autumn.

"Tacy!" she shouted.

Don came downstairs in an undershirt. "Is my shirt ready?" he asked, ignoring me.

Mary lifted it off the ironing board, and he grabbed it and put it on.

"Get tomorrow's done too, will you?" He had to wear his hair short now, because of rules on the base. He didn't look like Ricky Nelson or Paul McCartney anymore—more like my old crew-cut Ken doll.

Mary arched her eyebrows at me and then made a face behind his back as he leaned over, picked up Autumn, and swung her around. She squealed with delight.

"Daddy will see you tomorrow," he said. "Be good for Mommy." He kissed her.

"Want to go!" she shouted. "See airplanes."

"Soon, baby. When they have visiting day." He placed her gently back on the floor. "Don't wait up," was all he said to Mary as he left. He didn't kiss her.

Mary ironed the other shirt, hung it on the banister, and unplugged the iron. Then she turned off the TV, which meant I wouldn't see *Dark Shadows* after all, but she put on some cool records. The Mamas and the Papas, Jefferson Airplane, Bob Dylan. Autumn "sang" along, and pounded her blocks on the floor.

"I'm going to wash my hair while you're here, if that's okay," Mary said. "I have to write a paper tonight after Autumn goes to bed. That's one good thing about Don being on night shift." Mary was taking a correspondence course from the state university, the school she would have gone away to if she hadn't gotten pregnant.

Someone knocked at the door. It was Mary's neighbor, Olga. She lived in a yellow house across the court. Mary had told me she was from Spain.

"May I borrow some oil?" she asked. "I am cooking Jerry's dinner. He will be home at six."

"Sure." Mary headed for the kitchen. "Do you need a ride to the grocery store tomorrow? I'll have the car because Don's on nights, and I have to go anyway."

"Thank you, yes," Olga said. "Hello, little one." She squatted down and kissed Autumn and said something to her in Spanish. Olga was so exotic. She wore big gold earrings and skinny black stretch pants.

Mary came back with a bottle of Wesson. "Not much left, so you may as well take it, and I'll get more tomorrow."

"Jerry will work at nights next week," Olga said. Jerry worked as a proofreader at the local newspaper while writing his novel, Mary had told me, and he did different shifts like Don did at the base. "I asked him again about a job because I am legal resident now. The newspaper needs a typist. He says no." She looked downcast. "Maybe you should try."

"I would, if I weren't taking this class right now." Mary sounded frustrated. "I need to earn some money. This is the last correspondence course I can take that will count toward a degree. Maybe I can get a job in a store or something when we're settled. But we haven't even talked about that yet, and we're still waiting to hear where Don will be sent."

I hated to think about Mary moving away. But Don had finally enlisted in the Air Force, and they would be leaving in June. The only good thing was that Dad had said we'd go visit them no matter where they ended up.

"You know I would watch the little one," Olga said. "But you are going."

"Thanks, Olga. Daisy's offered too, but you know . . ."

"Oh, Daisy." She said something in Spanish again, and she and Mary both laughed.

Olga kissed Mary on the cheek, then me and Autumn. "I must go and finish dinner for Jerry."

"What did she mean about Daisy?" I asked after Olga left. Daisy and her friend Helena lived in the other half of Olga's duplex. They were real hippie girls who wore granny dresses and feather earrings. Daisy played the guitar.

"Daisy's a lovely girl, but maybe not the most responsible person to look after a kid," Mary said. "Head in the clouds."

"You're moving away anyhow. I hate that. I'll be old enough to watch Autumn by myself soon, but you'll be who knows where."

"Well . . ." Mary hesitated. "I'm not sure I'm going anywhere."

I stopped building the tower I was making with Autumn. "What do you mean?"

"I mean I don't want to go with Don. You can probably tell things aren't exactly great right now, and I'm about to go crazy even with you and Mom and Don's mother to help me. I can't imagine being someplace like Minot, North Dakota, with a toddler and not knowing anyone, and not being able to go to school. And—well, this is important too. I'm really, really against the war. I don't want Don to have to go, if it comes to that. I don't believe in the cause. It's stupid and wrong. Don doesn't really think it's right either, but he's from a military family and he says when you're in the service, you do what you're told. I know I could never be a good little military wife and pretend it's all okay. And that would hurt Don's career. I won't do that to him." She sat down and put her hands over her face, the way she had before her wedding. "I shouldn't burden you with all this. Olga's the only person I've talked to about it. She's not happy either. Jerry controls everything she does. We're both prisoners. I know I can do more with my life. I want to finish school, no matter how long it takes. I almost never see Don now, and once he's in training, forget it. If we're going to end it, now is the best time."

I didn't know what to say, but maybe it didn't matter. Mary looked relieved now that she'd spilled it. "Guess I better wash my hair while you're still here."

"I can stay a while. I just have to go home at five to set the table."

She nodded and went upstairs.

Bob Dylan was yowling on the stereo about a lady artist with a mind of her own. I stared at one of Mary's paintings on the wall. She'd fixed up this little house so beautifully. Mom thought it was too "informal" and colorful, but I loved it. The bright wooden blocks Autumn and I were playing with looked like part of the décor.

When she had finished, Mary came back downstairs with a bag of rollers as big as soup cans and set her hair. It seemed funny that now she used rollers to make it straighter, not curlier. She wore it long now. I had grown mine out a little after rebelling against the short cut Mom had insisted on for years, sort of a cross between a bob and a pixie. But my hair was wavy and not long enough yet for those big rollers.

"Hey, listen," she said, "I don't want you to have to lie or carry secrets. But don't say anything to Mom and Dad just yet. Don and I are going to have a serious talk this weekend and make some decisions, so until then nothing's really set. This could go either way. Okay?"

"Okay," I agreed. Autumn was tired of the blocks and was pulling some picture books out of the toy basket in the corner. "Hey, Autumn. I can read you one book before I have to go. How about *Ping*?"

·······················

I thought about it all as I walked home. Mary was talking about a divorce, really. My parents knew a few—very few—people who were divorced, and it was always portrayed as strange and sad. But Mary seemed kind of resigned about it. She was only about to turn twenty-one, the age a lot of girls were when they got married. I wondered how old Olga was. Mary said she'd met Jerry when he was backpacking through Europe, which I thought was romantic. They hadn't been married very long either.

At dinner, nobody noticed how quiet I was as Matt carried on about the start of baseball season and Tommy about the senior class play.

"Don't forget, we have to go over that college acceptance letter one more time this week," Dad said, interrupting Tommy. "You really should have sent it in by now."

Tommy put his fork down and sat back. There was still food on his plate. "I guess I need to say this now." He looked at Dad. "I don't want to go to college. Mrs. Grant told me about this traveling summer stock company. She did that for a few years while she was in school, and she helped me get in. That means I'm going away this summer, after graduation. It's great experience. And after that, I want to join another theater company and keep touring, if I like it. Or go to New York. Acting is all I want to do. I'd never get this kind of experience acting in college. It would be wasting time."

"Wasting time?" Dad seldom sounded so mad. Mom had stopped eating and had a look of horror on her face, but really, that could have been any night. "Getting a degree in something *useful* so you can get a good job is a waste of time?"

"For me, yes." Tommy drummed his fingers on the table. "Every time I think about four more years of school, I want to run away. I know the career I want. I'll work hard and do whatever I have to do. Worst case scenario, if I find I don't like touring, I can come back in the fall and get a job for a year and *then* go to school. Or five years from now, if I go to New York and don't make it. There's plenty of time."

"Thomas, you know the rules," Dad said. "We're happy to put you through school now, but once you leave this house, you're on your own. Your sister had to learn that the hard way."

I had stopped eating too. Only Matt was still shoveling mashed potatoes into his mouth.

"I know. That's why I said I'd get a job and take care of myself. You can use the money for Matt and Stacy, when it's their turn."

"Or give it to Mary," I heard myself say, and everyone looked at me. "I mean, she knows taking a correspondence course here or there won't be enough for a degree."

"Yeah, that's a great idea," Tommy agreed. "She wants college more than anything. And I don't. So she deserves it."

I was thrilled until Dad said, "Mary will be moving away soon, and then she'll be an Air Force wife, with a child. She won't be able to manage going to school."

Holding on to my secret was agony. But to my relief, Dad reminded Tommy, "And we're not talking about Mary now, we're talking about you and your future. If you don't go to school, you're eligible for the draft. Did you think about that?"

"Yes, actually. My number's pretty high. After this summer, I can join the National Guard. It will mean some sacrifices of time here and there, but I think I can work around that." Tommy had it all figured out. "I've already turned eighteen. So I can join the theater company without parental permission, and the Guard too. But I'd like my family's support."

"I support you!" I jumped up. "As long as you don't have to go to that stupid war, you should do what you want."

"Stacy, sit down," Dad said. "This is not your concern."

"He's my brother," I pointed out. "You guys didn't give Mary a choice, and now she's—well, Tommy's right."

"I vote with Tommy." Matt finally ran out of food on his plate and spoke up. "He's a good actor. He could be in the movies or on TV someday."

"Or the unemployment line," Dad argued, but clearly he was losing control of the discussion.

Mom put her hand on her forehead and walked out of the room. Tommy looked sorry for a minute, but then he got up and started stacking plates. I gathered the ones at my end of the table. Dad went after Mom.

For once, I didn't have to fight with my brothers to help with the dishes. We did them together, knowing Mom was crying her eyes out a couple of rooms away.

"Thanks for the help, guys." Tommy hugged me and punched Matt in the shoulder.

"We're a family of black sheep," Matt said. "Wouldn't it be funny if I was the only one who did what they want?"

"Yeah, that'll happen," I said, using my most sarcastic voice.

Matt laughed. "After you and Mary, Stace and I will have it easy. Anything'll look good now."

·····················

By the weekend Tommy had our parents over a barrel. He wasn't even asking for any money, because he'd saved some from his part-time job and knew he'd get more for graduation presents. Nothing they could do would stop him.

I was edgy all weekend, jumping whenever the phone rang. I didn't want to go over to Mary's in case they were still talking. Or fighting. I wondered if she'd let us know right away.

"Are Mary and Don doing something this weekend?" Mom asked me on Sunday. "She hasn't brought Autumn over or called all week."

"When I saw her Wednesday, she said they had plans." This was as honest as I could get. "And sometimes Olga watches Autumn for her."

Mom gasped. "Not that awful girl with the frizzy hair?"

"No. Mary said she's not responsible enough. Olga is the Spanish lady, with the big earrings. She's nice."

"Well, I hope everything's all right."

I hoped so too.

·····················

I couldn't wait to get off the bus on Monday and race over to Spruce Court. Mary and Olga were drinking tea in the kitchen, and Autumn was having her own tea party on the floor with her dolls.

"Tacy, have tea," she urged. Mary and Olga laughed, but they looked like they'd been crying earlier. "Yes, Stacy, have some tea," Mary said. "I suppose you're here to get the news."

"Well, um . . ."

"It's okay. I called Mom today and said I'm coming over tonight, for dinner, and I'll tell everyone then." She sighed. "Tommy called me last week to get my opinion on his bombshell. I hate to make this announcement so soon after his, but maybe it's just as well."

I blew on my hot tea. "So I guess if you think Mom will be upset, you're staying here?"

"Yes. Don hasn't been happy either. Since he turned twenty-one in January, he's been hitting the bars out by the base pretty hard after work. I knew it. It'll be easier for him to start training and not have to worry about me. Of course, he's pretty broken up about Autumn. That part's killing us both." She looked at her daughter. "She doesn't really understand yet. I don't want her growing up without her dad, but I also don't want him to get drunk and stay away from us because he doesn't want to come home. That's not a life."

"It is easier for me and Jerry," Olga said. "We have no children. He will go to New York now, and finish his book."

"Olga's moving in here this summer," Mary said. "That's the only way we'll be able to afford it. We both have to get jobs, and figure out what to do about Autumn when we're working, and I guess I'll be postponing school for a while." She put her head down on the table. "God, I'm so mixed up. Relieved, but sad. And scared to death."

"Mommy." Autumn was at Mary's side. "Go outside with Tacy?"

Mary lifted her head and forced a smile. "Sure. Stacy, you don't mind, do you? Take her down to the playground for a little while."

A new playground had been built on the empty lot at the corner of Cedar and Birch. Too late for me to enjoy, but Autumn liked the swings and the spinny thing. We played around for twenty minutes and then I brought her back home.

"We'll be over in a little bit," Mary said. "Can you hold out one more hour or so?"

"Sure," I said. I hugged her before I left.

....

It all went about as well as you'd think. For the next month, I never knew whether I'd come home to find Mom lying on the couch or shut up in her bedroom, and Mrs. Brooks in the kitchen with a casserole for me to heat up for Dad and the boys. Dad was grim for a few weeks, but he always seemed to be able to work things through. He spoke to Mary about her plans, and to Don about his responsibilities to Autumn, and talked a lot about "making the best of it," and eventually Mom came out of the bedroom.

Don and Mary agreed that he'd stay at the house until he left for training in June. They seemed to be getting along a little better, smiling more and being kind of polite and careful with each other. Sometimes, when they played with Autumn or sang along together to the radio, I'd wonder if maybe love really could conquer all. But they went ahead with their plans. Don was leaving Mary the old Pontiac, and Jerry gave Olga his car, too, because he wouldn't need it in Brooklyn.

Olga got a job as a secretary at Fine Foods. She was on the lookout for another opening for Mary.

But first Mary had to figure out what to do with Autumn, since Olga had to work and Don was gone now. I wanted to take care of her, at least for the summer, but Mom and Dad didn't think it was a good idea.

I walked over one day in June to see if I could at least watch Autumn for a little while so Mary could go to the store or something. She thanked me but said no.

"I need more than just an hour or two," she said. "I have some job leads, but I have to figure out what to do long term. Funny, Mom and Shirley Kozicki both used to love to have Autumn. Shirley used to call and tell me to go get my hair done or something so she could watch her. Now the door's closed. Mom says she can't handle her for more than one or two days a week, and that's probably true. But Shirley—well, apparently getting my hair done is fine, but getting a job or going to school is not an acceptable reason to get a babysitter." She shook her head. "I'm afraid she might even try to sue for custody. Don had a long talk with her before he left and told her to butt out, but she's hysterical every time I talk to her now. I don't want to deprive Autumn of her grandparents, but she's making it tough."

"Could she really do that? That's so awful."

"When it comes down to it, I know she couldn't handle it. Karen's going off to college in the fall and can't help her, and Walter's been looking forward to an empty nest. I don't think he'd go along. But Shirley's kind of like Mom. If she can't get her way, she'll make your life hell. And Mom and Dad want me to 'face the consequences of my behavior' again. So I have to work this out myself."

"It's so unfair." I felt helpless. "First you have to drop school *again*. Then they won't even help you."

"Moral of the story, watch what you do when you get older. Don't end up in a trap."

··················

I moped around for a few days thinking about it all. Tommy had gone off to be a dancing, singing cowboy in *Oklahoma*. He'd worked it out somehow. There had to be a way for Mary.

She came over for dinner on Father's Day. We gave Dad his gifts, and Mom made roast beef. We were finishing up dessert when Mary said, "I have an announcement."

Mom put down the dishes she was picking up and sat down with her hand over her heart, like nothing good ever came out of that phrase. At least Mary had waited until we finished eating, unlike Tommy.

"I have a job, starting a week from Monday. The lawyer who's handling my divorce knows another lawyer who needed a typist, and they hired me. I called Shirley, and she'll take Autumn on Fridays. I'd appreciate it if you'd take her on Thursdays. The other three days, I've found someone to keep her. The lady lives in town, and she has a nice house and yard and she takes care of three other children. It's going to be tough financially, but I got some office clothes at Goodwill yesterday, and Olga says she'll pay a little extra on her share of the rent for a while to give me a break. I won't be going to school or doing much of anything else, but I think we can make it." She looked at Dad. "So I won't be moving back home, Dad. It wouldn't be right. You wanted me to stand on my feet, and that's what I'm doing. All I'm asking is for Mom to take Autumn one day a week, which she does most weeks anyway."

I jumped up and hugged Mary. "You did it!"

"Not yet, I haven't." She stared at Mom and Dad.

It was just like when they realized Tommy wouldn't back down. Dad said, "Sounds like you've made the best of a bad situation. But I still think Autumn needs her mother since her father's gone."

I could see that got to Mary. She swallowed and said, "I hate leaving her. You know that. But it's just three days a week she'll be away from family, and she'll enjoy playing with the other children."

They had no choice but to accept it. Dad even gave her some money for clothes, the same way he'd given Tommy a hundred dollars before he left.

....

Mary dove into her new life. She said typing up contracts was boring and the lawyers were kind of snotty, but she loved going to work because she was providing for herself and Autumn beyond what Don could afford to send back.

She and Autumn had dinner with us on Thursdays, the day Autumn stayed with us. Mrs. Kozicki calmed down, but she was still pretty frosty to all of us if we ran into her at the shopping center or something.

One Thursday in August, I took Autumn out back to push her on the swing set, which Dad had left up just for her. She squealed,

"Higher!" and I thought about how much time I'd spent going as high as I could so I could see way down the block. The neighborhood trees were bigger now, and shaded some of the houses from view. Autumn was already asking the kinds of questions I used to ask: "Who lives there? Can we go see that dog? What is that lady doing?" and I tried to answer her the way Dad had done for me, and take her for little walks and show her things. I told her about the orchard, too, but she was too young to make sense of it yet.

As we sat on the stoop drinking lemonade after we'd tired ourselves out with the swing, Autumn looked up and said, "I want to do *everything!*"

I tried to respond like a grown-up. "Nobody can do *everything.*" But when she frowned, I added, "But you should always *try* to do all kinds of things, even if they say you can't do it because you're a girl, or if other people will be looking at you, or even if they won't help you." Then, because I wanted to be honest, I added, "Just don't make a mistake."

This was all too confusing for her. "What's a mistake?" she asked, but she was already getting up to chase a butterfly, not waiting for an explanation.

"I don't know," I replied, even though she was now on the other side of the yard. "But they'll tell you when you make one."

5—1968

··········· ·· ······· ·

I was about to turn thirteen—finally, a teenager. But I was still in junior high, so it didn't count for much yet, other than being able to watch Autumn without being supervised myself and picking up a few other babysitting jobs around the neighborhood.

One spring day as I was playing with Autumn in our backyard after school, she pointed to a yard down on Maple. "Why are those people dark?"

I looked at where she was pointing and saw a woman and two little kids. "It's because they're Negroes. Or I think they like to be called black now. They're just a different color."

"They're not black, they're brown," Autumn declared.

"Well, that's what they're called. And we're white."

"White." She giggled, pointing at one of Mom's hyacinths. "*Those* are white."

"It's just what it's called. You've seen black people on TV, and in town. Remember?" Looking at the woman and her children, I saw only one thing: dollar signs. The kids appeared to be in the sweet spot to babysit, around four and six, maybe. I took Autumn's hand, marched down the utility easement between fences, leaned over theirs, and introduced myself.

The lady's name was Mrs. Andrews. She said they'd just moved in and her husband was in the Air Force and if she needed a sitter, she'd definitely think of me. The little boys waved at Autumn and she shyly waved back.

I told Mom about it when we went inside. She sighed. "Stacy, maybe you shouldn't get involved with those people."

"Why not? She's nice. Her husband's from the base."

Mom gave me a look and went back to chopping vegetables. I knew it wasn't over, just a not-in-front-of-Autumn thing.

We drank some grape juice and then I said, "I guess I'll walk Autumn home now. Olga should be home from work. We can wait outside or go over to Daisy and Helena's house if she's not."

"Wait outside," Mom said firmly. She still didn't think much of Daisy or Helena.

Mary wouldn't be coming straight home after work because she was taking a night class at the local college. Somebody she'd met at work had put her in touch with somebody to talk to there about financial aid, and Dad had caved and given her the rest of the money she needed. So she'd taken a course there in the fall, and now she was taking another one. She was so ecstatic about it that nobody gave her open grief about even more time away from Autumn. And at least Olga could watch Autumn while she was at class since it was at night.

Mary had her time organized down to the minute. She complained that it would take forever to finish school, but she was working on some possibilities. They might let her "test out" of some things, she explained, like the foreign-language requirement. She'd taken Spanish in high school, and living with Olga had improved her skills enough that she thought she could pass.

Olga's car wasn't in the driveway yet, so we sat on the front stoop. Mary kept forgetting to give me a key.

Helena came out of her house to fetch the trashcan. She called out, "Peace!" and gave me the V-sign, and I gave her one back. I had drawn peace symbols all over my school notebooks. Helena was pretty. She had on an Indian-style headband.

Olga drove up. "¿Como estuvo tu día?" she asked Autumn, and Autumn giggled back, "Bue-no."

I couldn't wait to take Spanish in high school. I was getting such a great head start.

"Will you stay to eat with us?" Olga asked.

"No thanks. Mom's expecting me."

Daisy came outside. Her blond hair was always a mess, and she was wearing somebody's old Army jacket. "Want to come over tonight?" she called to Olga. "Timmy and Arch are bringing their guitars."

"I have la niña tonight." Olga said, gesturing toward Autumn. "Maybe tomorrow?"

"Usual Friday shindig," Daisy replied. "Hey, Stacy, you want a quick lesson?"

"Well . . ." I looked at my watch. "Just a few minutes. I have to get home."

Daisy had a folk acoustic guitar with nylon strings, and she was teaching me some basic chords out of her Bob Dylan songbook. She had a lovely voice and liked to sing Joan Baez songs. I wished I could sing, but at least I was learning to play.

I strummed along to a couple of records. "You're doing so well." Daisy beamed at me. "Did you get a guitar yet?"

"Not yet, but my birthday is soon and I have my parents talked into it. I think my mom wants me to take real lessons somewhere though. So I can play at the guitar mass."

"I've showed you all I really know myself." Daisy tapped her lower lip. "Maybe Timmy could teach you. He's pretty good."

Timmy smiled all the time and wore round wire-frame glasses, like John Lennon. I didn't think my mom would like him.

Helena came downstairs. She had something small and white in her hand that she tried to hide, but I knew what it was.

"I have to go now," I said. "Thanks for the lesson."

They both smiled.

"Come by again," Daisy said.

· ·

I got my birthday guitar, bought some songbooks with my baby-sitting money (Mrs. Andrews did end up asking me to watch the boys a few times), and set about learning more. I didn't tell anybody but Julie Gardner that I really wanted to progress to electric guitar. I wanted to play like Keith Richards. Even if girls didn't do that.

Finally, school was out. I should have been happy, but I was bored senseless. Matt had a part-time job, and Tommy was off touring with another theater company now that he'd finished his first National Guard stint. Mary wasn't taking a class, but she still had work. And Julie's family had rented a Winnebago to drive all the way to Tahoe to camp, so she wouldn't be around for weeks.

Mary let Autumn sleep over some Saturday nights, and that was the best part of my week. She slept in the twin bed that used to be Mary's, and sometimes in the night she'd climb into mine.

One evening Dad said at dinner, "Well, looks like that deal for the Oakley place went through. They were surveying over there when I drove back from a call today."

"That's such a shame," Mom said. "It's nice having a farm so close by."

"What are they surveying for?" I asked Dad.

"Houses, sweetheart. A development called Oakley Estates. Looks like Mary will get some new neighbors. Of course, Mrs. Ramsey's field will be a buffer for the people on that side of the Park."

· ·

The next day I rode my bike down Cobbs and checked it out. There were indeed survey crews there, putting sticks in the ground with flags on them. The old Oakley house had been empty for a long time, ever since Mr. Oakley had died. One of his sons had kept the farm going, but he didn't live there, and Dad had been saying for a couple of years that he thought it would be sold soon.

I looked closely at the Oakley house. We passed it now and then, but I'd never paid much attention to it. Now I realized how shabby it was. Would they tear it down, or build the houses around it?

"They'll tear it down," Dad said when I asked that night. "Or burn it."

"*Burn* it?"

"They do that sometimes with old abandoned houses. They've probably taken everything of value out already, any copper pipes or fixtures. They let the fire department burn it as a training exercise. Easier and cheaper than tearing it down."

I was still horrified. It was bad enough they'd plow up all those fields and build more houses. Why couldn't they just fix this one?

"Old houses like that are expensive to keep up and heat." Dad was reading my mind again. "Oakley's son tried to rent it, but it's too big and needs too much work. So it will go along with the barn and outbuildings."

I didn't care about the barn or the other buildings, but I felt bad for the house.

• • • • • • • • • • • • • • •

A couple of weeks later, the local paper ran an article about Oakley Estates, with drawings of what the houses would look like. Some of the larger models had two-car garages. They all had extra bathrooms and family rooms and walk-in closets, and they were designed in a "neo-Colonial" style, whatever that was.

Mom didn't throw that section of the paper away. It stayed in the living room for a few days, and she kept looking it over.

"Maybe we should think about one of those places," she suggested to Dad one night. "They're so spacious. And we'd have an extra bathroom."

"Why do we need more space?" Dad asked. "We're down to two kids, one in high school. We needed another bathroom ten years ago, but we've gotten by."

"But it will be a *new* neighborhood. With the right kinds of people," she argued. "Goodness knows what's happening in this one. Negroes and Puerto Ricans and Filipinos moving in. Groups of airmen renting a place and treating it like a rooming house. There's an *abandoned* house over on Beech near the shopping center. And those awful people on Mary's street—I can't stand to think about it. If we got a larger place, maybe she'd consider moving home. And even if not, we'll still need the space for Autumn if she's going to keep staying with us."

"Hold on, Evelyn." Dad raised his hand. "First, Negroes have the right to live where they please, as long as they can afford it. Most of the ones here are Air Force, and they're fine people. They keep their houses up as well, or better, than some of the white families. I can't say I approve of everyone who's moved here the last few years, but that's true of any neighborhood. The problem is that people can't be satisfied to fix up their own place and set down roots. They have to keep moving to the next exciting thing, and that's what Oakley Estates is. In a few years it'll have the same problems. It's the nature of life nowadays."

Mom didn't say anything more then, but for the next few weeks she kept dropping hints about Oakley Estates.

I, meanwhile, kept an eye on the Oakley property every time I went to Mary's. I knew better than to walk through the Ramsey bean field for a closer look (I never forgot Dad's lecture about private property), but I would ride or stroll down Cobbs Road to see if anything was happening yet.

One Sunday morning I walked Autumn home after she'd spent the night. Sometimes Mom took her to church with us on Sundays, but this weekend we'd gone to the Saturday afternoon guitar mass instead.

To my surprise, Daisy's friend Arch was sitting in the living room when we got to Mary's. I wasn't sure I liked him. He was more intense than Mary's other hippie friends, who were always smiling and friendly. Mary said he was serious about politics and social justice, and that he was very smart. He was handsome, too, in a kind of hippie way, with dark hair and a beard. His guitar was leaning against the stair banister.

"I didn't expect you yet." Mary seemed flustered. She hugged Autumn. "Did you have fun at Grandmom's?"

"We toasted marshyellows!" Autumn exclaimed. "Pop-Pop made hamburgers outside after church, and me and Stacy had marshyellows. Matt made one on fire and ate it!"

"That's nice, sweetheart," Mary said. "Stacy, you've met Arch before. He's friends with Daisy and Helena . . ."

"I know," I said. "Hi."

He just nodded to me.

"Where's Olga?" I asked.

"She stayed with a friend," Mary answered.

"I thought both of you were going to a party last night." I tried not to sound like Mom.

"We did. In town." Mary was turning red. "Do you want something to drink?"

"I'll get it." I went into the kitchen and checked the fridge for the pitcher of water that was usually there. The pitcher was there, but it held a few pieces of fruit and some smelly red wine. I ran tap water instead.

Back in the living room, Autumn was spreading out junk from her toy basket, and Arch was standing by the door holding his guitar.

"Thanks for the advice," Mary said as she followed him outside. I saw her whisper something to him. He touched her hand and then went over to Daisy's house.

"It stinks in here," I said to Mary when she came in. "Like Daisy's stupid incense."

"She gave me some." Mary opened a window. "Arch is helping me decide what course to take in the fall." I noticed a college course catalog on the coffee table. "He's a grad student, in sociology."

"What's sociology?" I asked.

"It's the study of human social behavior. Not individual behavior, like psychology. More like our social institutions, and how we organize ourselves."

"That sounds interesting," I said. "Like neighborhoods?"

"Yes, that would be one example."

"I think you should take it, then."

Mary smiled. "I think I will."

·························

Something told me not to mention Arch's visit to my parents. They didn't like some of Mary's friends anyway, and something weird was going on. Well, I had a whole boring summer to investigate.

But spying on Mary and the Oakley property both proved un-illuminating over the next week—until I dropped in on Daisy one day to show her how much I had progressed with my guitar, that is.

We played some things together and strummed along with some records. She sang "Little Boxes" and giggled. "That's this street," she said, waving her hand.

The door opened, and Helena walked in with Arch. He looked at me sort of funny.

"Thanks for the lift," Helena said. She gave him a smoochy kiss, and they used their tongues. It was both gross and fascinating. He left, and I felt relief that one of the theories that had been nagging at me couldn't be true. He must be dating Helena. So there couldn't have been any funny business with Mary.

·························

The next week, my two spying projects converged.

"They're burning the Oakley house on Saturday morning," Dad announced. "Anyone want to come watch?"

"I do!" I said, jumping out of my chair.

Dad laughed. "I thought you were against this whole development process."

"I am. But I want to see what they do."

On the day of the fire, part of Cobbs Road was blocked off, and the closest we could get was across the street. Several people had gathered to watch.

The firemen went inside. Soon they came out, and puffs of smoke appeared from all corners of the house.

Dad put his arm around me. "Sort of feels backwards, doesn't it? Firemen setting the fire, then leaving the building. Now they'll just make sure it doesn't spread where it's shouldn't, and put it out when enough of the structure has burned down."

The firemen moved on to the barn, and we watched the house burn for a while. When we'd seen enough, Dad said, "Let's walk back. We'll stop in and see Mary."

My heart began to pound as we approached Spruce Court. I hoped Daisy and Helena weren't around with any "incense," and that stupid Arch wasn't either. He wasn't nice like Timmy.

To my relief, just Mary and Olga were there, playing with Autumn and cleaning the house. We told them we'd been to see the fire, and Mary laughed.

"We saw the smoke. You mean Matt isn't over there trying to walk on the roof?"

"He's at Indian River, camping with the Bakers for the weekend," Dad said. "We're down a man, if you want Autumn to come over."

"Autumn, do you want to go to Pop-Pop's tonight?" Mary asked. "Dad, you really don't mind taking her again? Olga and I are hosting a potluck."

"Of course not." Dad picked up Autumn. "We'll take her to the church carnival tomorrow and bring her back by dinnertime. Do you have her things ready?"

"You don't have to take her now," Mary said. "I'll run her over, or maybe Stacy can come by . . ."

"I will," I said. "I can check on whether the house has finished burning on the way."

. . . .

I walked back over at four. An acrid smoke cloud hung over the whole area, discouraging me from detouring up Cobbs Road.

When I got to Mary's I looked out the kitchen window across the field. All I could see through the trees on the far side of the field was smoke.

Olga was cooking something that smelled delicious, competing with the smoke. "People will bring food tonight," she said. "But I know what they do. They all bring desserts!"

Mary came downstairs with Autumn's overnight bag.

"Not much of a night for a dinner party, with all that smoke," I said.

"Guess we picked the wrong one." She shrugged.

"Who's coming, anyway?"

"Some of Olga's friends, the neighbors, Timmy and Arch . . ."

The door opened, and a young man rushed in, holding a bottle of wine. Mary smiled. "She's in the kitchen."

The man handed the wine to Mary and lunged at Olga, who had run into the room. They did some of that tongue kissing, with Olga murmuring something in Spanish I didn't catch. He gripped her face in his hands. "I followed the smoke until I found your flame," he said.

I rolled my eyes at Mary. She just said, "Stacy, this is Ron."

Ron didn't acknowledge me. He seemed to be trying to swallow Olga's face.

"Let's hit the road, Autumn," I said, and took her hand.

She wrinkled her nose when we got outside. "It stinks."

"It's the fire over on the farm."

"Did the animals get hurt?" Her eyes filled with tears. I put down her bag and knelt next to her. "No, honey, the animals went to live on other farms, and the fire was on purpose, to get rid of some stuff. They're going to build houses there."

"I love houses!" she squealed, her tears forgotten.

I hugged her. "Me too. Maybe I'll learn to love the new ones."

When we got home, Mom and I had to close all the windows and run the air conditioner in the living room because of the smoke.

"Those houses in Oakley Estates will all have central air," she said to Dad.

The smoke was giving me a headache. I was glad Autumn fell asleep early.

·····················•

I still felt lousy the next morning.

"Let her sleep," Mom cautioned Autumn at the door of my room. "She has a bad headache." She came over to me and said gently, "Stacy, we're taking Autumn to church and then the carnival. So you can rest all day if you need to." She patted my cheek.

I slept for a couple of hours. Then I got hungry, so I got up and made some toast with peanut butter. When I opened the kitchen door, the air seemed clearer, though there was still a trace of smoke. I closed the door and swallowed a couple of aspirin.

Sunday morning TV was boring. Despite my headache, I felt like going for a bike ride. I pedaled east, away from the smoke. As I approached the abandoned house on Beech, I slowed down and looked at it—peeling paint, grass nearly a foot tall. Why would someone abandon a perfectly good house in Arboria Park? This wasn't a farm.

I decided I wanted to see the burned house after all. I cruised by slowly. Yellow police tape stretched across the front of the property, and the house and outbuildings were just piles of blackened rubble.

My curiosity satisfied, I headed for Mary's to see how the party had gone and maybe find out what the deal was with Olga and Ron. I was also trying to swallow my dislike of Arch enough to see if Mary or Helena could ask him about why someone would abandon a perfectly good house, and if Dad was right about why people like Mom wanted to move somewhere else. Maybe *sociology* held the answers.

Nobody answered when I knocked on the door, but Mary's and Olga's cars were both in the driveway. I thought maybe the party had run late and they were sleeping in. I turned to go, but just then Olga opened the door, wearing a baby-doll nightgown. With no jewelry or red lipstick, she looked so different. Her hair was disheveled, and she still had on some smeary mascara.

"Mary is not here," she said, and started to close the door.

"Where is she?" I asked.

Olga sighed and held the door open a crack. "She is out."

I heard a man's voice inside. "Who is it, baby?" It was Ron.

"She will be back later." Olga shut the door.

....

Back home, I lay on the couch and tried to read. My head hurt again.

Mom and Dad came home around three. Autumn ran over to me and babbled about the carnival and the pony ride and the cotton candy.

"How are you feeling?" Mom asked, leaning over me.

"A little better. I just took some more aspirin."

"Get Autumn's things and I'll run her back home," Dad said to Mom.

"I'll take her." I sat up. "I kind of feel like getting out."

"The wind did blow the smoke away," Dad said. "But are you sure you feel like it, sweetheart?"

"I'm sure." I took the overnight bag from Mom. "Come on, Autumn, let's go tell your mom and Olga about the carnival."

Autumn chattered all the way over. She'd had way too much sugar at the carnival. When we got to her house, Mary and Olga were in the kitchen, cleaning up from the party. Autumn threw herself at Mary, still yammering away.

"I have to go," I said, and fled. I couldn't look at them.

Olga followed me outside. "Stacy, may I walk with you?"

I shrugged, and she strolled down the court with me. "There are things you need to understand. Your sister did not want you to know about them yet, because you are young. But you see things and wonder, so you have to know." She stopped at the corner and clasped her hands together. "That man Ron is from my work. He is good to me. We go to dinner and to dance. Then I forget Jerry and how he made me feel like a nothing. The same is for your sister. Her heart was broken. She is lonely. She needs to heal."

"It's Arch, isn't it?" I said. "She's been, well, *sleeping* with Arch. What kind of name is *Arch*, anyway?"

"Yes, Arch. And why? She talks to him about her education, and the war and the politics that those others"—she waved her hand back at Spruce Court—"those others are too silly to know about. They listen to their music and they think that will change the world. They call the soldiers bad names, when Mary is afraid for the father of her child."

I nodded. This I understood. Don was on a flight crew now, and there was some talk that they might be sent to Southeast Asia. I knew Mary was scared for him.

"Arch studies to learn to make the world better. Mary wants to teach and help people. So they are both like that. But she doesn't want a heartbreak again. It's too soon. He cannot break her heart, because she will not fall in love with him. He is not what she wants in other ways, and she does not want to be with him for long. And he will not love her, either. He has been with Helena and so many others . . ." She trailed off, and we walked silently for a moment toward Maple. "He is finished at the school in August, and then he is going away. She knows. So he makes her feel good for the summer, and she has fun, and then she will work hard and study again."

It did make sense, in a way. But I couldn't imagine why Mary would want to sleep with someone she wasn't in love with. At least she thought she'd been in love with Don.

Olga put her hand on my arm and said in a low voice, "Don't

worry that she will have another baby. We know ways to prevent the pregnancies."

I couldn't believe she was talking about condoms and sex to me. Europeans sure did things differently.

"For me," she said, "now my life is for fun. And freedom. For Mary, it is for her child and becoming educated. We both will help her, yes?"

"Tell Mary I won't tell anybody, and that I'm okay," I said.

"Yes. She will want to talk to you herself, later." Olga turned to go back home. "And please know she never does wrong things when the *niña* is home. She loves her more than life. And Ron does not stay with me when she is there."

·······················

Dad was coming out of the house when I got home. "I'm going to Strommer's to get barbecued chicken and potato salad for dinner. We ate at the carnival with Autumn, so we're not that hungry. I told your mother not to bother cooking tonight."

"I'll go with you," I said.

As we drove toward the shopping center, I said, "Can we drive by that house on Beech? The abandoned one?"

"I suppose." Dad turned on Beech. "But why?"

"I don't know. Something about abandoned houses gets to me. I mean, I understood about Oakley's. It's like you see those houses out in the country with trees growing out of them when people get land poor, like you told me. But why would someone abandon a house in Arboria Park?"

Dad slowed down so we could look at the house. "Could be a lot of things," he said. "The owner might have died and not left a will, or maybe left one that takes time to sort out. Maybe the owner couldn't pay for it and just left. Maybe they want to rent it and they don't have a tenant yet, and for some reason they're not taking care of it."

"What if everybody feels like Mom does, and they all move

to Oakley Estates or some other new place they're building? What happens then?"

"I hope not everybody feels like your mother does, and they'll stay. Some won't. They want the central air and the big garage, and they'll go. Nothing wrong with that as long as another family moves in who wants a smaller house, or who can't afford a bigger one."

We got to the shopping center but sat outside the deli in the car.

"There's something you have to understand about your mother," Dad said. "We both came from small towns where people worked hard for very little. She's from coal country, and my relatives worked in the steel mills. People died young. The war—World War II—was a terrible thing, but it did provide some opportunities when it was over. It meant we didn't have to live that life. I learned skills in the Army I could use at home. Lots of the boys did, or they used the G.I. Bill to go to college. We could afford to buy nice houses and raise our children with more than we ever dreamed of. For me, that's enough. But for some folks, it's not."

"Like Mom?"

Dad rubbed his head. "Your mother has always been afraid that we're all being judged by what we have, and that what counts is what other people think about us. And she's a perfectionist, and sometimes she takes that out on you kids without meaning to. Her vision of life doesn't allow for any bumps or wrong turns. Every time one of you makes a mistake or veers from the path, she's sure it's because we didn't provide enough for you, somehow, and that if you had just been exposed to the 'right' people and experiences, you'd have turned out better. Well, Mary was a model daughter in every way, had the best kinds of friends imaginable, dated a boy we all approved of. And things went haywire anyway." He opened the car door. "Come on, let's get some chicken."

....

Over the next week, I thought about it all some more—what Olga had told me, and Dad too. I told Mary I would never tell on her and that I understood, even though I still didn't completely get it. And she told me what Olga had: Arch was going to Chicago to get his Ph.D. And Daisy and Helena were leaving for California in a VW bus with Timmy.

"Sometimes people and things come along when you need them," Mary reflected. "Olga and I had a terrible time last year, and we needed some fun in our lives. I guess we had some things to get out of our systems."

The week before school started, someone finally cut the grass at the house on Beech, and workmen fixed the sagging gutter and painted the trim. A "For Sale" sign went up. By then, though, I'd noticed another empty house on Maple getting the same overgrown look. Through the fall, the houses started going up on the Oakley farm, laid out on long avenues and short cul-de-sacs, out to Foster Road.

6—1970

. . . .

"Anastasia Louise, you are not leaving this house looking like that."

I glared at Mom and stomped back to my room. I was on my way out to Julie's, wearing a loose T-shirt Tommy had left behind after a brief visit home. It said PROPERTY OF NEW YORK AESTHETIC CLUB, and almost covered my denim cut-offs.

In my room, I rooted around. Most of my stuff was in the washing machine in the basement, and there were a few new "school clothes" hanging in the closet. I couldn't believe school started in only two weeks.

I put on my favorite blouse, the one with a tiny floral pattern. It was two years old and getting tight under the arms, so this summer I was getting the last out of it. I'd about finished my growth spurts, I figured. At age fifteen, I was now five foot seven, and I didn't have to worry about my weight. I kept the shorts on. Mom didn't like me wearing cut-offs, or anything too short, but this was my most "acceptable" pair. Mary had helped me embroider flowers on all the pockets.

I looked at myself in the mirror and decided it wouldn't hurt to clean up a little. After all, Julie and I might decide to walk to the shopping center or something. I put on pink Yardley lipstick and some mascara. People said my dark eyes were my best feature. Lord knew I didn't have many. My chestnut hair still wouldn't go straight, though I now wore it at chin length. Some tiny gold earrings and I was all set.

With the lipstick and my latest wad of babysitting cash in my pocket, I made a second attempt to get out of the house. Matt's bedroom door was closed. After graduation, he'd started working as a hospital orderly in the emergency room, and now he was studying to be a paramedic. And he'd been right: our folks actually approved of his choice. But I knew he just wanted to speed around in an ambulance.

I twirled my way through the living room in front of Mom. "Acceptable now?"

She sighed, which I took as an okay. I beat it out the door before she could change her mind.

The day was warm and breezy, without the killer humidity we'd had all week. Its beauty exacerbated my restlessness. Summer hadn't been that interesting, and now that it was tumbling to an end I wanted something to happen.

Being a teenager wasn't anything like I had hoped. Times had changed. Most people didn't care about things like proms and dances, and boys didn't ask you out on real dates. You just hung out, and that wasn't easy. The Soda Spot had closed down, and now it was a paint store. The new fast-food places didn't encourage kids to hang around. You had to buy something, eat it quickly, and get out. I knew my parents were watching me closely because of what happened with Mary, but they didn't have much to worry about. I'd managed to just barely clear the hurdles of being asked out and kissing, but I was a long way from having to make any decisions about sex. Julie and I were neither popular nor outcasts, and the average kinds of boys we liked hadn't quite realized yet that they weren't going to get the it-girls and turned to ones like us.

As I slowed down my bike approaching Julie's house, I noticed Richie Oliva and another boy playing basketball on

Richie's driveway. Richie lived next door to Julie and was kind of a jerk. I didn't recognize the other boy, who had dark hair and eyes. Though he wasn't that tall, he was outmaneuvering Richie, running around him to sink basket after basket and laughing. Richie was stocky and lumbering; this boy was quick and sort of graceful, almost, and his arms looked strong.

How would they feel around me? I nearly fell off the bike. I made myself stop staring before they saw me.

Julie hadn't mentioned any new boys in her end of the neighborhood, and that was something she'd notice. Had she been holding out on me?

As soon as I got inside the door I asked, "Who's the guy playing basketball with Richie?"

"What guy?" She leaned out the door, but I pulled her back. Conveniently, one of the windows in her room overlooked the Olivas' driveway. I dragged her to it and we stood just to its side, peering around the white café curtains. Through the open window we could hear the boys joshing each other.

Julie shrugged. "Beats me. I've never seen him before. Should we go talk to them?"

"Won't it look weird if we go talk to Richie? We're usually trying not to."

The boys stopped bouncing the ball and went inside Richie's house. I collapsed on Julie's bed.

"You okay?" she asked.

"I don't know." I didn't. Julie was the boy-crazy one, not me. Not that I didn't get crushes, but not on sight, and not this hard, this fast.

"Look what we bought for school," she said, pulling clothes out of a shopping bag. We looked them over and talked about what went with what.

I heard the Olivas' screen door slam, and I ran to the window. The guys were walking down the driveway.

"Come on," Julie said. "Let's follow them."

"Isn't that a little obvious?"

"It's a free country. Maybe they're going to the shopping center."

We dashed outside. The boys were walking away from us, toward the corner. "Act natural," Julie cautioned, like we followed boys around all the time.

At the corner they turned left instead of right toward the shopping center. "Now what?" I asked.

Julie made the turn too. "Maybe they're going to the playground. We can act like we are, anyway."

They stopped at Brad Staiger's house on Mimosa and knocked on the door. We had no choice but to walk past and head for the playground. Younger teens like us, carless and jobless, sometime hung out there if there weren't a bunch of little kids around.

"Hey, wait up." I heard Richie's voice behind us. "You guys going to the playground?"

"Yeah, just seeing who's around." Julie glanced back, acting totally casual.

"Brad's not home." Richie walked up to us. "His dad has a cool pool table in the basement. Man, it's boring around here."

The other guy sort of smiled at us and said, "Hi, I'm Greg."

"Oh, yeah." Richie remembered his manners. "This is my cousin, Greg Martinez. This is Julie from next door, and, um . . ."

"Stacy Halloran." I managed to get my own name out.

"We'll wish we were this bored when school starts." Julie walked toward Cedar.

I reluctantly followed. What if this was my only chance to talk to Greg? But she'd played it just right. They fell in step with us.

There were a couple of little kids at the playground, messing around on the spinner. We walked past them over to the igloo-shaped jungle gym. The boys climbed on one side of it and sat down on one of the metal bars, facing in. We got on the other side, facing them. Standard jungle gym etiquette.

"Are you visiting Richie's family?" I asked Greg. It came out wrong, and obvious. Of course he was.

"Yeah, my parents went to a wedding down at the beach. My older sister is working in New York, and my little brother's at camp. So they brought me along to hang out with Richie. We got here yesterday."

I let Julie ask, "Where are you from?"

"New Jersey. Not too far from Philly."

"I wish we'd gone to Jersey instead of you coming here." Richie climbed to the top of the structure.

"It's not so interesting there, either." Greg grinned.

"Next summer I'll have a car," Richie bragged.

"Then you can drive it to summer school," Julie taunted him, and they started bickering back and forth, like they always did.

"That's a pretty shirt," Greg said to me.

I felt myself turning red. "Thanks."

"My sister studies fashion design at Parsons. That's why she's in New York this summer. Some kind of internship."

"My brother lives in New York. He's an actor."

"No kidding. Broadway?"

"He wishes. Some parts in plays, some TV commercials. If he needs money he goes on tour doing musicals."

"That's cool. Do you want to do that too?"

"Not really. I don't know what I want to do."

"Me either. I like history and I like science, but I don't know what I want to do yet."

"I wish we could have talked your folks into taking us to the beach," Richie said, interrupting us.

"Me too," Greg agreed. "We go to the beach in Jersey sometimes. Wildwood, Margate, places like that. We even went to Atlantic City last summer, but it was weird and kind of sad. All these big hotels, falling apart, and this seedy boardwalk that probably used to be cool."

"Were any of the hotels abandoned?" I asked. Richie and even Julie looked at me like I was crazy, but Greg didn't, so I added, "Abandoned buildings fascinate me. I'd love to see a big, abandoned hotel."

"Some were," Greg said. "My dad trained in the Army there during World War II. They marched on the boardwalk. He says the hotels were grand back then."

"That's what gets me about empty buildings. Somebody went to a lot of trouble to design and build them, and make everything just right. Then suddenly nobody wants them anymore, and the same place that somebody loved falls apart. And new ones are built without fixing up the old ones." I stopped and felt myself blushing. What a way to impress a boy, babbling about abandoned buildings.

Greg leaned forward. "That's what fascinates me about history. Not what famous guy did what famous thing when. The way people lived, the things they used. Like when you walk around the old part of Philly, with Independence Hall and all the brick sidewalks. People lived there and walked around working and talking while the founders were doing their thing. And before them, Indians. They hunted and made stuff."

He got it. Not only was he not treating me like a nut job, he was into it. I was bursting to tell him more, about our historic district downtown with its own brick sidewalks, the farms turned into housing developments, Arboria Park itself.

But Julie stepped in, thinking she was rescuing me from total humiliation. "Ever been down to Ocean City? They have a big amusement park there and everything . . ." And she went on about all the cool things in Ocean City. Richie described all the different roller coasters he'd ridden, and I made a few brief comments to show I really was a regular girl and not some weird ghost hunter or something.

A car pulled up and Brad Staiger leaned out and yelled, "Hey, Richie!" I couldn't see the driver.

Richie hopped off the jungle gym, and Greg followed. Julie and I stayed put. I hoped she'd wait until we went home before telling me what a dork I'd been.

The boys conferred briefly with Brad, and then the car drove off. "Brad says a bunch of people are gonna be down here tonight,"

Richie announced as they came back over. "That was Darrell Smith driving, and he might even be able to scrounge up some beer from his old man's stash. You girls gonna come by?"

"Sure," I said before Julie could answer.

"We're going over to Brad's now," Richie said.

Julie did the right thing again. "Yeah, maybe we'll go to the shopping center," she said, so we got to walk with them as far as Brad's house.

We kept going on Mimosa until we were sure they were inside, then turned back to Julie's. Then, as I knew she would, she let me have it.

"Geez, Stacy, way to go. Better tune up your conversation skills with boys before school starts."

"I *know*. Listen, can I stay here tonight? I just know Mom won't let me out to go to the playground, and I don't feel like coming up with a bunch of lies. It'll be easier if I'm here."

"Sure. Come over right after dinner. We better figure out something cool to wear."

....

I raced home on my bike and told Mom I was spending the night at Julie's. She didn't put up a fight about it; Julie and I stayed at each other's houses all the time.

Julie and I had been to a couple of playground gatherings earlier in the summer. Just a bunch of kids hanging around talking about how bored they were, nothing much. But tonight Greg Martinez would be there. I took the laundry in from the clothesline and folded it up without Mom even asking me to, hoping to find the perfect thing to wear. But somehow nothing seemed quite right, not even any of my new clothes. I could wear my favorite pair of jeans, which had another embroidered flower on the front pocket, and a beaded tie belt. And Greg had complimented my blouse, so should I wear it again? No, I'd gotten it all sweaty.

I grabbed the first top I thought I could stand out of the clean laundry, then took a shower and doused myself with Muguet des Bois before walking back down to Julie's. It was the perfect summer night to hang around outside.

We got ready in Julie's room, playing songs like "Summer in the City" and "Cherry Hill Park" to get us in the right mood. I ended up wearing Julie's white peasant blouse, which showed off my tan, and fussed with my hair until it was as good as it would ever be.

"You look *fine*," Julie reassured me. "Your hair is beautiful. And it'll be dark, anyway."

"I know this is stupid," I said, putting on just a touch of lipstick again. I didn't want to look like I was trying too hard and overdo it, so I skipped the blue frosted eye shadow and big peace-sign earrings I'd brought. We both wore bead necklaces we'd made from kits we got at the shopping center; mine was blue and Julie's red to match her red-and-white-striped bellbottoms.

She tied on her fringed belt and said, "Let's go. The street-lights are coming on."

There were about a half dozen kids congregated over by the swings and jungle gym as we walked up. Richie and Greg were among them.

We all climbed onto the jungle gym again. This time Greg sat next to me. He still had on the black T-shirt and jeans he'd worn earlier. We didn't get a chance to say much to each other at first, though, because more kids arrived and everyone was talking back and forth. Someone brought a portable radio and turned it on to the Top 40 station, facing the field, not too loud. Everybody knew the rules of hanging out: Don't make so much noise that the people on Cedar or Birch got mad and chased us away.

Greg turned to me. "You look nice," he said.

I got red again. "Thanks." Tommy James and the Shondells' "Crimson and Clover" came on the radio. I was glad it wasn't "I Think We're Alone Now," because I just would have died on the spot.

Richie and a few others started clowning around and showing off on the jungle gym, hanging upside down and swinging

around. Most of the rest of us headed off toward a group gathering at the swings. Greg stayed by my side, but I was paralyzed:
Julie had promised not to interfere with my interactions with
him, but I was afraid of saying something stupid again.

Darrell showed up with the beer, but he hadn't been able to
swipe much. A few cans got passed around, so all I got was a sip
after Greg handed one to me. I was irrationally glad I got it after
he drank out of it.

Carolyn Fenner and her breasts arrived, and I was dismayed
as Greg's gaze fixed on them, along with every other guy's. You
couldn't *not* notice them—each one as big as your head, barely
contained in a halter top carefully chosen to look like it might fail
at its task any moment. I held my breath as she eyed us, but then
she flounced over to Darrell and two other older guys. Clearly,
they were the alpha males of the gathering; Richie Oliva's cousin
wasn't worth her time.

Once Greg gotten his eyeful, he turned back to me. "What's
that big field between the houses?" he asked.

I had to explain it properly, didn't I?

"This development, Arboria Park, used to be an orchard
that was part of a farm. That field is still part of it, and those lights
directly across are another development they put on another farm.
My mom wants to move there, but I don't like the houses. There
are no windows on the sides, only the front and back." I glanced
around to see if Julie was in earshot. She was sitting on the spinner,
kissing Gary Sampson. Julie had crushes on him and Mike Ippolito,
but Gary was here tonight and Mike wasn't, so that was that. Beth
Conley and Brad Staiger were making out on the other side.

Someone passed a lit joint to me. Greg took it before I could
and handed it to someone else, and I was grateful.

"A lot of New Jersey used to be farms too," he said. "Like
we were talking about before. There were probably Revolutionary
War soldiers walking around where they're building shopping
malls now."

I liked how he said "we" were talking. Together, we drifted away from the main group of kids, to where the edge of the playground met the field. Darkness had settled. Greg looked up. "You can see a little bit of sky over here, away from those streetlights," he said. "You can't where I live." He pointed. "Is that the Big Dipper? Over there, like kind of over those houses sticking out in the field?"

"I don't know the constellations very well," I admitted. "But my dad taught me the stars in the Big Dipper. Alkeid, Mizar, Alioth, Megrez, Phecda, Merak, and Dubhe," I recited. "Back before Arboria Park had streetlights, we could see the stars better. My dad had to memorize all the constellations during the war so he could navigate at night. He was in the Air Corps. Then they sent him to the South Pacific, and he had to learn all new ones because he was in a different hemisphere!"

"Maybe he knew my dad or my Uncle Miguel," Greg said. "They were in the Air Corps. My dad stayed in after the war, got his twenty years in. Now he's in charge of security for a big company. We moved around a lot when I was a little kid, but since he got this job we've lived in Jersey."

"I've never lived anywhere but here. My dad works for the phone company."

As I looked for the Big Dipper, I saw a shooting star. Before I could say anything, Greg grabbed my arm. "Did you see that?"

"The shooting star? Yeah. I saw one once before, when I was little," I babbled. "You're supposed to make a wish." As I said it, I made one—that this moment with Greg Martinez would never end.

"Tell me more about the farms and stuff you were talking about earlier," he urged.

So I talked about Mrs. Ramsey and the apple orchard, finishing up with, "That's why we're standing here on the edge instead of going into the field. I try to respect her property." I was sounding dorky again.

"Not quite a full moon." Greg looked up. "I think it's waxing, not waning."

We stood watching for a few minutes more, with the faint noise from the kids laughing and talking behind us, and the radio finishing the long version of the Guess Who's "No Sugar Tonight." I saw another shooting star over the Pines, and this time it was me grabbing Greg's arm.

He laughed. "Saw it too."

"My sister lives over there, in one of those houses," I told him. "With my little niece, Autumn. She's five, and I take care of her a lot. Mary works and goes to college part time and she's an artist too. Her ex-husband's in the Air Force, and he's flying cargo to Vietnam now."

"I don't like the war," Greg confessed. "I mean, I come from a military family, and obviously you do too. But this isn't like the other wars our fathers fought. I hope it's over before I have to make a decision."

I knew somehow that was something he probably didn't share with Richie or too many people. And he was taking a chance that I'd call him a coward or a communist.

"I don't like it. My brother Tommy, the actor I told you about, he went in the National Guard so he wouldn't get drafted. My other brother, Matt, has been okay so far. He's training to be a paramedic. I don't know if that makes him more or less desirable to the military. Even my father isn't that crazy about this war. He says we have to support the president and the country, but I know he doesn't want my brothers to have to go."

Greg touched my hand. "What are you doing?"

I'd unconsciously been fingering chords to Eric Clapton's "Let It Rain." It was playing on the radio. "Sorry," I said. "I play guitar. Well, I try to. I'm not too good."

"That's cool," Greg said. "What kinds of music?"

"I have songbooks for Bob Dylan and stuff like that, to learn the chords. But I'd like to be able to play like James Taylor. Not strumming chords, but like—"

And right at that moment, "Fire and Rain" came on. I laughed.

"Well, like *that*. Where the acoustic guitar isn't just background. He's almost like a classical guitarist, you know? But what I really want is an electric guitar, to play real rock 'n' roll. Girls get stuck playing the folky stuff, but I'd love to really play *hard*. I'm just not any good, though."

"Have you ever head this band from Detroit, MC5?" Greg asked. "They're really good. I bet you'd want to play like—"

"Yes!" I exclaimed. "I can't believe you've heard of them. It's not easy to hear stuff other than what's on the radio. I'm lucky my sister has friends who know about different kinds of music. And Tommy tells me about things in New York."

"Yeah, my sister in New York tells me about stuff too."

We stood there talking for I don't know how long, until the radio went off and a couple of cars drove up and people jumped in. Most of us had curfews of midnight or thereabouts.

"We better get back," Greg said. "Me and Richie have to be in by twelve fifteen."

"We're midnight, but sometimes Julie's dad is watching TV, and if you distract him he doesn't notice the time."

Julie was *still* kissing Gary Sampson, like it was the romance of the century. Greg rounded up Richie, and after Gary left with his friends, the four of us took the shortcut up Birch Street. Greg walked next to me, forcing Julie to walk with Richie. My heart and mind were racing. Would he kiss me good night? I'd never wanted to be kissed so much in my life.

Greg reached for my hand and slowed down, letting Julie and Richie get a little farther ahead. They were arguing about something, as usual.

Once again I was at a loss for something to say, but he wasn't saying anything either. The two-block walk was far too short.

In front of Julie's house, we all said good night, and Greg finally let go of my hand. "It was nice meeting you, Stacy," he said, and then he and Richie went into the Olivas' house.

I stared at Richie's door for a few seconds before following

Julie into her house, where her dad was watching *Twelve O'Clock High* on TV. He didn't notice that we were a few minutes late. He just told us not to stay up all night talking, and let us go to Julie's room.

Julie talked for a while, though. She was already worried that Gary Sampson might not call her, even though she gave him her number, and if she didn't actually go out with him before school started people would gossip about her making out with him all evening. I made sympathetic noises, even though I thought she should have known better. But if Greg Martinez *had* kissed me, would I have done the same? Or more? I turned my face into the pillow.

Finally, she whispered, "So what's up with you and Greg? You guys went off for a while there."

"Just talked. He didn't kiss me."

"Maybe he didn't kiss you good night because Richie and I were there. Listen, I got from Richie that they're going to church tomorrow morning and then meeting Greg's parents at some restaurant for brunch, and then they're going home."

Julie's parents weren't Catholic, and who knew which mass Richie's family would attend? And what restaurant? It didn't matter. He hadn't kissed me or gotten my phone number or address. Still, he didn't have to hold my hand walking home, but he had.

I lay awake on the daybed in Julie's room long after she went to sleep. I thought about Greg next door, maybe in a bunk in Richie's room, or in a guest room, or on the sofa. Was he thinking about me at all?

·····················•

The Olivas must have gone to church early, because the car was gone by the time we got up. Julie promised to work some info out of Richie when she saw him again.

But very little information was forthcoming. Richie hadn't heard from Greg by the time school started. Gary Sampson hung out at Julie's locker a lot, so she didn't have to worry about looking easy. Over the next few months, I studied all the boys in the hallways, and none of them appealed to me anymore.

Finally, after Christmas, I got up the nerve to ask Richie about Greg. He shrugged. "They just moved to California. His dad got a new job."

So it was just that one night—a touch of hands, a conversation in a field under shooting stars and a waxing moon. But I never forgot it, or him.

7—1974

····················

I lay on my bed with the fan on the dresser blowing on me. It was mid-July, and I had just gotten home from my summer waitressing job. Lunch shift. Dad was at work, Mom at the mall. A rare moment of quiet in a hectic week.

Mary was getting married again, on Saturday. This time it was on her terms. She was happy.

Mary had finally graduated from college in late 1971 and gotten a job teaching art in a high school a couple of towns away. She still lived in the pink house on Spruce Court with Autumn. Olga had moved out, but they were still best friends. Mary and some other young teachers at the school had banded together, helping each other out. One of them was JC Harris, the assistant band director. Since Mary taught art and loved music and he taught music and loved art, they were a perfect match.

JC Harris was about Mary's age, and some of his family was local. JC stood for "Josiah Clark," his preacher grandfather's name. His father had served in World War II. (JC had made sure to drop that fact the first time he visited our house, since Mary had told him it would score points with Dad. Dad had asked, "Tuskegee Airmen?" and JC had said no, the infantry.) After the war his father had studied dentistry in Baltimore and stayed there, serving the black community. The Harrises were all musical, and JC had started picking up various instruments as soon as he could walk. His favorites were piano and saxophone. He had a degree in music education from the University of Maryland and a master's in musicology from Reed, and was working on an Ed.D.

You couldn't not like JC. He knew all about every type of music: classical, jazz, blues, opera. He was the first person I knew who listened to Stanley Clark and Gil Scott-Heron, and to own a record by Sam Cooke's brother, but he could get misty-eyed singing along with Mary to Joni Mitchell's "Morning Morgantown," too.

It was great to see them together; they were like two peas in a pod. Mary held her head high when people gave them dirty looks at the mall or made remarks about race mixing. They never acted angry or hurt, just rose above it all. I think JC's family was as flummoxed as ours at first, but they were good people. And now everyone would attend a big, joyful wedding. I was maid of honor, Olga was a bridesmaid, and Autumn had her own special dress and role in the ceremony. They had rented a hall for the ceremony and reception; there would be a DJ and dancing and a bar. Everything Mary had missed the first time around.

Mary wasn't wearing white ("I look too washed out in white," she told me), but she wanted a long dress this time, and lots of flowers. And music. JC's Aunt Mona would sing a gospel solo and play piano during the service, and a string quartet of JC's students would play at the reception during dinner, before the dancing started.

Mary had wanted me to play the guitar during the ceremony, but I'd talked her out of it. I wasn't playing much these days.

Actually, the mere word "guitar" was enough to set off an anxiety attack. Lots of ordinary words did—"grow up," "amateur," "virgin." Even the phrase "first time," used in any context—like, "It was the first time we went to that restaurant"—could send me looking for a door, a restroom, a place to run to.

I knew it wasn't normal. It wasn't normal to cut my arm or leg on purpose and watch the blood, either, or to cross streets without looking, or to steal my mother's unused, expired Valium from the cluttered medicine cabinet. *I'll see a therapist when I go back to college in the fall*, I told myself.

If I went back.

I forced myself to go in the kitchen and make a fancy salad for dinner. Mom was frazzled, as usual. Mary and JC were handling all the wedding details themselves, but Mom still had to clean the house within an inch of its life and worry about things like Tommy driving from New York and what everyone would wear to the wedding. And of course, the big elephant in the room: Her daughter was marrying a black man in front of God and everybody. Well, a hundred guests, anyway.

Matt strolled into the house while I was chopping vegetables, wearing his paramedic uniform. He lived in town now; he'd rented a room in a house full of messy guys. "Make enough for leftovers," he said.

"Begging food again?" I asked. "I can tell it's the middle of the month."

"Yes, I'm broke, but it's because I had a major car repair, smartypants. Transmission, four hundred bucks. Not the bar or scuba-diving lessons, I swear. I get paid next week."

"What about the horse track?" I asked.

"No horse track. I don't go anymore unless Dad wants to, once in a blue moon. To make any money you have to really know about horses, like Gil did. I don't have the patience for it."

Another elephant in the room. He and his "friend" Gil had gone everywhere together for six months; now Gil was gone. But nobody would dare talk about it, not even on pain of death, in front of Matt or otherwise.

Matt reached for a slice of tomato I had cut and startled me, and the tip of the knife I was using to chop onions sliced into my finger.

"Damn!" I held it under a stream of cold water.

"Let me see." Matt alternately wiped off the blood and held my finger under the water, then dried it off and told me to press on it with a paper towel while he found a bandage in his carry bag. It was nice having a paramedic in the family.

Mom came in just as he was wrapping it up. "Oh, my God, what did you do, Stacy?"

"She's fine," Matt said. "Doesn't need stitches or anything. Just a cut finger."

Mom stared at my hand. "How long will she need to wear that?"

"She can probably take it off tomorrow, if you're worried about the wedding," Matt said. "You'll be holding flowers anyway, right, Stace?"

"Honestly, Stacy, you're so accident prone these days. Please be more careful."

Matt winked at me. He knew better than anyone, having tended my cuts and bruises all summer.

"When's Tommy getting here?" Matt rooted in the fridge for a beer.

"Around five, I think," I said. "They're renting a car."

"I can't believe he's bringing that girl to the wedding," Mom said.

"His girlfriend, Mom," I said. "Jenny. She has a name."

"He's living with her, Stacy. That may be fine in New York, but what if people here find out? And they're staying in a hotel. *Together.* You know that will get around."

"It's 1974, Mom," Matt said. "Not the dark ages."

"Did you find some shoes at the mall?" I tried to distract her.

"Yes. They're not quite what I wanted, but they'll do. It's so hard to know what to wear to this wedding. The bride in turquoise, Autumn in pink, you and Olga and JC's sister in purple . . . Lord knows what the rest of his family will wear. I asked his mother what color she was wearing so we wouldn't clash, and she said her dress was multicolor. I don't know what that means."

"It probably means she's found something that combines all the wedding colors," I said. "Clarice is very tasteful. That suit she wore to the engagement party was gorgeous. You said so yourself."

"We're the hillbillies in this wedding," Matt said, and belched on purpose.

"Hand me the sponge," I said. He tossed it at me and I tried to catch it with my bandaged hand, and missed. Mom sighed.

"You afraid she can't catch the bouquet?" Matt asked her.

"I got the flowers from her first wedding, when I was nine," I said. "So I don't need them again. Olga's practically engaged to that doctor now, anyway. She'll probably catch them." I managed this banter with bile rising in my throat. *Take it easy*, I thought as I wiped up the counter.

Mom and I got dinner in the oven before Tommy and Jenny arrived. We'd all been curious about Jenny, because she was a model. "Just catalogue, and some ads," she told me as we all sat outside having drinks. "I'm not tall enough for high fashion. You have to be a giraffe!"

I hadn't even bothered to change out of my waitress uniform, and I felt greasy and sloppy next to her. She just wore jeans and a T-shirt with a scarf around her neck, but she looked so *chic*.

"How was the trip down?" Dad asked Tommy.

"Not bad. Glad we didn't wait until tomorrow and the weekend traffic."

Mom wasn't saying much, just being super polite and serving drinks and peanuts. Jenny turned to Tommy. "Honey, shouldn't we go check in to the hotel and change for dinner?"

"You just got here," Dad said. "And you don't have to dress up for us." As usual, he was doing a far better job than Mom coping with the situation. "We're all family here."

Mom jumped up and said something about needing more ice.

Tommy grinned. "So, Stace, how's the working world?"

"On lunch shift, not great. Somebody tipped me a whole *quarter* today on eight bucks' worth of food. At least at night, people have the mindset of going out for dinner, and sometimes they've had a drink at the bar first. That loosens up the wallets a little."

"Well, that's why you're going to college," Dad said. "So you won't have to do that for the rest of your life. It's good for a summer, though. Builds character."

"Decide on a major yet?" Tommy asked. "You dropped psych after one semester."

"I don't have to declare until midyear. Maybe sociology," I hedged.

"I thought JC would have you talked into music ed," Tommy said.

I faked a smile, like Mom. "No, *definitely* not music."

Tommy looked at me for a moment, then turned to Dad. "So how are the tomatoes this year?"

"See for yourself, son. We may get a ripe one while you're in town."

Mary and JC arrived with Autumn, and in the flurry I went inside to change clothes and swallow another Valium in the bathroom. We got dinner on the table, and everybody seemed to be having a good time, except for Mom. And maybe me.

After dinner, Tommy and Jenny left for the hotel, and Mary, Autumn, and JC went over to check on the house they'd just bought down on Mimosa. It was one of the four-bedroom models.

"I don't understand why you didn't buy in Oakley Estates," Mom had said when they announced the purchase.

"We looked there. But we couldn't afford what we want. We'll get more house for the money here, and it's just been redone," Mary had explained. "Finished basement rec room, two bathrooms, and space for JC and me to have a studio. And this neighborhood is more diverse. So much better for when we have children."

"You're having more children?" Mom asked, as if the possibility had never occurred to her.

Mary had laughed. "Of course. I'm the age I always wanted

to be to get married and have kids. I want at least one more, and so does JC."

Mom's anxiety had increased exponentially after that conversation. Not enough for her to get a new Valium prescription, though. I wondered if anyone would notice if I removed the bottle from the bathroom, so I could carry it with me. Maybe it was because they were expired, but the relief I got didn't last very long.

I told Mom I'd clean up and load the dishwasher. She and Dad watched some variety show, too loud, in the living room. Matt had a ballgame tuned in on the smaller TV down in the basement. I went down there after I finished cleaning up.

We watched the game in silence, me in the armchair, Matt sprawled on the couch. The basement door opened, and Tommy came down the steps, carrying a plastic bag.

"What are you doing back here?" I asked. "I thought you went to the hotel."

"Forgot my sunglasses," he said. "And I wanted to see you. I have something for you." He handed me the bag.

It was full of tapes, and my heart sank. From the time I was in kindergarten, the thought of so much music would have sent me into spasms of ecstasy. Not now. I forced a smile. "Thanks."

"Okay, now I know for sure," Tommy said, shoving Matt's feet off the sofa so he could sit down. "Something's wrong, Stace. When Mom told me on the phone, I figured she was just overreacting as usual. Then Dad said tonight he hoped I could cheer you up, because you've been down in the dumps all summer. And now you're not rooting through those tapes and jumping up to play them. Something's not right."

"I had a bad semester," I said. "Let's leave it at that. Music doesn't appeal to me anymore. Nothing does. Maybe I'm just depressed."

"Is there something to play these on down here?" Tommy asked.

"Yes. Matt's old tape deck."

Tommy took the bag from me. "Listen to this."

It was a tape of the New York Dolls singing "Trash." Live. In spite of myself, I got all prickly.

Matt turned down the TV. "Man, that's pretty good," he said to Tommy. "Who is it?"

"New York Dolls. Bunch of hairy, macho guys who dress up like women, and they tear up a room."

The tape segued to the Dictators and Television, and then a woman reciting poetry. "That's Patti Smith." Tommy beamed. "The guy who performs next is named Jim Carroll."

Together we listened to tape after tape. They drew me in and carried me away. It had been months since I'd felt that way about any music, and I hadn't listened to any good rock and roll for even longer.

"This is amazing," I told Tommy. "I needed this."

"Why aren't you playing at Mary's wedding?" he asked.

I struggled to explain myself. "I just don't play anymore. I made a detour with folk rock, and it didn't go anywhere for me. This is what I really love. What we're hearing right now."

"Then that's what you should start playing," Tommy said. "You used to talk about it all the time."

"I wasn't any good on folk guitar. I'd be even worse trying to play like . . . like those guys."

"Tom Verlaine and Richard Lloyd? You're right, nobody can play like that. But I think you'd have some fun if you tried. Besides, you liked Johnny Thunders too, and his technique is really terrible if you compare him to somebody like Verlaine. It's raw, but it works."

"I can't waste time on music," I said, pulling at a thread in the chair. "I need to figure out what I'm going to do and be. You guys all just knew. Mom says Mary taught school to her dolls when she was four. You knew you wanted to be an actor when you played one of the Three Kings in the church pageant. And Matt, well, he practically *lived* in the emergency room growing up. He had to become a paramedic."

"You used to love so many things. Like drawing. Why did you stop?"

"Because I couldn't draw as well as Mary. *She's* the artist."

"You drew *differently* than Mary," Tommy said, blowing out an exasperated breath. "Different style. You tried to force yourself to be like her, instead of developing your own style. I have a hunch something like that is going on with the guitar playing. Maybe you couldn't play like Leo Kottke, so you gave up the acoustic. You can't be Tom Verlaine, so you won't even try the electric. But who cares how good you are? You don't have to be a professional to have some fun with it. And I'm sorry, Stace, but you look like you need some fun in your life. Bad. And if you don't want to tell us why, okay, but we're not going to watch you be miserable."

He put in another tape: Lou Reed singing "I'll Be Your Mirror." I'd heard the old Velvet Underground version with Nico, but this was different. I burst into tears.

After a couple of minutes, though, I found myself feeling better—lighter, somehow. Tommy handed me a tissue, and I blew my nose. "Thanks. I guess I needed to do that."

"Don't worry if you can't figure your life out right away," Tommy said. "You're only nineteen, for heaven's sake."

I looked at the clock. "Don't you need to get back to Jenny?"

"She'll be okay. She's gone to sleep already."

The tape moved on to another odd-sounding girl.

"Debbie Harry, from The Stilettos," Tommy said. "Nobody playing in New York right now has what you'd call any kind of traditional talent. They just make it up on their own."

We listened some more, and I felt calm, like the first half hour after taking Valium.

"So how are things going with you, Matt?" Tommy asked.

Matt shrugged.

"You ought to be a paramedic in Manhattan, if you want some real action," Tommy said. "All the life-threatening situations you could ever hope for. And that's just walking to work."

Matt laughed.

"You might find other things more tolerable too," Tommy added. "You could be yourself up there. Homosexuals don't have such a hard time where there are a lot of theater and art communities, and there's a whole gay subculture in the city."

I gasped. Nobody had ever dared utter the word "homosexual" out loud around Matt. Least of all Matt himself. I wondered if he'd punch Tommy in the face.

"I don't think so," Matt said, as calmly as if Tommy had suggested he start rooting for the Yankees. "I was born here. I like it here. And I'm hoping to be accepted in my own community someday, not be part of a subculture. Let's face it—I like sports and beer and I'm an adrenaline junkie, for better or worse. I don't fit the stereotypes on either side. I'd like to just be myself around my family, though. Mom and Dad aren't ready, and who knows if they ever will be. Mom can't even handle you guys and your relationships. So I'll let her keep trying to fix me up with girls if I have to. But among ourselves, we can stop pretending."

I jumped up and hugged Matt. Tommy grinned and threw his arms around both of us. I didn't feel alone anymore

"I better get going," Tommy said. "We have a wedding rehearsal and dinner tomorrow, people."

"Me too. Good idea to blast the music while we talked," Matt said. "Although I suspect Dad couldn't have heard us anyway, with how loud he has the TV on. I think he's going deaf."

"He's not old enough," I said. "He's only fifty-three. He just seems older because he's been a grandpa for so long."

"Now he gets to be father of the bride again, and this time it's not shotgun," Tommy said. "Matt, we have to behave better this time, for Mary."

"I swear to God, Matt, if you make *any* faces while I'm walking up that aisle, even at the rehearsal, you're a dead man," I said.

Tommy hugged me again. "Feel better?"

"A little. I'll be all right."

"Listen to the music, and let it out some more."

We all went upstairs, and I followed the boys out on the porch.

Tommy paused on the bottom step. "Stacy, you realize none of us would be what we are without you, right?" he said. "You always stuck up for everybody, even telling off Mary's mother-in-law." He chuckled. "That was one of the greatest moments of all time, by the way. So if you need help from us, we're here. We owe you."

· ·

Inside, Dad was still watching TV. "You kids turn off the lights downstairs?"

"Yes, Dad."

"It's nice when you can all get together like that. Even if you all have to listen to that crazy music."

In the bathroom, I looked at the Valium, then poured the remaining pills into the toilet and flushed them. I threw away the bottle, along with a congealed jar of Vaseline and some Maalox from the 1960s.

"Why did you throw out all those things from the medicine chest?" Mom asked me the next morning.

"Because they're almost as old as Autumn," I said. "It's just junk."

"We have to run over to the optometrist this morning," Mom said. "Your father is getting drops in his eyes, so I have to drive. Why he would schedule that on the day of Mary's wedding rehearsal I can't even—"

"Because it's a day I have off," Dad said, walking into the room. "Stacy, can you stick around in case Mary calls and needs anything?"

After they left, I busied myself by doing a full manicure for the wedding. One thing about not playing guitar for five months: my nails had grown out nicely. I replaced Matt's bandage with a smaller Band-Aid and listened to one of Tommy's tapes, letting it pull me along.

I heard the roar of an engine over the music and looked outside. Don Kozicki was in the driveway, sitting astride a huge, loud motorcycle. I sighed. You never knew what Don would be like since he'd gotten out of the service. Sometimes he was drunk, sometimes just surly, other times almost as nice he used to be. I hadn't seen him since Christmas. I inspected him through the window. He was unshaven and overweight, wearing a dusty leather jacket in the July heat.

"Where's your sister?" he growled at me as I went out on the porch.

"How should I know? Uh, home, maybe?" I wondered if he was so drunk he couldn't remember where Mary lived.

He shut off the engine. "She's not there."

"Well, I don't know. She and JC probably have a lot to do today."

"Marrying that—I don't what's got into her. You think I'm gonna stand by and watch my kid being raised by—"

"Stop right there, Don," I snapped. "I'm not going to listen to your racist bullshit. Go back to your mother's and sleep it off."

"I'm not drunk." He looked right at me, and to my surprise, I realized that he was telling the truth. The bluster disappeared like air out of a balloon. He got off the cycle and sat down on the porch step, like he had almost ten years before on the day of his own wedding.

"You think I enjoy being the walking cliché of a fucked-up vet?" he asked. "I didn't even see combat. Just flew weapons in, bodies out. Some of 'em right here to the morgue at the base. Not even a pilot like my dad, just a crewman. I was a failure before I even got into the war, so I can't blame that for my life, but I do have nightmares about those bodies in the cargo hold, for what it's worth."

I sat down next to him. "The war messed up a lot of people's lives."

"I wish Mary well, I really do. I never really knew her at all, and this wedding proves it. I hardly know my kid, either, and my mother looks at me like I'm yesterday's trash." He put his head in his hands. "Drunk's soliloquy, and I haven't even had a drink yet today."

"You're still Autumn's dad. Mary wants you to spend time with her. Just not drunk."

"They're both probably better off with Mr. Smooth there. Honestly, I don't care that he's black, I care that he's better for my family than I am. I spend hours riding around, trying to think of what I can do with myself. Never can figure it out."

"I hear you," I said. "But you're not even thirty yet, and you've dealt with a lot of heavy stuff already."

"Yeah. Mostly of my own making, but damn, do I have to pay all my life for a mistake I made at eighteen?"

I flinched and almost jumped up. He looked at me. "Maybe you do understand. Because that look in your eye right now? It's the one I see in the mirror the morning after one of those cargo-hold nightmares. Whatever it was, we have the same choices. Over, under, around, or through. Or run away, but that hasn't done much for me, as you can see."

We sat quietly for a minute. I couldn't believe I had more faith in Don Kozicki's ability to get his sorry life together than I did in my own.

"I better go," he said. "Tell Mary I stopped by to wish her well, but leave out the details, if you know what I mean."

"I will. Don, Autumn will always need you. You're her dad. And Mary worried about you every single day you were over there. She cared what happened to you. She still would, if you let her."

After Don left, I wished I hadn't flushed away the Valium. To distract myself, I put the final coat on my nails and waited for it to dry. As I sat there, my eye fell on the newspaper I'd spread out on the table under my manicure supplies—the classifieds section. And there it was, in the center of the page: "Yard sale Fri/Sat: Moving. Furniture, household, lawn mower, Fender Stratocaster with amp . . ."

Fender Stratocaster. The address was right in Arboria Park,

one of the houses fronting Cobbs. I grabbed my wallet and checkbook and ran out of the house.

A few people were browsing the yard sale. Some nice antiques mixed with household junk. But what caught my eye was Don Kozicki, talking to a ponytailed man who seemed to be the homeowner.

"Hey, Don."

"Stacy. What are you doing here?"

"Hoping to look at a Fender guitar. I'm trying to go through."

He looked at me like I was crazy for a second, then laughed. "Me too. See this armoire here? I'm buying it for your sister. Wedding gift."

The armoire was lovely, with an inlaid design on the doors. "Solid oak, handmade," Don said. "No veneer. Maybe she could use it for her art supplies or something."

"It's beautiful," I said. "She'll love it."

"My new pal Bob here is letting me have it for what I got on me because we're both vets, even though I told him he could fetch three times that if he took it to the auction. He'll even deliver."

Bob grinned. "My wife and I ran into some bad luck the last couple of years, but it seems to be changing now. I got a new job on the West Coast, and we're starting fresh. So, you want to see the Fender?"

"I sure do."

"Haven't played it in years, and it could use some work. But it's a good one, if you get it cleaned up. Buying it for your boyfriend?"

I froze. Once upon a time I might have argued with him about how sexist that was, or made a joke. But now I just wanted to run away.

Don looked at me and back at Bob. "I'm pretty sure this young lady can play hell out of a guitar all by herself, pal. She's smart as a whip and has more balls than half the United States Air Force, so don't even try to overcharge her."

"Wouldn't dream of it." Bob looked impressed.

"You think it's okay if he delivers the armoire to Mary's house on Spruce?" Don asked me. "I don't know her new address. And you don't need to tell me, or keep it from me either. I'll wait until Mary tells me herself."

"She isn't moving until they get back from their honeymoon in Montreal," I said. "The old address is fine. I'll tell her to expect a gift."

"Thanks, kid," Don said. "You have a good day."

"I will," I said, and turned to Bob. "I'm ready to see that Stratocaster now."

8—AUTUMN, 1979

······················•

It's tough being named after a season you hate. I mean, I shouldn't hate it. The weather's nice and it's pretty. And every year I look forward to school starting, but the last few years that's just let me down, and maybe that's why I don't like the fall.

I guess I got my hopes up for high school, but freshman year wasn't going so great. The friends who'd drifted away during junior high hadn't drifted back. The only one left was Brenda Randall. She still stopped in front of my house every day on the way to the bus stop and sat with me on the bus. But we didn't have anything in common anymore, so the march to the bus stop, the wait, and the ride were usually silent. She knew I couldn't even pretend to be interested in her Christian youth group activities, and I didn't have any activities of my own to discuss with her. We didn't like the same music anymore, or the same TV shows.

I appreciated Brenda's loyalty. She didn't have to stand out front of my house every morning in her long, dowdy skirts and wait for me, especially when her family so clearly didn't approve of mine. So I kept up the friendship charade from my side, smiling and scooting over for her to sit with me on the ride home from school. We didn't share any classes or even a lunch period, so we should have had something to talk about on the ride home, but we never did.

At lunch I'd grab something I could carry and then roam around so I wouldn't have to sit alone. You weren't supposed to be anywhere but the cafeteria during lunch, but I'd memorized Vice Principal Stewart's route as he patrolled the doors and the parking lot, looking for kids who were sneaking off to their cars or the 7-Eleven. I knew how to avoid him.

Once I wandered as far as the bleachers by the football field, but it skeeved me out. My mom said I might have been conceived there. "It was either there, after the prom, or in the car over by the lake the weekend before, I'm not sure," she'd told me, even though I hadn't asked. "Your father forgot the condoms both times. We thought it was safe. So remember, if you're going to have sex with anyone, always have protection ready . . ."

I was pretty sure I was the only girl in school whose mom openly talked about things like sex and drugs. That should have been cool, but it was just embarrassing. Besides, I'd never even had a boyfriend. Once back in eighth grade this one guy, Raymond, who was really nice and funny, had kissed me, and we'd hung around sometimes at lunch. But he'd moved away after about a month.

You'd think people would be over it by now. My mom had been married to JC for five years. There were interracial couples at school, and most kids didn't bat an eye at that—but for some reason my family being mixed had set off a thing somewhere around sixth grade, when it seemed like everyone was looking for any reason to hate somebody else, and now nobody even remembered why they hated me, but they did. I'd left fifth grade with plenty of friends, but on the first day of sixth it was like they'd all held a secret meeting. The boys had called me names, and the girls had wanted to impress the boys by treating me like dirt—all of them except Brenda, and she was undergoing her own transformation. She wouldn't wear jeans or listen to rock records anymore, whereas by eighth grade I was beginning to embrace my outcast status and dress in jeans and T-shirts.

My mom never cared about how I dressed. She said Grandmom used to criticize whatever she and Aunt Stacy wore, so she never bothered me. Honestly, the same girls who wouldn't give me the time of day were envious of how much freedom I had. I could have worn a face full of makeup and tube tops in February if I wanted to. But I never wanted to.

After school I always dumped my books in my room and left to wander around, the same way I did at school. I felt guilty about not wanting to be home. After all, our house was, on paper, the coolest place ever. Mom and JC were always playing some kind of great music and having artists over to talk about politics and stuff. I was expected to clean my room and help out because "that's what families do, they help each other," but I didn't get a lot of grief otherwise. My little sister, Ruby, was three, and Jason was a year and a half, and they were cute. But they got on my nerves. Rubes was always getting into my stuff and wanting me to read to her or something. And Jason was constantly squalling or whirling around like a tornado. I watched them whenever Mom asked me to, but I didn't play with them much otherwise, which made me feel guilty, but not guilty enough to do something about it.

One Saturday in October I was finishing up the breakfast dishes, staring out the window and wondering why it was so quiet—I mean, Jason was shrieking, as usual, and Ruby was singing along with the TV, which was on way too loud, but nothing was happening, really—when Mom came into the kitchen.

"JC's taking Jason for the day to run errands and wait in the gas line, and I'm bringing Ruby with me to painting group," she said. "It's the day where we bring the kids and let them paint too. So if you don't have plans, maybe you should go see your Grandma Shirley today."

Grandma Shirley was my dad's mother. She and Gramps lived a couple of blocks away. Gramps was okay, but Grandma got my back up. She never hid her contempt for my mom, but Mom insisted I see her regularly anyway. I felt sorry for her because of my dad being such a jerk and probably an alcoholic, but she didn't have to take it out on us.

"Maybe I will," I hedged. I had no plans at all. Zero.

Mom hugged me. "She'd really appreciate it. And then have Brenda over if you want."

She hadn't seemed to grasp yet that Brenda didn't come over anymore. But maybe that was because sometimes I lied about going to her house. Well, not lied, exactly—but I let Mom *think* that I was there so she wouldn't find out what I was really doing: drifting through the half-vacant shopping center by myself.

Once everybody had clattered out, the house really was quiet. That was rare. In addition to the usual racket of two toddlers and a musician stepfather, the house was often full of people, because Grandma Shirley wasn't the only relative who lived right in the Park. Grandmom Evelyn and Pop-Pop Tom were also nearby, Uncle Matt was a few blocks away, and JC's Aunt Mona and Uncle Clarence lived in the Crescent, so they were all popping in and out constantly. And then there were the people who didn't live there but might as well have (because our house was such a cool place to be if you weren't me): Stacy, my mom's best friend Olga, and JC's sister Gracie Ann. Somebody was over for dinner at least twice a week.

So I had the house to myself for once, but I didn't know what to do. I didn't feel like watching dumb cartoons or even reading, which was usually why I craved some quiet time. I thumbed through my records, and even JC's and Mom's, but somehow nothing hit the spot.

Might as well visit Grandma, then. I debated what would piss her off more: throwing on the jean jacket Stacy had given me, or wearing one of Matt's old flannel shirts over my T-shirt. Whatever fashion criticism my mom didn't offer, my grandmothers made up for in spades.

I decided on the jacket and headed over to Oak Street.

To my relief, Gramps's car was gone and nobody answered my knock. I figured they must have gone to the mall or something. Only Gramps and Grandma would go there that early.

I thought about going to Grandmom Evelyn's instead, but she might try to take me shopping for dumb skirts I'd never wear. So instead I cut over to the Pines to see where we used to live. The house had been vacant for a while, and I wanted to see whether anybody was moving in yet. Stacy and I always cared about stuff like that. She told me how she used to ride around on her bike and wonder about all the people in the houses. I felt like I was related to half the neighborhood, but sometimes I did wonder about the other half. I wished I had a camera to film all the people, doing whatever their daily thing was, and splice it all together. To embarrass some of my classmates and show the others that people weren't really so different.

Somebody was living in the other side of the duplex, but our side was empty. Nobody was around, so I went around the back to peep in the kitchen. It didn't look much different from when we lived there.

"Hey!" I heard a guy's voice behind me and my life passed before my eyes as I turned around.

The guy approached me. Not a grown-up, but older than me. He wore heavy lace-up boots, ripped jeans, and a denim vest covered with studs and patches over a ratty sweatshirt, but what really caught my attention was his hair. It was an actual sprayed-up Mohawk. I'd never seen a real person with one, and I thought punk rock was a novelty that had run its course.

"You movin' in?" he asked.

I backed away. "No. I used to live here, a long time ago."

"That house has been vacant for ages," he said. "Same landlord owns the one I live in. Owns most of the Pines. Word is he ran out of money buying up the houses and can't fix 'em now." He squinted at me. "What are you staring at? You think punk is dead? You listen to The Eagles or something?"

"No," I said, and I felt my face reddening. "I mean, I've never seen any, um, punks around here."

"You ain't been looking, then." He spat on the ground. "Wanna see some more, hear some music?"

"Maybe."

He stuck out his hand. "Kip Vanderwende, disgraced heir and family fuckup."

I shook his hand and said, "Autumn."

"Yeah, it's fall, so what?"

"It's my *name*. Autumn Kozicki."

He pulled on my hand. "Come on."

Every part of me knew I shouldn't go off with a stranger, and yet I just had to. I followed him over to Pine Court, to a green duplex. One side looked empty, the other had an old sheet over the living room window. The screen door nearly came off in Kip's hand as he opened it.

"Hey, Sylvie," he yelled. "We got company."

"Fuck you!" a female voice called down the steps.

Kip grinned at me and beckoned me into the kitchen. A guy with short, spiky hair sat at the table, eating cereal and drinking a beer. He looked up at us. "We're outta Lucky Charms."

"Fuck that, Nox," Kip said. "You seen my tape box?"

Nox shrugged. I heard footsteps on the stairs, then a girl appeared in the doorway. She had blond braids, and one side of her head was shaved.

"This is Autumn," Kip said to her. "She doesn't believe punk rock exists. Even with that great punk name."

"I'm Sylvie," the girl said, lighting a cigarette. "You looking for a room?"

"Um, no. I live over on Mimosa, but I just went to look at my old house on Spruce . . ."

Kip pushed past Sylvie and stomped up the steps. She stared at me. "How old are you, anyway?"

My face burned again. "How old do I have to be?"

She laughed, but there was a bitter edge to it. "Well, you just beat Kip to the punch line."

Kip returned holding an old boom box and a leather pouch. "Come on."

He led me out the back door and into the field. It seemed like he was cutting across toward the playground, but then we veered away and along the edge of the woods, where the fall wildflowers were in full bloom.

Kip sat on the ground and fumbled with the tape player. "Batteries should be okay," he said. "Just stole 'em last week."

And then I heard that amazing intro to "Sonic Reducer," and I knew my life had just been divided into before and after. I'd been looking for that song; I just hadn't known it. Between JC and my mom and Stacy and Uncle Tommy, who visited from New York occasionally, I thought I'd heard everything. I remembered there being a big flurry about punk rock and the Sex Pistols when I was in junior high, but it had all died down pretty quickly. You didn't hear that kind of thing on the radio. Even Tommy said the New York punks had all died of heroin or something. It had barely been a blip on my radar.

But now, as Kip's tape player segued from the Dead Boys to the Ramones, from the Clash's "White Riot" to Sham 69's "If the Kids Are United," and then the Germs and the Avengers and the Damned, I understood what I'd been missing. Kip announced the band name as each song started, and I realized that some of them, like the UK Subs and the Misfits, were represented as patches on his vest.

"This is great," I said. "I guess I never realized . . ."

"Punk was just a bunch of degenerates having a costume party in 1977," Kip said. "That's what they want you to believe."

"Well, you don't get exposed to much around here."

He laughed. "You gotta get out more. Record store downtown has a punk-rock section, and the guy will order whatever you want. We get a lot of stuff from there and tape each other's records. Even that shithole record place at the mall has *some*. You just gotta look. Maybe in *high school* they're still listening to disco or something," he said with a sneer, "but there's a whole world out there."

On one level I thought that was pretty big talk from a fuckup who lived in the Pines. But on the other hand, being a punk in Arboria Park had to be harder than being one in New York.

"Okay, I'm still in high school. What do you do?"

"Nothin'. Sylvie was going to college but she's broke and took a semester off. Her lease ran out a few months ago, but that land-lord is still in Florida up to his neck in shit, so a bunch of us are just squatting here. Nox can't decide if he's into school or not. Me, I'm not college material. Graduated high school with a D average three years ago, and my dad threw me out the day after. Pretty much fuck up everything I try. Deal a little pot, unload stuff at a warehouse with a guy I know."

"You're not a musician?"

"Not unless punk-rock harmonica becomes a thing. What, you a groupie or something?"

I blushed again. "No. I just wondered."

"I know some. People from Sylvie's college. They can't play much around here though. You gotta catch a ride to the city, Philly or something. As soon as I get it together, I'm outta here."

We listened to more tapes, until I could hear Kip's stomach growling over the music. I was getting hungry myself.

Kip shut off the machine and stood up. "Let's see if Nox left anything to eat."

·······················

Nox had indeed finished the Lucky Charms, but he'd left the Rice Krispies and a tiny bit of milk. It tasted like it had started to go bad, but I didn't want to say anything.

Kip started out the back door as soon as he finished, and I followed. He glanced back at me. "You got anywhere to be?"

I remembered I had a watch and checked it. Mom and Ruby would be back soon. "Yeah, I guess I better go home."

"Come here." He took my face in his hands and kissed me, hard and sloppy and long. It felt awesome. When he let go, he pulled a Rezillos pin off his vest, stuck it on my jacket, and said, "Come over any time if you want to hear some more music."

I went home in a stupor that, oddly, made the rest of the day more tolerable. I could deal with anything now. I had an escape, somebody to be with who could show me things the kids at school couldn't even imagine.

....

After that, every chance I got—after school, weekends—I went over to Pine Court. There were usually three or four other people around, listening to music and talking. Sometimes Kip and I hung out there, him with his arm around me. Other times we went out to the field and made out, kissing as the boom box played. Most of Kip's friends had some connection to the college, either students or dropouts, but some high school kids stopped by occasionally too—a shy Asian girl I'd seen on the bus, and a couple of boys who didn't look like punks, but one said he played the guitar. So when I'd see them around school, we'd smile at each other, like we had some secret handshake.

My mom never questioned why I was spending so much time out of the house or buying punk-rock records with my allowance. She'd never gotten her head out of the '60s, so she was politely tolerant of my music, but no more than that. JC was a trained musicologist, though, so he was always listening and pointing things out. "That's your basic Chuck Berry rhythm. Know where that came from?" he'd ask—and then he'd tell me. Even though I wasn't sure it was punk to talk about it, I'd always tell Kip what I'd learned. Sometimes he'd sneer, but sometimes he'd say something really thought-provoking back.

Three weeks after I met Kip, on a gray, chilly Saturday morning, I headed over to Pine Court. Mom had painting group, JC was conducting his high school orchestra somewhere, and Gracie Ann wanted the kids for the day. I was free until three.

Kip and I listened to music for a while, and then we went outside to walk around. Over on Spruce Court, both halves of my old duplex were empty. I felt something wet hit my face and looked up. It was starting to rain.

"I seen a truck over here, like a handyman," Kip said. "Maybe they're fixing it up."

"I wish I could go inside."

"Let's go, then. Out of this rain." Kip pushed on a living room window. "Should be able to get into one of these. Or pick the lock." He turned the knob on the front door, and it opened. He grinned at me and we dashed inside.

They had done some work on the place, mostly the kitchen. There were new countertops, the cabinets had been painted, and the old-fashioned porcelain sink had been replaced.

"I grew up here, until I was nine and my mom married my stepfather," I told Kip. "My dad left when I was two. He has all those Vietnam vet problems. Drinks a lot, and I can't depend on him. JC, my stepdad, is all right though. They have two kids, and I just get tired of having little kids around. And the house is always full of relatives."

"My house was full of people too," Kip said. "I'm second youngest of twelve, and my old man was an Air Force sergeant who couldn't shut it off at home. I've been a fuckup since birth. How about you?"

"I don't think of myself that way. There are things I hope I can do." I went back into the living room. "Glad they're pulling up that ugly shag carpet. *That* wasn't here when we lived here."

"What's upstairs?" Kip asked.

"My old room, for one." We climbed the steps and I showed him the small back bedroom. Outside the window, the rain poured down.

"Guess we're stuck here until it stops." Kip put his arm around me and led me away from the window.

"We shouldn't stay here. Somebody might see us, and we're trespassing."

"Trespassing is punk." Kip pulled me down. We sat on the floor, and soon he was on top of me. With the rain on the roof, and the quiet semi-darkness of the room, it felt great. Not romantic, exactly. I wasn't really sure how to describe it.

Suddenly Kip unzipped his jeans, and out popped an erect penis. I'd never seen a real one before and almost laughed. Instead I said, "Hey, wait a minute. We need to talk about this. No way unless we get a condom."

Damn, I was my mother's daughter. "Use a condom" was tattooed on my brain.

"Or," I said, and felt my face getting red, "if you want to do something else . . ."

Kip fumbled in his pockets and fished out a wrapped rubber. "I may have gotten kicked out of Boy Scouts, but I'm always prepared."

I stared at it. "What's the expiration date?"

"Hell, I just stole the box two weeks ago."

Maybe it was nerves, but that got me laughing, and him too. We lay back down and started kissing again. I was distracted, trying to figure out about taking clothes off and stuff. My mom had left some sex books on the hallway bookcase right outside my bedroom door, high enough that Ruby and Jason couldn't see or reach them but within obvious range for me—*Our Bodies, Ourselves* and *Joy of Sex*, among others. I wouldn't have asked her any questions about the contents in a million years, or let her see me looking at them, but I hadn't been able to resist reading them, so I kind of knew how things were supposed to go.

Only Kip didn't seem concerned with getting my clothes off, or his. He just unzipped my jeans and wriggled them down just past my hips, rolled on the condom, and dove in.

It hurt, like I knew it would. I hoped I wasn't bleeding too much. What would I clean up the floor with if I did? When the handymen came back on Monday, I didn't want them to find blood.

It was over pretty fast. Kip pulled out after a couple of minutes and sat back. "Hey, rain's stopping. Better get out of here."

He got up, went into the bathroom, and took a loud piss. I scrambled to my feet and checked for blood. None on the floor, thank God.

Kip followed me downstairs and out the door. I walked ahead of him back over to Pine Court, through the remaining sprinkles of rain.

"Hey, wait up." He caught up and kissed me. "You gonna be around tomorrow?"

"Yeah, I guess so."

He kissed me again, and I headed home, hoping to get a little time alone to remember and process it all. We'd used protection. He still wanted to see me again. It hurt and hadn't been very interesting—not as good as making out in the field—but first times could be that way, according to what I'd read.

....

I ached a little that night and in the morning when I showered, but it was a cool kind of pain, somehow. Luckily everything at home was chaos, with Gracie Ann stopping by after her church service for brunch, and then Olga popping in, and a neighbor coming over with one of Ruby's playmates. It wasn't hard to holler "I'm going out, be back later!" around one o'clock and escape.

Kip seemed glad to see me. We hung out for a while in the room he shared with Nox, as Sylvie and her friends went in and out downstairs. We listened to the Ramones singing "You Should Never Have Opened That Door," and then Kip pushed me down on his mattress and we had sex again, just as fast as the day before, but this time it didn't hurt much.

I left myself enough time to detour to the shopping center

for a bottle of cranberry juice on the way home. One of the sex books said if you did it too many times close together at first you could get something called "honeymoon cystitis," which sounded nasty. The book said cranberry juice would prevent it.

I chugged the bottle, then cursed myself for not bringing my backpack. I usually didn't drink cranberry juice, and if I brought a bottle into the house my mom would just know what it was for and ask questions. I'd have to sneak over to the 7-Eleven before school or during lunch to get another one.

....

On Tuesday when I went to Kip's, he started to shove me down on the mattress again.

"Wait a second," I said, and sat up. "I don't have to be home for a while. My folks are taking the kids someplace after work. We don't have to rush it *again*."

Kip looked puzzled. I pulled off my T-shirt and unsnapped my bra. "Come on, let's enjoy this."

He groped at my boobs, uncertainly at first and then with more enthusiasm. We kissed, and I guided him down my neck and to my chest. Geez, he was twenty-one years old; hadn't he ever read a sex book? I pulled his sweatshirt off too.

Soon we were naked on the mattress, and it got a lot more interesting. Kip licked my stomach and moved down between my legs, and this time it was me having an orgasm in less than a minute. My first one. He put a condom on, and this time not only did he last a little longer, it felt pretty good, too.

"There," I said as we lay sweating on the mattress in the dusk. "How was that?"

"Pretty punk rock," he said, laughing, and we lay there as the room darkened. I dozed off for a little while.

I woke when the light came on. Kip was up and stumbling into his jeans. I could hear people downstairs. "What time is it?"

"'Bout six thirty, I think."

"Geez, I better get home in case my mom calls." I sat up and reached for my clothes, and my eye fell on Kip's arm as he grabbed his shirt. It was swollen and had lines on it, like cat scratches, almost. How had I not noticed earlier? Too distracted.

"Hey." I gripped his arm. "What's up with this?"

He pulled away and yanked on his shirt. "Nothin'. Just played around with some stuff with my buddy from work. No big deal. I'm not a smack addict."

"You should be careful." I bit my tongue, not wanting to lecture. We'd smoked pot a few times, and once Nox had bragged about taking some prescription pills he got out of somebody's medicine cabinet, but I'd never seen them with anything else.

"Hey, quit worrying. Don't get like Sylvie. I quit fucking her because she was always whining about something."

I grabbed my shoes and started to walk out the door, but he stopped me. "Hey." He kissed me, tenderly. "Don't be mad. That was super, just now. We got a good thing. I may be a fuckup, but I'm not a drug addict. Sam from work got ahold of some stuff, and we tried it out. Sylvie and Nox and the others aren't into that shit. I just scratched an itch, that's all."

"Okay," I said, because I didn't know what else to say. On the way out I snagged the bottle of cranberry juice I had hidden in the back of their fridge, glad Nox hadn't poured it on his Lucky Charms.

I scolded myself on the walk home under the streetlights. What had I gotten myself into?

....

But I was back the next day, and we made love a few more times over the next week or so.

"My punk-rock friends are all I got," Kip said as we sat in the field one afternoon. "And you. You understand."

Sylvie met us at the door when we walked back. "Hey, Autumn, you wanna go to a show next Friday? Somebody managed to book The Cramps at the college. People with school IDs can bring guests, and I think we have enough to go around because my ID's still valid."

"Yes!" I shouted. "I'll have to figure something out with my mom, but I'd love it."

I raced home. I told Mom that Sylvie was the sister of somebody from school, and named a couple of other younger kids who were going, including the Asian girl, Rosie Thanh.

Rosie and I had done little more than wave to each other on the bus and talk a couple of times at Kip's house but I asked her to come over after school on Thursday, when Kip had to work. Mostly I wanted Mom to think I had this nice new friend so she'd be okay about the show, but I was curious about Rosie too. She had never said much when I saw her at Kip's house, just read every word on every album cover and sometimes wrote things in a notebook.

Rosie's family was from Vietnam, she told me as we sat in my room playing records.

"I hate when they call me 'boat people girl,'" she said, her eyes filling with tears. "We were here before all that. Those people on Pine—well, they're the first ones that have been nice to me in a long time."

"Me too," I said. I wished I could sit with Rosie on the bus, but I didn't want to hurt Brenda's feelings.

·····················

The evening of the show, we met up at Pine Court. When we got there, Sylvie said Kip was sick.

I ran upstairs to check on him. His eyes were glassy, and he seemed to have a fever. He was huddled in bed wearing a sweatshirt and jeans.

"Sucks to miss this," he said. "Have fun. Tell me all about it after."

Rosie and I crammed ourselves into Sylvie's old car with Nox and Billy Persinger, the guitar-playing boy from school, and we drove over to the college.

The show wasn't in the auditorium or on a stage or anything, just a room in the back of the student center. The second we got inside, Rosie and Billy and I ran up close to where they were setting up for the opening band and watched. Sylvie was nearby, telling a friend she might have enough money to go back to school full time in the spring. Nox sat on the floor with another guy, talking about putting together a zine. More college kids filtered in. I loved the energy in the room, and wished Kip was there.

Billy was telling us about what he was learning to play on his guitar when someone tapped my shoulder. "Autumn?"

I nearly jumped out of my skin. It was my Aunt Stacy. I never thought in a million years anybody from the family would be at this show, unless somebody got a concussion moshing and they called the paramedics.

She hugged me. "I guess neither one of us expected to see the other here. I haven't seen you in so long! Every time I've stopped by lately, your mom says you're out with your friends. I remember being your age, never wanting to be home . . ."

"Um, yeah. Those are my friends, Rosie and Billy." I waved toward them. "Sylvie over there, she's a student here, and she and her friends invited us."

I hoped Stacy wouldn't flip when she saw Sylvie and the punk girl she was talking to. But then again, she was a social worker, so she'd probably seen a lot of weird-looking people before.

She just nodded. "Oh, she's talking to Patricia. She's a student too, and an intern and peer mentor at my office; she's the one who invited me. Your mom said you've been listening to punk rock, and I've just been dying to talk to you about it. It's so exciting to have an actual show to go to right in town."

I knew Stacy loved music, like the rest of the family, but this was still a surprise. She looked different than usual, too, wearing black eyeliner and dark red lipstick.

"I'll let you get back to your friends," she said. "Looks like they're about to start anyway." She and Patricia headed back to the other side of the room.

The opening band started their first song, and my attention swung back to the stage. They were locals—not really punk, just loud. I watched the drummer intently. Whenever Kip and I listened to records, I always found myself pounding out the rhythms. JC had some percussion instruments around, and I'd always been attracted to them as a kid. Kip and I sometimes talked about how it was the beat that held a punk song together.

The band finished and took down their equipment so The Cramps could set up. The room had filled, and I couldn't see Stacy and Patricia too well anymore.

Once The Cramps hit, everything went crazy. They started with "New Kind of Kick." That was Kip's favorite Cramps song, and I was sorry he was missing it. Lux Interior shoved the microphone right at us, and Billy shouted into it, jumping up and down. I kept an eye on the drummer and Poison Ivy, wondering what it would be like to play to so many people.

It was over before I knew it; the lights came on, and college security told us we had to leave. I looked for Stacy to say goodbye, but didn't find her. I hoped Sylvie hadn't said anything about me and Kip to Patricia. My folks had been as cool about this show as they were about everything else, but I knew Kip would be another story.

....

It was barely past ten when we got back to Sylvie's. I'd negotiated a midnight curfew, so I'd have lots of time to tell Kip what he'd missed. I raced up the steps. His door was closed, and I didn't hear any music playing. But I could see light under the door, so I knew he must be awake.

I burst in—and froze. Kip was crouching next to his mattress, a piece of rubber tied around his arm, holding a syringe. A nude girl, a sharp-faced brunette I'd never seen before, sat on the mattress, something tied around her own arm. They both had a vacant look in their eyes.

"Kip."

He turned and stared, and it was like he couldn't even recognize me.

I spun around, ran down the steps, and blurted out, "Kip's shooting heroin."

"Not again! That son of a bitch!" Sylvie screamed, and she pushed past me. I walked toward the couch, but my knees buckled under me. Nox caught me and sat me down, then ran after Sylvie.

Rosie and Billy huddled around me. I was crying now, and Rosie was trembling. She whispered, "I didn't expect this."

"Let's go," Billy said. "You okay, Autumn?"

"I think so." Any minute that rat-faced girl was going to be thrown down the steps by somebody, and I didn't want to be there when she was. Billy and Rosie took my arms, and we walked out the door.

"Was he passed out, or overdosed, or what?" Billy asked.

Rosie glared at him.

"He was shooting up. With a naked girl in his bed."

Rosie went, "Ooooh," and Billy looked confused.

I stumbled. They caught me again, and I sat down on the concrete storm sewer on the corner.

"Don't you get it, Billy? Autumn was *going out* with him," Rosie explained.

"No, I wasn't, Rosie. I was just having sex with him. Like a sucker." I put my head down on my knees.

From almost a block away we heard a slamming door and Sylvie screeching. I pulled myself up. "We better get out of here."

"We'll walk you home," Billy said.

"I should have known," I said as we headed down Cedar. "I saw marks and swelling on his arm and asked him. He said it was a one-off with a guy from work. But then he also said Sylvie used to get on his case, so I should have realized."

"I don't think I want to go over there anymore," Rosie said, and sighed. "I'll miss it."

"Why don't we ever hang out in school?" Billy asked. "What lunch period are you guys on?"

"A," Rosie said. "I sit at a table where no one talks to me. I hate it."

"I'm on A too," I said. "I go out and walk around."

"I'm on A too," Billy said. "Me and Benny Aquino sit at the corner table by the window and draw pictures of the Ramones. We could squeeze you guys in."

"Thanks," Rosie said. "Now I won't mind Monday so much."

"Me and Benny want to start a band. We could all trade tapes, too. We don't need those guys anymore."

We turned up Mimosa, and I stopped under a streetlight. "Rosie, how much do I look like I've been crying? My parents will still be up."

She scrunched up her face, and I had my answer. So we sat down on the curb again for a while. Rosie and Billy talked about the show and made plans for hanging out at school. I just wanted to lie in the gutter and die.

When we finally walked to my house, Rosie said, "I'll call you tomorrow, okay?"

"It'll be all right," Billy said awkwardly.

"Thanks, guys." I almost broke down again as they both put their arms around me, but I managed to hold it together as I walked inside.

"Hey, you're early," Mom said. "How was the concert?"

"It didn't go very late," I said, hanging up my jacket so she wouldn't see my face.

"Did you get something to eat afterwards?" she asked. That gave me my out.

"No, Sylvie had to get back, so Billy walked us home from her house. I'm kind of thirsty." I went in the kitchen and made a lot of noise opening the refrigerator and stuff, hoping Mom and JC would go to bed or go back to watching TV and leave me alone.

Finally I came out and deflected any more questions by telling them I'd seen Stacy. Mom looked amused. "Well, I'm glad to hear she has a social life. She works too hard."

I headed for my room.

"Don't play your records without headphones," Mom cautioned. "The kids are asleep."

I didn't even want to listen to music. Maybe I never would again. A few hours before, as I watched the show, I'd been thinking about getting some drums and asking Billy if we could jam together. Now I couldn't imagine listening to any of the records I loved. I lay in the dark, wondering how I'd tell Rosie and Billy I didn't even want to be a punk anymore. Maybe they wouldn't want to hang around with me anyway, once they thought about it. I was just a dumb slut who'd had sex with a heroin addict.

·····················

Things still looked glum in the morning. But I was actually glad for once that everybody was around. Mom didn't have painting group, so she and JC decided to clean the house top to bottom. They played music that was anything but punk—high-energy stuff like Santana and War—and periodically they danced around in the living room, with Ruby joining in. As I scrubbed the bathroom, I realized I didn't want to leave the house anymore. I had such a great family; why didn't I appreciate them more?

Because I didn't belong. I didn't belong anywhere.

Most recent Saturday nights I had sat alone in my room, aching to be with Kip and wondering what he was doing without me. Now I ached not just because I'd never be with him again, but because it was all so meaningless. I listened to Lou Reed singing "Heroin" with the Velvet Underground, and wondered if Kip had done it to be like his heroes, or if it was because he really was hurting, and I hadn't tried to help him. Maybe I still could.

I considered looking for him on Sunday. But then I thought of that creepy girl. All those Saturday nights I tortured myself in my room after kissing him good-bye in the field, was she in his bed? Or was someone else?

Sunday looked to be interminable, until Stacy came over around one. After talking to Mom and JC and fussing with the kids for a while, she said, "Hey Autumn, I really came to see you. We haven't talked for ages. Want to go for a walk?"

That was the last thing I wanted to do, but I put on my jacket anyway and followed her out.

"Let's go to the playground," she said.

Stacy always wanted to go to the playground when we hung out. Maybe because she used to take me there when I was little, or because it was the closest thing we had to a park, I didn't know. I did know it was too close to Kip's house for comfort, and anyway that corner—the playground, the field—was kind of tainted now.

"Do we have to?" I asked. "We could go to the shopping center instead, get some sodas."

"Well, okay," Stacy said. "But there's really no place to sit and eat or drink up there since Strommer's and the five-and-dime closed, and it's so sad now, with all the empty stores. How about we pick up sodas at Thriftway and drive to the lake?"

The lake. Possibly my place of origin. It fit, somehow. I nodded my agreement, and we climbed into Stacy's car.

As she drove, Stacy talked about the show and all her favorite bands, while I pondered whether to tell her about Kip. If anybody I knew was going to understand, it would be her.

At the lake, leaves swirled in the breeze and geese flew in V's overhead.

"So tell me about how you got into punk rock," Stacy urged as we strolled. "I tried to get you to listen to the Ramones a couple of years ago, but you said they sounded like a cartoon."

I took a deep breath. "Stacy, can we go sit down at the picnic tables? This is kind of a long story, and you're not going to like it."

And I told her everything—meeting Kip, the way the music made me feel, the way he made me feel, and how it all got mixed up together. I confessed to not having many friends at school, at least until now, and how I wasn't sure they'd stick by me. She listened and asked a few questions with her social worker face on, not judging, just taking it in.

Finally, when I kind of ran out of steam, she said, "I remember Kip Vanderwende. Such a bratty little kid, and that family is so screwed up. The father's a head case, always yelling. And their mom is so put-upon, never a word for herself. She was always too busy to socialize with your grandmom or the other neighbor ladies, and I think she was afraid of her husband. Lord knows what he did to her or the kids in terms of physical violence. And the place was a damn baby factory, even by Catholic standards." She glanced at some people walking by and waited until they had moved on. "One of Kip's sisters told your mom once that the father would make the mother drop whatever she was doing, cleaning or cooking or whatever, and go in the bedroom with him whenever he wanted it. Can you imagine what that did to the kids? And they were all competing for everything—money, attention, not getting slapped around—so they turned on each other, like wolves. Half of them turned out to be super overachievers, like Stevie, who was in my class. He was an Eagle Scout, but you couldn't even admire him because he was so smug and arrogant. The rest—well, one of his sisters is in jail, and another has been in and out of the state mental health system. Kip probably felt overlooked."

She'd told me more about Kip's family than he had. I felt sorry for him again.

But she added, "It doesn't excuse his behavior. Addicts are very manipulative. They know how to push buttons to get what they want. An alcoholic will steal your wallet, and a junkie will steal your wallet and then help you look for it. And I'm going to tell you something"—her face lost the sympathetic, professional look—"something I haven't fully told anybody, except my therapist a few years ago. Your mom knows a little of it, but not all." She stopped for a minute, looking out at the sparkling lake. "Getting involved with older men before you're an adult with a few years under your belt is never a good idea. Because any adult male who goes for young girls, especially underage ones, has an agenda. Sometimes it's about control, sometimes it's about feeling inadequate sexually and needing to dominate. Sometimes they just want an audience to admire them. It's never healthy."

She made Kip sound like Charles Manson. I was going to tell her he wasn't so bad. But something about her dead-eyed stare stopped me. She might be using social worker words like "agenda," but something else was going on, something deeper.

"And so," she said, still looking away, "here's my story. I was a little lost when I landed at the state university. I wanted to be there, but I was overwhelmed. I know I'm the family joke, always changing majors and never figuring out what I wanted to do. I never had a talent or direction like your mom and the boys. I thought college was a chance to try new things, figure it out. Instead I felt surrounded by people who were smarter and more together than me. I went to a local coffeehouse a lot and watched people sing. They'd do Linda Ronstadt, Jackson Browne, stuff like that. They had these jam sessions anybody could join, and I started bringing my guitar sometimes. There was this guy there. He was thirty-one, I was eighteen, and kind of a young eighteen at that. I mean, your mom was *married* at eighteen. Anyway, we got to talking, and he asked me to play along with him at shows he did, people's parties, small bars, stuff like that. I was thrilled. I didn't think I played that well compared with the other people there, but he made me feel like I could do it. And I went out with him a few times, and at first that made me feel special. I hated being this dumb virgin loser, and I thought maybe he was my chance. But something about him made me uncomfortable. I didn't like the way he told me what I was supposed to think, what music to listen to or not, and how much he drank. So I kind of broke up with him and he said okay, let's be friends. And for a while, we were. Then one night . . ."

She stopped again, for a while. I waited.

"One night in February, he called and asked me if I wanted to go see his friend play at a bar in Philly. It was raining, kind of sleety, and I had a test to study for, but somehow he talked me into it. He was my friend, right? So I go off with him, and I figure out pretty quick we're not going to Philly, unless it's the most indirect, backwoods way imaginable. He drove out in the country and stopped the van, then grabbed my wrist and told me to get in the back. And then . . . it was my own fault. I should have fought or run or something, but it was pouring rain and I didn't even know where I was or how to get back to town."

What she was describing sounded like rape, almost. Could you be raped by somebody you knew, somebody you went out with? She must have asked herself the same thing.

"So he finishes in about five minutes, and I'm hurting like hell, and then he says he wasn't sure he should do that but clearly I 'needed' it so I could grow up. Then he drives me home and says, 'See you around,' like we've just had this lovely evening."

I hated to imagine her in the back of that van, listening to the rain. That sound had been a nice backdrop when Kip and I were lying on the floor of my old room. But it must have been a nightmare for Stacy.

"So, not surprisingly, I don't hear from him for a few days, and I'm totally freaking out. Your mom always gave me the same condom lectures you get, and he hadn't used one, so I was in hell until I got my period. I couldn't bring myself to go to the coffee-house or see anyone I knew from there. Then out of the blue, he calls and says he doesn't want me to play with him that weekend. Honestly, I'd forgotten about it, it was just somebody's party or something, and he says don't bother to come because he doesn't want to play with 'amateurs' anymore." She picked up a red maple leaf that had fallen on the table. "I don't know how I got through that semester, frankly. I had to avoid every single place I might run into him. Until right before I came home for the summer, somebody mentioned that he'd left for Nashville to make it big. He'd already been spit out in New York and LA. Never heard anything more from him or about him after that. Never wanted to."

I put my arms around her. "Stacy, that's so awful."

"It was tough." She pulled back. "So I want you to tell me, honestly. Was there any kind of force or coercion involved?"

"No. Unless you count what you were talking about before, I guess. I was a thousand percent willing. Heck, I even pushed *him* into doing some things, sexually I mean."

She nodded. "Still, I think you're facing some of the same things I did. It's not just that you don't trust people now. You don't trust yourself and your own judgment."

"I think you're right," I said, nodding. "You're pretty smart, you know."

"Yeah, I can figure out everybody's problems but my own," Stacy said with a snort. "That's why I'm a social worker, I guess."

"How did you . . ."

"Get past it? Therapy, for one. And I went through a bad spell with music. Didn't want to play the guitar anymore, didn't even know what I wanted to listen to. And men . . . well. It took a while. But music was what brought me back. Tommy helped me, though I don't think he realized it. He came down for your mom's wedding with all these bootleg tapes for me. New York glam rock, the roots of punk. Hearing Johnny Thunders made me remember how I always wanted to play something that really rocked, not strum a folk guitar in the back of a coffeehouse. That music was healing. And I know it sounds weird, but I had an interesting conversation with your dad the day before your mom married JC. We were both at loose ends, and he was kind of perceptive. I bought my Stratocaster that day, and even if I never play for anyone else, I play for myself. Punk rock. And that's something else I want to tell you. Don't let Kip Vanderwende take your music, if that's what you love. If you just listened to it because he did and it really wasn't you, maybe it's best to walk away, but if that's the music of your soul, don't let him keep it."

"I won't." I looked out at the ducks waddling along the other side of the lake. "My friends—Rosie and Billy—we want to listen to music together, and maybe learn to play."

"That's the spirit," Stacy said. "And that's what I wanted to talk to you about, actually. You remember Patricia, from the show? She was one of my first clients. Chronic truant, runaway, alcohol, bad boys, the works. Her stepfather beat her and her mother black and blue. But she always had something—something that helped her rise above her circumstances. She got the help she needed, and she blossomed. Her mother left the bastard and she reconciled with her, and then she finished school. Now she's in college, and she wants to get an MSW. When we started the peer mentor program, she was the first girl I thought of. And she's a punk rocker through and through, so I guess that's how she knows your friend."

"Sylvie," I said. "Sylvie's all right. She actually warned me about Kip, in a way. I just didn't get what she was saying at the time."

"Well, Patty's trying to get some local kids together to organize a space where they can go to hear and play music, without drugs or alcohol. She says she'd love to talk to you, because you and your friends are just the kinds of kids she wants to see involved."

"That sounds neat," I said. "Maybe I will."

"Okay." Stacy started to get up, then sat again. "One more thing. I'm going to sound like your mother now, but I have to. Did you use protection? I'll take you to get tested for pregnancy or STDs, but if there is anything, we'll have to tell your mom."

I squirmed. "We always used condoms. It's in my DNA, remember? He stole them from the drugstore."

"Just making sure. And remember, if you ever want to go for any other birth control and you don't want your mom turning it into a big feminist ceremony, you can ask me."

"I think it's going to be a long time before I need to. But thanks anyway."

Stacy peered at me. "It's good to be careful, but don't let what happened with Kip shut you down from caring about people who do deserve it." She got this faraway look. "Listen. I know this is going to sound crazy, but . . . when I finally felt ready to start dating again, I was still worried. About trusting my own judgment, like I said. Then I thought about this boy"—her eyes lit up—"who I met in high school. I only knew him for a few hours. But he gave me this feeling that I didn't have to pretend to be someone I wasn't, that I was free to say things right up front to him about being against the war and wanting to be a rock musician, or talk about nerdy stuff like constellations and abandoned buildings. I never saw him again after that night—he was just visiting—but I used him as a lesson. Now I don't bother with anybody who wants to change me, or patronizes me, or tries to have power over me. I look for guys who are good and genuine. They're not always easy to find. I know everybody in the family thinks I'm destined to be an old maid, but I'm selective. I haven't gone out with that many guys, but the ones I have, I don't regret. Things didn't work out for other reasons, but they were decent people, and I took something good away from the relationship." She paused. "Maybe there's still something you can take away from this. Only you can figure that out."

As we drove home, I thought about Stacy's story, and Patty's, and even Kip's. I had it so easy and hadn't even realized it.

"About your mom," Stacy said. "Acting like the condom queen is how she dealt with her own sexual traumas. She never had a chance to figure out how she felt about sex because everything got wrapped up in getting pregnant and being shamed. So you and I got the birth control lectures, but no warnings about some other things to consider about sex and relationships. She got swept up by a cute, nice boy she thought she was in love with, and ended up a pregnant housewife when she should have been at the freshman mixer. So she's tried to protect us by making sure we didn't get knocked up."

That was probably true. And in trying to make sex sound so matter of fact, Mom hadn't let me in on other factors. Like how you could fall so hard for someone that you couldn't see their bad side. Stacy had given me a lot to think about.

When she dropped me off, Ruby was alone in the front yard, glumly kicking a ball around. "Hey, Ruby," I greeted her. "Where's Mikey and Amber?"

"They're sick. They can't come out."

"Well, I can play ball with you, if you want." Stacy had played with me for hours when I was a kid, yet I never made time for Ruby.

Ruby's face brightened. "First you kick the ball to me, and then I kick it to you."

I kicked the ball softly toward her. She swung her leg at it and it shot past me, hitting the door of JC's car. I laughed. "Okay, Rubes, maybe we should play in the backyard instead."

....

On Monday, I woke up as I had the previous two days, with a feeling of loss. At least I'd see Rosie and Billy at school. But first I had to do something.

When Brenda arrived at my house, I said, "Hey, listen. I've been really bad about never talking to you. Just because we're not best friends anymore, and we like different things . . . well, we don't have to keep walking and sitting together if you don't want to. But if we do, we should try to communicate. I mean, even if we don't like the same stuff, we still go to school together and have some of the same teachers and subjects."

"That's true," she said. "Like Mr. Coyle in English. He's such"—she lowered her voice like she was about to swear—"such a *jerk*!" She giggled.

"Yeah, he is," I said. "Listen, I never told you how great it was for you to stick by me all this time. Thanks for being so nice to me."

She shook her head. "I don't understand people sometimes. Why is there so much hate? Why does everybody look for ways to not get along? We all used to be friends. Jesus wants us to love one another. And judging people is definitely *not* Christian. At least, I don't think so."

"Well, it means a lot to me that you stuck around."

Spontaneously we both dropped our books to the ground and did this dumb fist-and-hand-slapping routine all the kids used to do back in fourth grade.

Brenda laughed. "That felt good."

I picked up my stuff. "It did. We don't have to be best friends—but we can still talk. Maybe once in a while, we could even go to the shopping center and get a soda, like we used to."

"I'd like that," she said.

As the bus approached, I added, "And you don't *have* to sit with me every day. But when we do sit together, I promise to listen and talk to you."

"Deal," she said. "Um, is it okay if I don't sit with you this morning? Wait, that sounds awful. It's just that Mr. Skeene assigned me and Todd Healy to do a history presentation together, and I'd like to talk to him about it . . ."

Todd was an earnest black kid whose family went to the same holy-roller church as Gracie Ann. Sometimes he read the Bible on the bus. He and Brenda were going to get along great.

"Sure," I said over my shoulder as I boarded the bus. Brenda headed over to Todd, smiling, and I plunked down next to Rosie.

"Everything all right?" she asked me.

"No. But I'm working on it," I said. "Thanks."

"Billy and I have stuff to tell you at lunch."

••••••••••••••••••••••

I barely paid attention in any of my morning classes, too full of curiosity about what Rosie and Billy had to say. When the lunch bell rang, I hustled to the cafeteria. Once I found Billy and Rosie, I demanded, "So? What stuff?"

They'd gone over to the Pine house on Sunday, out of curiosity, to see if Sylvie was okay. Kip was gone; Nox had helped her throw him out, and they didn't know where he'd gone. The girl in his bed was some sixteen-year-old dropout skank from downtown who'd been fucking both Kip and Sam for drugs. Sylvie was planning to leave Pine Court anyway; the landlord was back.

"She's moving in with a friend from school," Billy said. "That girl she was talking to at the show. Her punk name is Patty Melt."

"There's more about Kip," Rosie interrupted. "Sylvie said she and Nox were missing some records. They didn't think too much of it at first, because they're always trading and lending them to friends. But they figured out that the ones they couldn't account for were all expensive imports. Kip was stealing them and selling them back to the record store downtown. And Sylvie had some cash hidden in her room, and he stole that too."

"I really fell for that jerk. I guess I should be grateful it wasn't worse."

"Patty and Sylvie and some other college kids are going to rent another house, one with a basement, and make it a place for kids to hang out and play music and do art and stuff," Billy said. "They'll let us know when they have a meeting to set it up. No drug addicts or parasites allowed, they said."

························

Stacy came to see me again Friday evening. She told Mom she was bringing me some records, but I knew she was checking on me.

This time we did go for a little walk, but not toward the Pines or the playground. She said she'd given my phone number to Patty and discussed the punk house project with Mom and JC to get their approval for me to participate.

"Let me know if you ever want to mess around with the guitar," she said as we headed home.

"Thanks," I said, "but I want to play drums. When I can afford some."

"Well, Christmas is coming."

"I know, but I already asked Mom and JC and Dad to go in on a movie camera for Christmas. I want to make films too, of bands. I guess I'll start saving my allowance for drums. JC can teach me the basics."

"Tell you what," Stacy said. "Let's check the classifieds for a used set, or see if JC knows somebody with one, and I'll match whatever you can save."

I hugged her. "Thanks, Stacy."

"We'll play together sometime," she said. "But we'll need a bass player."

"Rosie wants to play bass. She's saving up too. And Billy already has a guitar."

"Then you're well on your way."

· · · · · · · · · · · · · · · · · · · ·

The next few months were better. After school, if I wasn't with my friends I was trying to finish my homework so I could go to the punk house over on Beech Street for a few hours. Or sometimes I was playing with Ruby and Jason.

One cold Saturday after Christmas, I walked over to Pine. Everyone was long gone; the house was being fixed up. I filmed it with my new camera, then walked over to Spruce.

People were living in both halves of my old house. On our side, it was a mother and her little girl. The mom laughed and said yes when I asked to film them; her daughter was riding a pink tricycle around the court, the way I used to. I hoped they were happy.

I saw Sylvie sometimes at the new punk house. Nox, too. He said Kip's dealer, Sam, had gotten word he was about to get busted, and the two of them had taken off out west. Stacy had talked to me about being prepared if things didn't end well for Kip. Maybe he'd die alone, but that was his choice.

And Patty Melt told me her own secret. "I got involved with Kip briefly about a year ago," she said one Saturday as I helped her paint the basement of the Beech house. "Then I realized he was doing drugs and sleeping with teenage girls, so I broke it off—but I stuck around for a while after. I thought I could help him. That social worker urge, I guess. Stacy says I'll need to learn when it's worth expending the extra energy and when it's not or I'll burn out, and she's right. He was Exhibit A. He did clean up for a while, but only because his dealer got busted and he was too scared and too lazy to stand on a downtown corner at midnight. Then he met Sam at work and started using again, probably around the time he met you. Sylvie's a soft touch, so she gave him a place to stay, and then she just couldn't get rid of him. Maybe there's a scared little boy or a potentially decent man hidden under there somewhere, but right now, he's a predator. The scene is lucky to be rid of him."

By spring, I had let it go. I had tons of stuff to do and people to do it with now. There was a nice new boy at school, too. Billy introduced us. But I was taking it slow, just being friends for the moment.

I claimed back "Sonic Reducer." That was the hardest song to listen to at first. But I realized that Kip introducing me to the music had been a good thing; it's just that he wasn't. If I'd been older, stronger, felt I belonged somewhere, maybe I could have thanked him that day he played it for me, then gone on my way. Sometimes, I pretend that's just what I did.

9—STACY, 1980

When I saw him again, I was playing guitar in the basement of a rental house on Beech Street, wearing a Dead Kennedys T-shirt and Scarlet Slasher lipstick, on a Friday night in September.

Autumn and her friends had formed a band called the Parkers, and they were the last of four groups playing the Beech House basement that night. Shows were usually over around eleven, to lessen the chances of a neighborhood noise complaint. Benny couldn't play that night, so Autumn had begged me to fill in. They'd mostly just wanted some additional noise, so it had been enough to do a quick run-through before the show.

The spectators were mostly neighborhood high school kids or college students on their way out to late-night parties or townie bars. That's why I noticed him at first. Midway through our set, a man a little older than the others descended the stairs and stood in the back, in front of the hand-lettered "Respect the House" sign. Some things about him had changed: the military-style haircut, for one, and his upper body was more muscular, more powerful now. Some things hadn't: the black T-shirt and jeans (with a brown suede jacket added), the dark eyes that danced as they met mine, the smile that made me lose track of what I was playing.

Billy didn't notice my error, just kept yowling and flailing away on his own guitar. I put my head down to catch my breath and stared at the concrete floor as Billy announced our next song, a Ramones cover.

When I dared look up again, I fucked up a chord change. I kept looking away until we finished the set. Then I busied myself unplugging my guitar from the house amp. I was still crouched over the amp when I felt a hand on my arm.

"It *is* you." He smiled. "Stacy Halloran. I thought I'd never see you again. And playing a song from my favorite band."

"Greg." Everything was kaleidoscoping now: Autumn and her friends, some kids trooping noisily up the steps, others arguing about which record to play. Greg Martinez, with his hand on my arm, was all that mattered.

He shook his head. "Ten years, and here you are, a block from my house. All I had to do was follow the sound."

Autumn danced up to us, pulling me back to reality. "Hey, that was so cool."

"Thanks for letting me play with you. Do you need a ride, or are you hanging out here?" I tried to remember my responsibilities.

"We'll walk," she said. "We can get home in time for Thriller Theatre." She looked at Greg. "Hi, I'm Autumn and this is our band, the Parkers. Stacy's helping us out."

"Autumn, this is Greg Martinez. I knew him in high school," I managed to say. "This is my niece and her friends, Rosie and Billy."

They all shook hands with Greg and then headed for the steps. Greg and I followed.

"We watch all the horror flicks on TV because we're writing our own film," Billy explained over his shoulder. "Autumn's gonna direct it."

"It's a punk Ramones horror movie," Rosie said, giggling.

"We'll film it over at the shopping center, around all the empty stores," Autumn said. "All the guys get killed first, and

Rosie has to fight the monster all by herself. It's called *You Should Never Have Opened That Door.*"

"Then if we do a sequel, it'll be *I Don't Wanna Go Down to the Basement,*" Billy added. "We'll film it at school, 'cause the basement's creepy there."

Outside the house, they all hugged me and took off down the street, laughing and talking a mile a minute.

"So," Greg said. "You want to take a walk and catch up on the past ten years? Unless you have somewhere to be."

"Nowhere. Nowhere but here." I tried to calm myself. "Start by telling me why you're here."

"Here, Arboria Park? Short version, I'm finishing up my last few months in the Air Force. Stationed right here, until the end of the year. I live on Holly with a couple of other guys from the base."

Holly was a short street that ran between Beech and Elm. "Which house?" I asked automatically.

He grinned. "Stacy, you haven't changed. North side, corner of Beech and Holly. I'm on graveyard shift, working base security, and my sleep habits are screwed. I had tonight off, slept part of the afternoon, and was too groggy to go out but not tired enough to sleep again. So I went for a walk, and when I got around the corner I heard some music and followed it. Saw some kids coming out of that house and asked them if it was a party, and they said no, it's a punk house, go on in. Good thing I did."

"So you've been back here for a while."

He looked sheepish. "I looked for you as soon as I got here. All I found in the phone book was your parents' number and address. I thought about calling them, but it seemed too creepy. I figured you'd left town, maybe gotten married or something."

"I'm a social worker, and if we list our numbers our clients will never leave us alone."

"So you're not married or anything?"

I blushed as I placed my guitar in the trunk of my car and pulled out my denim jacket. "Nope, just a spinster aunt."

He helped me with the jacket and took my arm. "Let's go."

We headed up Beech to Holly. He pointed to his house. "We're all on different shifts, so basically somebody's always asleep and somebody else is always cooking something smelly."

"That house used to belong to the Albrights," I said before I could stop myself.

"You still live here in the Park?"

"No, apartment complex out on the highway. But my parents are here, and Autumn's mom remarried and lives on Mimosa, and my brother Matt is on the other end of Beech. So I'm around a lot."

"Give me the tour, then. I know your parents are on the Circle. I drove by a few times, like a stalker."

We headed over that way, and he explained, "I asked Richie about you occasionally. He always said he didn't know exactly where you lived."

"Like hell. Anyway, he could have asked."

"That's Richie. We're an Air Force family but he had to be different, so he joined the Marines. Making a career of it, and it's been good for him. After we moved we didn't get back to the East Coast for a few years, except for a couple of visits to New York."

"I asked Richie about you too, but all he ever said was you were in California."

"San Diego. I went to college out there for about two and a half years and then got restless. Hadn't settled on what I wanted to do. The war was over, so I enlisted in the Air Force. Always kind of wanted to. Took a few more college courses when I could. Now I've had enough, and I'm ready to go back to school next year and finish a biology degree. Then I want to get a master's in ecology."

"I graduated from the state university and put off a major as long as they'd let me. I had more history credits than anything else, so I went with that, but with no plan whatsoever. I got into social work because they're always desperate for somebody, especially if they can speak a little Spanish. I work mostly with families of teenagers, runaways, stuff like that."

"Do you like it?" Greg asked.

I shrugged. "Sometimes. It's been three years, and I'm feeling myself starting to burn out. They say most people flame out around five, and if by some miracle they make it to ten they're usually hopelessly cynical and maladjusted themselves."

We approached the Circle and I pointed to my parents' house. "They're still there, even though Mom always wants to move. First it was Oakley Estates, then every development that went up west of town. But Dad's got the house almost paid for, and he's not budging."

We continued down Elm. After a few steps, we asked each other simultaneously, "How did you get into punk rock?"

Greg laughed. "California. Some stuff from LA dribbled out. I still have buddies there that send me tapes. Went up and saw a few bands. And my sister's still in New York. She writes for one of those fashion magazines, about what colors you should wear and stuff. So I got a taste of NYC punk when I visited. Your brother still there?"

"Yes. He gets parts in TV shows sometimes, lots of off-Broadway stuff, and commercials. He introduced me to New York glam and punk."

We reached Mimosa and I pointed east. "Mary, my sister, lives down there. She and her husband JC have two other kids besides Autumn. Ruby's four and Jason is two and a half. You have a younger brother, right?"

"Yes, Alex. He's finishing college in LA. He quit halfway through too, to volunteer in Central America for a year." He motioned down the street. "Let's go past Richie's house."

"His parents are still here," Greg said as we stopped in front of it. "So I get a decent Sunday dinner once in a while. Richie's at Parris Island. Does your friend still live next door?"

"Julie? No, her parents moved. We're still in touch, off and on. She's a nurse in Atlanta now."

I knew where we were going next, and so did he. He took my hand.

The playground had changed over the years: The jungle gym was gone. Now all the equipment was made of wood. We walked past it to the edge of the field.

Greg was still shaking his head. "I can't believe it. Stacy Halloran, most unusual girl I ever met. The beautiful one with the beautiful name."

"It's Anastasia Louise, actually."

"That's beautiful too." He dropped my hand and bowed slightly toward me. "Gregory Roberto Martinez. We'll need all that for the wedding vows." Then he laughed as he saw my face. "Sorry. Getting ahead of myself here. Well, we're back where we started. Pick up where we left off, or start fresh?"

"Where did we leave off, exactly?" I needled him.

"I was such an idiot, not getting your address or phone number. When you're fifteen, you don't understand what a long-distance relationship is."

"I know. New Jersey seemed like California to me. And California might as well have been the moon."

"Probably just as well. At that age, we'd surely have found a way to mess up a good thing. Are your niece and her friends the same age we were that night?"

"Yes. And you realize she'll want you in her movie now, to die a bloody death in front of the Thriftway. She wants Matt to wrap himself in bandages and be a zombie, and Tommy to play the owner of the shopping center. After the monster dies the punk kids come back to life, and the owner lets them use the empty stores for shows."

"So what part are you playing?"

"I think I just have to run and scream. So, as you can see, I haven't progressed much in ten years. Still hanging around with fifteen-year-olds."

"Good thing, too. If you were, I don't know, off sipping cocktails at the country club or something, how would I have found you?"

We gazed out across the field toward the lights of Oakley Estates. They had never seemed so beautiful before. The stars were like exploding fireworks. I could almost hear a cheap radio playing the Top 40 from 1970.

"We got a waxing moon again," Greg said, putting his arm around me. "Think we'll get any shooting stars this time?"

"You never know." I slipped my arm around his waist.

"You can't see any stars at the base. Too many lights. When I'm on swing shift, sometimes I drive a few miles over to the bay after work, watch the stars from the beach. We'll have to do that soon. Bring some tapes and blast 'em for the gulls." He looked behind us at the playground. "No jungle gym to sit on here anymore, huh?"

We climbed up on a wooden playground structure with platforms and tunnels. Greg leaned back against a low wall and pulled me down next to him. "There. Wish we had a bottle of wine or something. Or, if we really wanted to re-create our first evening, a sip of warm Schlitz and a badly rolled joint."

I leaned into his shoulder. "Why did you take that joint away from me?"

"Because I'd smoked a couple of times before, but I could tell you hadn't. And I didn't want that to be what you remembered about that night."

And just like that, a shooting star flared over the Pines. "This is too much," Greg said.

"Last time I think we caught part of the Perseids, but I don't know what that one was."

"Did you make a wish?" he asked.

"I didn't have to this time."

We shared our first kiss then, light but lingering. Greg smiled as we finally drew apart.

"Oh, boy. Gotta decide here: go slow and enjoy letting this thing build, or give in to the inevitable and run away together tonight?"

"Life's a journey, not a destination. At least, that's what everybody tells me when I'm flailing around." I leaned back against him again. "Anyway, you figured your life out, obviously. Tell me about that."

"I told you I loved science and history. Well, reading about the industrial revolution and stuff like that, I thought about how all that affected the environment. Americans have always thought we have more land and water than we could ever use, so who cares if we dump our waste and destroy some of it? That's all come home to roost now, and I guess I finally decided science was the way for me to make use of what I learned in history."

"That does make sense. I've never been able to coalesce my interests that way. Or see how everything fits together."

"You will, Halloran. I have faith in you. God, I don't know what to talk about first. Chronological order, or free association?"

We spent hours talking, and sometimes not talking. I don't know when I fell asleep, but when I woke I could hear mourning doves and see just a bit of light, enough to illuminate the dew on the field. I sat there a moment, still in Greg's arms. The improbability of it all hit me, and I could feel tears even as I wanted to race into the field and scream for everybody south of Cobbs Road to wake up and share my joy.

He woke then too, and looked startled. "Oh, boy. I'm stiff. What time is it?"

"Quarter after six. We're facing the wrong direction for sunrise."

He stretched his arms out. "I could use some coffee and breakfast."

"Don't even look at me," I said, crawling over to the ladder. "I can't imagine what I look like now."

"You look fabulous. Come on, we're not finished. Let's get breakfast. The diner near the base is open."

"My car is *all* the way over on Beech."

"Let's get walking, then. At least we'll be facing the sunrise."

We made our way across the Park, holding hands. The streetlights went off, a few cars drove by. We walked past Mary's house, and Matt's. Finally, my car came into view. In the pinkish light of the sunrise, Beech House was as quiet as the others on the street.

The diner was quiet too, just a few sleepy airmen coming on or off a shift. We found a booth, and I told Greg to order coffee while I went to the ladies' room.

"And a cinnamon roll," I added. "The cinnamon rolls here are divine."

"I really will have to marry you, Halloran," Greg said. "I dream about those cinnamon rolls sometimes. I couldn't be with someone who didn't understand."

After the food came, Greg said, "Seriously, I want to see you again. Might be tough while I'm on nights. Next one off, though, I'm taking you to dinner."

"Just so you know, I'm on call some weekends. I can go out, but I have to keep checking my messages."

"We'll do what we have to." He leaned across the table and kissed me again. It tasted of coffee and cinnamon and possibilities.

·······················

It was hard to stop when I kissed him good-bye at his house. I tried to sleep when I finally got home, but a wrong number and a Jehovah's Witness working the building were the least of my problems. At a decent hour, I called Mary.

"Hey there," she said. "Autumn says you guys had a great show last night. I would have loved to see it, but of course she'd rather *die* . . ."

"I wanted to make sure she got home okay."

"Are you kidding? The one thing in life I never have to worry about is where my daughter and her friends are on Friday nights. At eleven thirty they have to drop everything and watch those awful monster movies on Channel 8. And in our basement more often than not, because, Billy let slip, we 'have the best snacks.'"

I heard Autumn in the background. "*Ask her about the guy!*"

"Oh, yeah. Autumn says you ran into some dreamboat from high school."

"No. I mean yes, kind of. Mary, it was Greg Martinez. From the playground when I was fifteen. *The* guy."

"What—*oh*. The one from New Jersey you never saw again?"

"I knew it!" Autumn screeched.

"Autumn, *please*. So what happened?"

"He's been back here for a while. Stationed at the base. He's getting out of the Air Force in a few months and going back to school to finish his degree and get a master's. Mary, my head is spinning. We talked all night and then went for breakfast."

"*Well.* I'm glad you found him again, but right now I think you need to settle down, maybe take a nap."

"I will. I'm not crazy. Really."

Mary laughed. "I know."

······················

Greg called me that night before he left for work. "Hey. Got a few minutes here. After you dropped me off I slept the sleep of the righteous, and when I woke up I realized I'd crossed off a *huge* thing on my to-do list."

"That's how I felt too," I said. "Except I couldn't sleep, only a short nap this afternoon. I'm in bed now, reading and fading fast."

"Tell me you're wearing that DK shirt again, and I'll go AWOL."

"Sorry. Just one from a charity walk I did with Matt."

"Well, I'll wait until tomorrow afternoon, then. I'll have a few hours before I have to go to work. Until then, good night, my queen of the punks, goddess of the suburban starlight. We still have a lot to talk about."

······················

Over the next few weeks, we got together every chance we could, catching up, listening to music, and making out like we were fifteen again. One chilly, clear evening we drove down to the bay to check out the stars. We walked the sand, listening to the gentle lap of the waves and gazing at the full orange moon.

"I wish tonight wasn't a work night," Greg said. "At least I'm on days this week." He put his lips to my ear. "We're both off next weekend. Why don't we drive down to the beach, get a hotel somewhere?"

I tensed involuntarily, and he loosened his hold. "Hey, sorry. No rush, if you're not ready."

"It's not that. I've never wanted to be with anybody as much as I want to be with you. I got myself on the pill the Monday after we reconnected, just so I'd be ready."

"Stacy, you're like an endless box of Crackerjacks, with a different surprise every time."

"It's just . . ." I cast around for the right words. "I'm never sure I'm doing that right. I don't want you going to a lot of effort with hotels and things, and then I screw it up."

"Stacy, seriously. You could never screw it up. We will be amazing together."

"I can't help it. I always feel like I'm doing something wrong, like I missed something along the way, and now I can't catch up. Like everything else in my life, really."

Greg gently touched my face. "I know something or some-one happened to you to make you think that way. It's all right if you want to tell me."

"Not here. It's too nice tonight." I looked out at the lights of a barge on the water. "But soon. And yes to the weekend, but let's just keep it low key."

"Anything you want." He pulled me close again. "We'll just get together Saturday, see what happens. No pressure. And you don't have to tell me the bastard's name, if you're worried about a jailhouse wedding on death row. But now I really wish I'd found you sooner."

I wished he had too, but I said, "It's not your job to rescue me."

"Maybe not. But I wondered for years how I'd feel if I saw you again, what you were doing, if you were okay. We'll work out all the tough parts."

We held each other in that spot for a while, almost like we were slow dancing on the sand. I relaxed into him as he kissed my hair, wondering if I should just let it happen now, on this moonlit beach, and not give myself a chance to spoil everything. But then a car sped past on the road above the beach, radio blaring Van Halen, reminding me we weren't far from civilization.

"Not quite private enough here." Greg laughed. "We'll find a better beach spot someday. The Caribbean, maybe. When the time is right. Okay?"

"Okay," I said. "Let's start at my house, Saturday night."

....

Despite what I told Greg, I did want it to be special. It had to be different this time. I fussed around—candles in the bedroom, wineglasses on the coffee table. Backup birth control ready in the bathroom. I agonized over what to wear: dress up special, or wear something easy to get out of? I didn't own anything sexy and couldn't imagine myself trying to be. *Normal people don't do this*, I thought as I plowed through drawers. *They just let things happen.* I found a shell-pink, long halter-style nightgown Mary had given to me that I'd always felt was too nice to wear. It was more elegant than sexy, but when I tried it on it made me feel pretty. That helped.

I knew I'd made the right decision when I answered the door. Greg's eyes moved up and down. "Wow, Halloran. I like this side of you." He thrust a bottle of wine at me and clicked two cassette tapes together. "One of these is Spanish guitars, very romantic. The other one is a California band called Black Flag, but maybe we'll save that for tomorrow."

It will be different this time. I settled next to him on the couch with a glass of wine, willing myself not to think about what

I was supposed to be doing. I trusted Greg. Enough to fall asleep with him that first night, enough that every touch he'd given me so far had felt right.

As we moved into the bedroom, with the candles and the Spanish guitars (he was right, they were romantic and not distracting), I knew I was in the right place.

Long after the candle on the dresser had burned down and the tape had clicked off, Greg reached over to snuff out the other candle on the nightstand. "I guess we can add 'sexual chemistry' to our list of what works," he said. "You didn't even get distracted trying to figure out the guitar chords."

"I had better things to do." I reached for him as he settled in again.

"Just wanted you to feel okay about it." He ran his fingers along my neck.

"I feel more than okay."

He grinned. "Then let's just sleep for an hour or two, and maybe do it all again."

....

I called Mary a couple of weeks before Thanksgiving in a panic. "Help me," I begged. "I'm stressed about bringing Greg to Thanksgiving dinner. You know, 'the Puerto Rican airman from the rooming house.' That's all Mom will see . . ."

"Relax," Mary said. "It shouldn't be that bad. But if you want to come over Sunday I'll invite Mom and Dad, get her off her turf so to speak, with no holiday pressure. Greg's met all of us and seen the chaos here, so it'll be easier for him too."

"Would you? That would be great."

"Of course. I remember how this can be. They'll like Greg just fine."

Mary was right. Having the kids around helped keep conversation light. After dinner, JC and Dad sat at the dining room table playing Legos with Jason. Ruby snuggled up to me on the couch and asked me to read her favorite book to her, *Bread and Jam for Frances*. Greg sat in the kitchen with Autumn, helping her learn the words to a song she wanted to sing for the Spanish Club's school assembly.

Each time I looked up from reading I could see how lost Mom seemed, her eyes flitting from place to place. Wondering how we'd all stepped off the path and left her alone.

"Hey, Stacy," Greg called from the kitchen. "Autumn's got that same accent and pronunciation you have."

"It's Castilian," I said. "We both learned from Olga. My Hispanic clients laugh at me, and my Panamanian high school Spanish teacher was always trying to fix it."

"Señora Hughes," Autumn giggled. "She *still* is."

"Mary and I want to go to Spain when the kids are a little older," JC said. "I've always wanted to see the running of the bulls."

"*Seeing* better be all you do," Mary teased him. "No bull running until all the kids are big enough to rescue you."

"I'm applying to a program for student filmmakers this summer," Autumn announced. "They go to Europe for two weeks. I probably won't get in this year, because most of the kids are older. But I thought I'd try."

"Never hurts to try new things," Dad agreed. "Jason, I bet we could put wings on that car we just made, and make it an airplane."

"Do they have punk rock in Spain?" Autumn asked.

"They do in Puerto Rico," Greg said. "My sister Lisa went there last year for a fashion shoot, and she sent me a record of a local band covering the Sex Pistols. You haven't lived until you hear 'God Save the Queen' in Spanish."

"Hey, that's an idea for the assembly," Autumn said. "Except Señora Hughes wouldn't like it. Maybe at the end-of-year assembly, and I'll just take French next year instead."

Ruby jumped up and got another book off the shelf, a collection of African folk tales. She took it over to Mom. "Let's read the one about the cow," she urged.

"Go on, Mom," I said. "She loves being read to."

Ruby squeezed into the chair with Mom. "See? The farmer loves his cow . . ."

Autumn and Greg walked into the room, singing. "*El cielo azul* . . ."

Ruby yelled, "Everybody shut up! I'm reading to Grandmom."

Mary looked at Mom, and back to me. "Welcome to the United Colors of Arboria," she said. As Greg and Autumn finished their song, he smiled at me. It was going to be all right.

10 — 1983

....

I had a wedding to plan. Nine-year-old me was doing cartwheels in the backyard. Twenty-eight-year-old me was more pragmatic but still determined to enjoy the process, even with tight finances and the doleful face of my mother in the way.

Greg and I had been living together for a while in a house on Birch. We'd moved in together around the time he finished his Air Force hitch. Dad hadn't said much, but Mom had flipped.

"It's bad enough Tommy's shacked up with another one," she'd lectured me.

Now I knew how Mary must have felt.

"Mom, that is very rude. He and Megan are engaged. We're all going up to her uncle's vineyard for the wedding this summer, remember? And Greg and I will be too, someday, when he's finished with school and finds a job. And maybe I'll find something better by then too."

She shook her head. "Don't expect a big wedding or gifts when you do."

She'd been stunned when we finally set the date (to coincide with the Perseids) and people had started asking her what we wanted and where I was registered. Somehow the latter half of the twentieth century had eluded Mom.

Greg had been working away at part-time security jobs and a gig I found for him doing intake interviews for a veterans' substance abuse program. He commuted to the state university for his classes; he understood why I didn't want to move up there.

In February Autumn learned she'd gotten a scholarship to NYU film school. She was about to unveil her latest documentary at Beech House, the site where she'd premiered all her horror movies and music videos. We were all invited, even the grandparents, though they opted for a private showing at Mary's house the following Sunday instead.

Though some of the original Beech House inhabitants and regulars had graduated and moved on, more had come along who were involved with the project. Patty was still around, working on her MSW; Sylvie had a job that had required her to alter her hairdo, but she still liked to rock out on weekends. As we helped set up chairs in the basement for the film debut, new kids came in, looking as excited as Autumn and her friends had a few years before.

"Is Matt coming?" I asked Mary as she and JC and the kids sat down with us.

"He's working, so he'll come over on Sunday. Don, too."

"Don just came in."

He stood near the steps, a scowl on his face. Autumn rushed over to tell him to sit up front with us, and Mary waved to him, but he just barked at Autumn that he'd stay where he was, thanks.

Don was still unpredictable. Every long period of stability he'd managed—a steady job, a girlfriend, a regular address—had been punctuated by unfortunate slips: the brief biker gang stint of 1973, the DUI in 1978, the night in jail after the bar fight in 1981. Lately he'd been on a good roll, showing up for all of Autumn's school and film events. Now his face told me he'd fallen off the wagon again.

I tried not to think about it as the lights went off and Autumn's *Punx in the Park* unfurled on the sheet hung at the end of the basement. The footage ranged from shaky shots of early

Beech House shows to recent, more professional-looking ones, along with interviews of youngsters from the Park talking about their favorite bands. It was an entertaining half hour, and everyone applauded as the lights went on again.

Mary and I helped the house kids serve refreshments as a horde of younger kids surrounded Autumn, wanting to know more about film school and what it was like in the "old days" a scant three years before. I could see she was both flattered and flummoxed at having graduated from being just another Park punk to one of the scene's veterans.

Don didn't come over for our punk-themed cupcakes, or to congratulate Autumn. When I saw him going up the steps, I followed, and caught up to him at the front door.

"What's wrong, Don? Autumn was so happy to see you. We're kind of celebrating her NYU acceptance . . ."

He turned, eyes blazing. "Yeah, she called and told me right away. I should be happy for her, but it's just another punch in the gut. She's turned out great. All because I bailed out of her life."

I sighed. "Don, it's not always about you. Anyway, she thanked you in the credits the way she always does. You helped give her the first camera she used. And she wants you to go to New York with her this spring to check things out . . ."

"Let her mother take her, and that fag actor brother of yours can help her."

I pushed him out the door onto the sidewalk. "That does it, Don. I'm sick of trying to be nice to you." I shoved his chest again, and he stumbled backward on the lawn. "Stay away from all of us if that's how you feel. Tommy is an actor but he isn't gay, and you should know that. Matt is. Yeah, Matt, the one who pitches in the Police and Fire league and runs marathons. The one who could kick your sorry ass into tomorrow. Maybe you should stay out of Autumn's life, and ours, until you figure out who you really are."

The red color had drained from Don's face. Someone in the house must have heard me yelling and called Greg, because he ran out the door and caught Don's arm as he started to slump. "What's going on here, Stacy?"

Before I could answer Don said, "She's yelling at me for being a drunken idiot at my daughter's party. Which I am. So I'll go." He turned away.

Greg didn't let go of his arm. "Where's your bike? Think you'd trust me to ride it back to your house, and let Stacy drive you home?"

I was about to say I wouldn't drive him and he could smash the motorcycle into the nearest tree for all I cared when Autumn came out of the house.

"Dad." She looked calm but wary. "I wanted to thank you for coming. But maybe you should go now, and come over on Sunday and watch the movie again. Sober." She stood her ground, staring at him.

Don met her gaze. "You're right, honey. I'm sorry I ruined your party. Your movie was great. I should have stayed away."

"So what happened, Dad?" Autumn wasn't giving up.

"Nothing much." He looked at the ground. "Work's fine, Nancy's fine, everything's fine. Then you called me about NYU last night. Should've been the proudest moment of my life. Instead, I drove straight to the liquor store and called in sick today."

"Dad, it's okay. Well, not the liquor store, but it's okay if you feel weird about it." Autumn turned back toward the house. "But come by Sunday. We'll talk."

"I will," he called after her, and turned back to Greg. "Here's the keys to the bike, Sarge. I'll walk. I could use the sobering up."

"Too cold for that," Greg laughed. "Stacy, go get your coat before you freeze."

"I don't blame you if you don't want to drive me, Stacy," Don said. "Stay here with my girl so she knows people care."

"I'll drive you," I said reluctantly. "Autumn's busy with her friends and her mom. We'll come back after we drop you off."

We were silent in the car, heading for his house in town. Halfway there he spoke up. "I'm really sorry, Stacy. Not just about

Autumn, but you and your family. I had no right to talk like that. I like your brothers, both of them. Good guys."

I stared out at the road, where Greg was riding the bike ahead of us. "Don, you're so live-and-let-live most of the time. Why are you so irrational when you're drunk or angry?"

"Guess I'll be working that out the rest of my life. You'll be the first to know when I do." He was quiet again for a minute. "Actually, I do know what happened this time. All I could think about when Autumn called was when Mary and I got our college acceptances senior year. Did you know I got into Penn State, and Ohio? We both had a future."

I pulled into his driveway behind Greg. Don got out of the car, stumbling only a little, and shook hands with him. "Thanks, man. I'll go to a meeting tomorrow before this spirals any further."

"You know, I still volunteer with the veterans' substance abuse groups at work," Greg said. "Want to come along sometime?"

Don shook his head. "Thanks, but I got my own meetings."

"I didn't mean it that way. I thought you might want to lead a group. You've managed sobriety for long periods, but you've also fallen and gotten back up. People need to know that happens, that a stumble doesn't have to mean giving up."

"Maybe." Don walked toward his door. "I'll talk to you when I'm in a better frame of mind."

Greg got into the car. "Stacy, I know how he can be. He's sorry. We'll hope he gets himself righted again. I think helping others might be good for him. Take him out of himself a little."

I backed out of the driveway. "I guess I'm just tired of him."

"Well, from my general observations, he kind of depends on you to kick him in the ass once in a while. He wouldn't accept it from Mary, and she's too soft-hearted anyway. Autumn's old enough to see him for what he is, but she feels sorry for him and resents him and loves him all at once. His own family is ashamed and lets him know it. He doesn't have many people who can give it to him straight without an agenda."

As I parked near Beech House I blurted out, "I think what I hate about him is what I hate about myself. Both of us spinning wheels, watching everyone else get it together. I'm not an alcoholic, but if I were I'd be as bad as him, or worse."

Greg took my hands. "Stacy, you both have trouble seeing where you're going, true. Don's a guy who had it all going for him, then one mistake threw him off his path. You're afraid to even step on one, and I've never really known why. I know what happened in college, but that's not it." He touched my face so I would look at him. "The first time I met you, you were already putting yourself down, saying you weren't any good at playing guitar when clearly you were obsessed with it. I figured it was just how girls talked, trying not to look stuck up. But I've watched you for almost three years now, and talked to Mary and your brothers."

I pulled away. "So what should I do? They don't have twelve-step meetings for being a general fuckup who's afraid of everything. I try to help people, like you want Don to do . . ."

"Stacy, if anything you help other people too much. You'd walk through fire for your family and friends and clients. Just not for yourself." He opened the car door. "Come on. Let's get back to Autumn's party. She needs you."

. . . .

In May, after turning in his master's thesis, Greg interviewed for a job with the state environmental agency. When he got it, we celebrated with dinner out and a show at Beech House. Autumn had told us the band was not to be missed; they were called the Fading Scars and had played the "punk anti-prom" at the house the week before.

The basement still held remnants of the prom décor: black crepe paper and dead flowers. The Parkers were opening, and as they sound-checked there was a commotion at the top of the steps and someone hollered down, "Jeff's here."

Billy and Benny put down their guitars and ran up the stairs with a couple of other boys. A moment later, two kids came down half-supporting, half-carrying a young man whose legs appeared to be paralyzed. Behind them, Benny and Billy were helping bring down a wheelchair. Everyone moved aside as they settled the man down and he wheeled himself to a spot in front of the makeshift stage. He nodded to us. "Nice night for a show, eh?"

Before we could answer, the Parkers crashed into their set. As they played I periodically stole looks at Jeff, who was bobbing his head in time to the music, a half smile on his face.

Autumn rushed over when they finished the set. "What did you think, Jeff?"

"Inside, I'm moshing my brains out," he answered. "Gonna let me sing 'I Don't Wanna Walk Around with You' sometime? Or 'Dancing with Myself'?"

"You bet," Autumn answered, and turned to us. "Have you guys met Jeff? He's been coming here for a few weeks."

He offered his hand. "Jeff Gale. Journalist, music fan, gimp about town. Pleased to meet you."

Greg and I introduced ourselves and shook his hand.

"I heard about this place and decided to check it out for a story," Jeff said. "Then this young lady and some of the others explained that the location has to be kept quiet. So I figured, what the hell, it's a great place to hear some music now and then. Even if basement shows are inherently discriminatory." He winked at Autumn.

"This house was chosen because it backs up to the shopping center, so there are fewer neighbors to object," I explained. "And the basement keeps the noise level down a bit more. I guess no one ever thought about—"

"We could put a cellar ramp in," Autumn suggested. "The skateboarders would like that. Might be a bit steep, though."

"Fear not," Jeff replied. "For an old daredevil like me, the steeper the better."

Greg and I talked with him between sets. "I write and take photos for the weekly newspaper," Jeff told us. "Not exactly hard journalism. Sewer board meetings. Car wash openings. This week I'm taste-testing French fries. Someone has to."

After the Fading Scars set, Billy asked Jeff if he wanted to go upstairs. Greg helped with the wheelchair.

"Gotta call for the handi-van," Jeff said after everyone got him settled again. "Could be hours before they get here. I'm not exactly high priority."

He made his phone call and wheeled into the living room. The kids went back downstairs to play records.

"Mind if we wait with you?" I asked.

"My pleasure. I'm on a waiting list for a gimpmobile of my own," he explained as we sat down across from him. "After you total the first one, you're not at the top."

"What happened?" Greg asked.

"Swerved to avoid a cat and hit a mailbox. Of course, I was doing fifty on the Avenue and singing along to The Blasters at the time. And was maybe the teensiest bit drunk." He shook his head. "Little overcompensation, eh? And before you ask, no, I'm no war hero or anything remotely noble. I used to be a mighty terror. Climbed difficult mountains, skied tougher ones, even went cave diving. This"—he tapped his legs—"was not a result of those adventures. It was a simple water-skiing accident. They really need a warning on those things. Like, 'Don't let your drunk buddy drive the boat around the rocks.'"

After we'd talked for about a half hour, Jeff said, "Guess I better roll up to the Avenue in case they actually show up when they say they will."

"Any way we can help?" I asked.

"Thank you, no." He headed toward the front door. "If they give me a hard time, I play the cripple card. Some of the drivers think if your legs are damaged, your brain must be too. So I just . . ." He went limp in the chair, twisted one arm, and slackened his jaw. "And I say, 'I dunno, when was I supposed to be here?' and they have to forgive me."

We walked with him up to the corner of Cobbs and the Avenue. "I live in that new handicap-accessible complex near the mall," he said. "Most of the other residents are eighty-year-old women. I show up in the lobby at one A.M. with a six-pack, and the night desk guy says, 'Are we out a little late again, Mr. Gale?'" He rolled his eyes. "The place plays havoc with my social life, too. I was dating Sven, the stylist from Curly Q's, for a while, but he broke up with me because my neighbors kept wanting him to do their hair."

He said this with the same sardonic, matter-of-fact outrageousness that he'd used all evening. I got the feeling it was a test, to see if his new friends were capable of more than pity.

"There's someone I'd like you to meet," I said. Greg gave me a warning look, but I plunged ahead. "My brother, Matt. He's a paramedic and, well, an extreme sports guy."

Jeff smiled. "Good call. Yes, I miss my old life, but I'm not a shrinking violet who can't stand to be reminded of it."

"Play any wheelchair sports?" Greg asked.

"Some racing. And those kids with the skateboard and bike tricks—seems like there ought to be a way for wheelies to get in on that."

We exchanged phone numbers, and the van arrived. "See you at a show," Jeff said with a wink as the driver helped him in.

We turned to walk back toward Beech House.

"Are you sure that was a good idea?" Greg asked. "About Matt, I mean. Fix-ups don't always work."

"Just a feeling," I said. "Not a fix-up, necessarily. But they could both probably use a friend who understands."

....

Jeff had said he was participating in a charity stroll—"Well, charity *roll*"—the next weekend, and I knew Matt was competing in the 5K run portion. So I signed myself up for the stroll, and on Saturday I found Jeff and brought him over to where Matt was stretching and warming up for the race.

"Matt, I'd like you to meet my new friend, Jeff Gale. He's a reporter at the *Weekly Gazette*."

They shook hands, and Matt said, "I remember you. You covered that motorcycle wreck on King a couple of weeks ago."

"Yes, wasn't it lucky that the moron decided to flip his bike in front of an Amish buggy just as I was leaving the dentist? My editor was very impressed I got some breaking news photos. Doesn't happen often."

"You ever want to do an ambo ride-along, let me know," Matt said. "We just got the trucks outfitted with some new handicap stuff. Probably a good idea for a real wheelchair user to check some of it out."

They chatted until Matt had to start his race, and then Jeff and I went over to the starting line for the walkers.

"You wicked, wicked girl," he said, laughing. "I see what you're up to."

"Don't be ridiculous, Jeff," I said. "You have a lot in common, and you should be friends, if nothing else."

"We'll see about that," Jeff said. The countdown began, and he made some vrooming noises. "Let me know if you get tired and need a ride."

....

August was upon me before I knew it. Greg was working at his new job; Autumn was packing for New York. And Matt and Jeff were dating. Openly.

Mom, already at the end of her rope over my wedding and Dad's recent emphysema diagnosis, was beside herself. Matt was one of the groomsmen, and I'd invited Jeff.

"What were you thinking?" she raged at me.

"I was thinking that I want him there. And if I hadn't invited him, Matt would have anyway. With my blessing." I was at her house, trying to tally up the RSVPs. "Matt has a right to be happy, just like the rest of us."

Dad came into the dining room where we were working. He'd barely started enjoying his retirement when his out-of-breath spells got worse and the doctor had told him the smoking had to stop. But the damage was done.

"Got my new suit yesterday," he said. "After the wedding, you can put it away for my funeral."

It was Dad's way to make jokes, and Mom's to cover her face and leave the room. He wasn't on his way out just yet. Still, I knew how glad he was that he could walk me down the aisle before things got worse.

Dad sat down across from me. "You have to understand, these things take some getting used to for people of our generation. You kids take everything in stride." He looked at the pile of acceptance cards. "Expecting a good turnout, I see."

"Looks that way."

We had reserved the NCO club at the airbase for the ceremony and reception. The wedding would be a bit less stiff and formal than the coloring-book one that had guided my childhood fantasies. Autumn was my maid of honor, and Mary and Greg's sister, Lisa, were bridesmaids, all in cobalt blue. Greg's brother, Alex, was best man, and Richie, whom I hadn't seen since high school, was a groomsman. Fifteen-year-old me would never have believed that Richie Oliva would be in my wedding.

I rejected all the Princess Diana–influenced frou-frou knockoffs in favor of a simple sleeveless long white jersey gown, with just enough pearls and detailing on the bodice to mollify nine-year-old Stacy. The one area where I went with my traditional fantasies was the cake. It would be tall and tiered, and decorated with flowers. The cake from my coloring-book dreams, the one Mary and Don should have had at their wedding.

....

Stacys of all ages were excited on the day. And nervous. I tried to settle myself down by calming Dad, who was worried because he'd been wheezing at the rehearsal.

"It's not so long a walk," he said. "I think I can make it without getting out of breath or coughing."

"Don't worry if you have to stop. I won't care."

"Well, your mother . . ."

I sat down next to him. "Everything's going to be great. Megan's taking photographs, JC is playing the piano . . . I wish Mom were happy about this being a real family wedding instead of being so judgmental about who's in the family."

"You've done a nice job," Dad said. "I decided a long time ago with Ev that you just do your best, and it's up to her to accept it or make herself miserable."

"I told her last night she's lucky we didn't do a punk wedding at Beech House, the way Autumn wanted. We still have that to look forward to someday."

That made Dad laugh. He was still chuckling when the music started. Ruby in her white dress and blue sash went first, scattering her flower petals like a star, all but waving and blowing kisses. Jason went up next carrying the rings, grimly staring straight ahead until he reached his destination.

As Autumn reached the midway point I took Dad's arm. He was calm now.

"You'll be all right," he whispered. As we stepped forward, I looked at Greg and watched his expression change. He hadn't seen the dress before.

"You look beautiful, Halloran," he whispered as Dad stepped back and he took my hand. "What kept you?"

"You know Dad. He likes to check out the scenery."

The chaplain cleared his throat, and Greg grinned at him. "Feels like ten years since I've seen her. We're ready now."

The ceremony was simple, punctuated with musical pieces JC had helped us select and one he'd written himself. *Remember this*, I told myself. Like nine-year-old Stacy, I believed in love. I looked at Ruby, who was seven, and Autumn, the age her mother was when she had married so reluctantly. There were people of all races in attendance, my brother's boyfriend, Patty and some punks, and Greg's Air Force buddies. As I held Greg's arm, clutching my bouquet with one hand so I could peep at the new ring on the other, I knew he understood.

I'd asked everyone to submit songs they wanted to hear when they sent back their RSVPs, so the reception was a blend of Motown and merengue, Sinatra and swing, romance and rock. Everyone danced away the afternoon. Patty and Autumn slipped the DJ a copy of the Descendents' "Marriage," and Greg and I, along with Alex and Tommy, joined their little impromptu mosh pit. Don had requested Nick Lowe's "I Knew the Bride When She Used to Rock and Roll" for a dance with me.

"Thanks for inviting us," he said as we whirled around. "You didn't have to."

"I wanted you and Nancy here." He and his girlfriend had spent a fair amount of time talking to Mary and JC, and even Matt and Jeff, and they seemed to be enjoying themselves. "And thank you so much for the beautiful curio cabinet."

He beamed. "Autumn said you'd like it. Mary too. Nancy and I are getting pretty good at scouting and buying antiques. Started out going to tag sales on the motorcycle, and now we take the truck every weekend because we buy and sell so much. It's just a fun sideline, but we'd like to open a shop someday, or at least a stall at the auction."

"I'm happy to hear that."

He laughed. "And I'm happy for you and Greg. Maybe we're both getting better at managing our lives."

My parents had met Greg's a couple of times before and everyone had hit it off, so I was glad to see them chatting at their table between dances. My dream wedding was surpassing expectations.

After I finished my dance with Don, Greg and I approached our parents' table. He held out his arm to his mother, Delia. "Come on, Mom. We need to dance."

I sat down in her chair. Dad and Greg's father, Javier, were deep in conversation.

"Mom, this is so wonderful," I said with a contented sigh. "Everything worked just right."

The smile that had been pasted on her face all afternoon vanished. She leaned toward me and whispered, "I'm so embarrassed. To present Greg's family with this . . . spectacle."

"What do you mean?" I felt light-headed, like the champagne I'd been sipping had hit all at once.

Her lip curled. "Look at Autumn and those *people*." She nodded toward the punks' table. Autumn had changed out of her blue pumps and was wearing Doc Martens with her bridesmaid dress. "And Matt and . . . oh, Stacy, we can never live this down. Why did you have to do this to us?"

I jumped up. "I didn't do anything to anyone. This is my wedding, and Greg's, and these are my family and friends. Your granddaughter, and your son."

I walked away, tears stinging, heading for the ladies' room. But then I saw Jeff, sitting alone while Matt waited for drinks at the bar.

I sat next to him. "Can I sit one out with you, Jeff?"

He smiled. "Wish I could have a dance, Stacy. Thank you for inviting me. I know this is tough for Matt, and you, but we needed to get it out of the way sooner or later."

"I want you here. You're my friend. And more to Matt."

Matt came back with a couple of drinks. "Hey, Stace. Want me to go back and get you something?"

"No thanks. I'm afraid if I have more I might say something terrible. To Mom."

Matt shook his head. "Don't let her get you down. We're not.

Who's having fun at this wedding? Practically everyone. If she can't, that's tough."

"I didn't put you guys on the spot, did I? That wasn't what I wanted."

"I already told her she didn't," Jeff said, looking up at Matt. "We both decided that we're tired of hiding and lying. People like you, Stacy, accept it, and other people never will. That's as good as it's going to get."

Matt nodded. "What he said." He grinned at Jeff. "He's the word guy."

Megan approached with her camera. "Hey, I haven't got all you guys together yet."

I smiled. "Get a good picture, Meg." Matt sat on my other side, and I took both their hands.

I stayed with them until Greg found me. It was time for us to cut the cake.

"I can't believe it, but I just had a fight with my mother," I whispered to him.

He nodded. "Don't let it spoil things."

"I won't." I kissed him. "Are your parents okay with everything?"

"Of course. Everything's great."

After serving the cake, I threw my bouquet. Ruby rushed to grab it. "I don't want to get married, I just want the flowers," she explained. "I'm the *flower girl*, and I don't have any flowers."

I hugged her, thinking of myself at Mary's first wedding. "Now you do."

．．．．．．．．．．．．．．．．．．．．．．

The families and a few close friends gathered at Mary's for a post-reception wind-down. Javier and Delia talked about wedding customs in Puerto Rico, and Olga added stories about Spain. Even Dad chimed in with tales of the ethnic weddings he'd seen growing up near Pittsburgh. Mom was silent.

"You know what I wish?" I said. "That we could do a kind of parade through the village thing. Here."

Tommy laughed. "Like in *The Godfather*, when they were in Sicily?"

"Kind of. With music."

Mary turned to JC. "Could you lead this procession, with your sax?"

"Well, that sounds more like a New Orleans funeral than a wedding," JC answered. "But hey, I'm down."

"Me too." Tommy jumped up. "I could use a walk after all that reception food."

Dad got to his feet. "I can't go walking all over the neighborhood anymore. But I'd sure like to come for a block or two, if I can." He looked at Mom. "Ev?"

"Maybe you shouldn't," she said.

Delia went over and took his arm. "We'll come along for part of it too, and see that he gets back all right."

JC re-entered the room, with his saxophone. "Well, then, let's get started."

Outside the house, JC began the parade with Ruby and Jason. Then the wedding party, plus Tommy and Megan, Jeff, and Lisa's husband, David. Javier and Delia each held one of Dad's arms. Olga and her husband and son came along too.

We walked over to Beech, then headed north. JC played whatever love songs came into his head, and people washing their cars or sitting in their yards waved. Others popped their heads out doors and shouted congratulations. Ruby twirled around, showing off her dress and my flowers to her friends, with Megan and Autumn documenting it all.

At the punk house, some kids who were making show fliers greeted us. After a brief consultation with JC as to whether he knew any "punk love songs," they sang us an a cappella version of "Do You Want to Dance."

Dad, breathing heavily, came over and kissed me good-bye. "I wish I could go the whole way," he said, clutching my hand.

"I know," I said, tearing up again. "I remember when you walked me all around the neighborhood."

"This is your place," he said. "Your home."

Delia took his arm again. "We'll take care of him for you." She and Javier hugged and kissed us too. I stopped and watched for a moment as they walked back, supporting Dad between them.

"Your folks are wonderful," I told Greg.

"Your dad's the best. And maybe your mom will come around."

"Maybe." I didn't want to think about her.

We turned down Maple. Some guys drinking beer on a car hood saluted us, and one dashed over to Greg and handed him a 40, shouting, "For the honeymoon, my man!"

On Oak, a woman in an Air Force uniform getting out of her car did a double take. "Sergeant Martinez!" she yelled. "I served with you in Texas!"

Some of Jason's and Ruby's schoolmates followed for a while, and so did a couple of giggly pre-teen girls who gushed over the dresses. Even Rosie Thanh's family came along for a couple of blocks.

We took our time going around Arbor Circle. So many of the neighbors from my childhood—like the Brookses and Franchesinis—were long gone, but there were others who were friends with my parents. I thought about Mom again, alone at Mary's, choosing to miss out on something she probably considered another spectacle. Maybe I should have asked her to come. But I knew in my heart she wouldn't have.

By the time we hit Elm again, word had gotten around. More people joined us—a scattering of kids, some on bikes; a teen on a skateboard; a couple of folks walking dogs.

"Remember when we first walked through this neighborhood, together?" Greg asked. "I knew I'd found you again for a reason."

Richie ran up to his parents' house as we passed by. "Looks like we left the reception too early!" his father said to us as they came out and joined us. We doubled back to Mimosa so we could hit part of Cedar, passing the Pines and then circling back down for a circuit through the Crescent. JC's aunt and uncle were out watering their yard, and insisted on taking some photos.

Finally, we walked back up Birch to our own house. Everyone crowded into the kitchen, and we opened some champagne, pouring it into everything from our new wedding-gift crystal to mismatched coffee mugs. Greg held up the 40 he'd been given. "Who wants malt liquor?"

After a toast there were more hugs and laughter. As everyone drifted away, Greg and I looked at each other. "Sunset at the playground?" he asked.

. . . .

We stood at the edge of the field and watched the pinks and purples behind Oakley Estates.

"I wish we could stay here all night, and wait for the Perseids," I said. "But we have to be up early, so your parents can drive us to the airport."

Greg held me closer. "The Perseids will still be over us tonight, even if we can't see them. And maybe there'll be a few tomorrow night too, when we're standing on a beach in Puerto Rico."

We stayed until the streetlights came on, then walked toward home. "I just fulfilled another one of my childhood wedding fantasies," I said. "Wearing my wedding gown all day, instead of changing."

"Good job. Now I want to take it off you."

He carried me through the door, past the mess in the kitchen and the partially packed suitcases in the hallway, and into the bedroom.

Afterward, late that night, I got out of bed, leaving Greg asleep, and crept into the bathroom in the dark. I opened the window screen and leaned out, listening to the late-night sounds of Arboria Park—crickets and frogs from the woods and the creek, a dog barking in the Crescent, the faint hum of the highway, a car radio playing Duran Duran.

The light flicked on. "What are you doing?"

"Savoring."

Greg grinned. "Come on, let's get dressed and go back to the playground. Time to catch a star."

11—1987

Mona Harris nodded approvingly as I arranged the lilacs she had brought in a green cut-glass vase. "They'll scent up whatever room they're in, so you may not want them in the kitchen," she said.

"I'll put them where we can enjoy them. I'm so glad I'm over that stage where any type of smell makes me sick. I'd hate to miss lilac season. Are you sure you can't stay for some coffee?"

"Not today, Stacy. That old man of mine wants to get on the road, get down to Salisbury before noon." She headed for the back door. "You take care now."

"Thanks so much for the lilacs, Mona. Have a good trip."

I carried the vase upstairs to the bedroom. The violets I'd put there a few days before, from my own yard, were wilting. Before carrying them downstairs, I paused at the door of what would be the baby's room. Though the recent amnio had indicated I was having a girl (and I had believed that all along anyway), I'd decided against the cliché of a pink nursery and was going with soft yellow, lavender, and a light sage green. One window looked out the back of the house toward the creek; the other faced west. A west-facing room was better for the baby, we had reasoned. Not as much morning sun to wake her early.

Greg and I had moved into this Crescent split-level a year and a half before, in anticipation of starting our family. It was next door to JC's aunt and uncle, and just a couple of houses away from where Julie and Donna and I had crossed the creek. I'd achieved Mom's dream of 1960, but she had moved on. "Why not a nicer neighborhood?" she had asked. "Mary says Olga just moved to Fox Catch."

"Well, her husband's a surgeon. They can afford it. This way we still get a pretty wooded lot, backing up to a creek and a farm. We couldn't afford that in another neighborhood." The fancy new subdivision of Fox Catch, home of doctors and lawyers west of town, was Mom's latest obsessive marker of success.

I adjusted the back window to let in some fresh morning air, then went back downstairs and out the door. It was too beautiful to stay inside.

Time for a walk. When we'd first moved back to Arboria Park, I'd ridden my bike around the way I had when I was a kid. But since my pregnancy started showing, my sense of balance was off and I didn't feel comfortable riding. Instead, I walked all over the neighborhood, visiting Mary and her family on weekends, or Matt and Jeff, who had bought a house together on Cedar. Sometimes I'd pop in to the newest punk house, on Elm, to see how the latest crop of kids was getting along.

I also visited my parents, of course. But I'd been over the day before, and left on a bad note again. I could deal with being told I shouldn't be walking so much in my condition. I could face disapproval over whatever I was eating or not eating. That was just Mom stuff. It was the rest of it—the unspoken undercurrent—that always set me off.

So, instead of heading toward Elm and the Circle, I went the other way. Maybe I'd stroll up Beech and see what flowers were blooming on that side of the neighborhood. In addition to resuming my childhood habits of snooping around, I'd discovered a new love: looking at gardens. Mona had helped me plant bulbs in the fall that had turned into breathtaking patches of crocuses, snow-drops, and daffodils earlier in the spring. Now it was the azaleas and lilacs that were bursting with color. I had one lilac bush in my yard, but Mona had four—three different shades of purple, plus a white one. She was looking forward to her roses blooming in June, and so was I—she'd said she'd give me some cuttings to start my own. It was Mona I relied on for advice on my feeble gardening attempts—not my mom, who was also a green thumb.

At the corner, I looked toward the boarded-up Shell station and impulsively headed over to see the cider mill foundation. The creek was sparkling, the birds were chirping, and a pleasant light smell seemed to permeate the air, even this close to the highway. All my senses were extra sensitive these days.

"Can you smell the air, baby?" I asked aloud, a hand on my burgeoning stomach. "I wish we could take a country walk today. Maybe Daddy will go with us to the lake this weekend."

I looked through the trees toward the Ramsey farm. Edith Ramsey, now close to eighty, still lived in the farmhouse, Mona had told me.

As if pulled by some hidden force, I walked to the highway. I hugged the far edges of the shoulder for a few yards, until I reached the diagonal turnoff that led to the next town—and past Edith Ramsey's farmhouse. When I got past the trees by the road in front of the house, and the long gravel drive, I saw a dazzling display of azaleas, all colors, possibly a hundred of them. Scarlet and white and pale pink; deep crimson and fuchsia and a purply magenta. I stood at the edge of the road, drinking in the sight and wishing I had brought a camera.

"Get out of that road or you'll be run over." I jumped at the sharp female voice to my right. Out of the azalea grove walked Edith Ramsey. Her shoulder-length hair was pure white, and she wore a straw hat and carried a pair of clippers. Though she wasn't tall, she carried herself straight and erect, not hunched like many older women.

Suddenly I was eight again, afraid she'd threaten me with the clippers instead of a shovel. "I'm sorry, ma'am. I was just admiring—"

"Come over here, then, and get a better look." She beckoned. "I wait all year for the azaleas to be at their prime. Folks stop cars along that stretch of road to have a peek, so you'd better get out of the way."

I stepped over into the grass and tried to stare at the bushes and not at Edith. "All this started with a couple of bushes at the end of the drive. My late husband, Kermit, bought them to cheer me up. That must have been around 1948. I kept adding more, and folks who admired them told me about different types and colors. Now they're my spring obsession." She pointed with her clippers. "I still take care of these myself. These, and my roses and some other perennials. But I need help dividing and propagating them sometimes now because I'm not as young as I used to be."

"They're so beautiful. I have a couple of the standard ones." As she leaned over to clip off a dead branch, I said, "Mrs. Ramsey, my name is Stacy Martinez. I live over on Willow Drive, across the creek. My parents knew you—Tom and Evelyn Halloran. Once, when I was eight, my friends and I trespassed on your property. My dad scolded me and told me the history of your place, and of Arboria Park, and I've always been careful not to trespass again. Until now."

Edith looked at me. "Tom Halloran. The phone man? He installed a new phone for me probably thirty years ago. Before they had all these new-fangled ones. This place once had a party line, with the Oakleys and the Cobbs. Those were the days!" She laughed. "Well, you're not trespassing, because I invited you out of the road. And you're welcome to come back any time and see the azaleas while they last."

"I can't believe some of these colors." I leaned down to look at a coral-flowered bush. "My neighbor has a lot of different-color lilacs. And roses."

"Would that be Mrs. Harris?" Edith asked. "Very fine lady. We've both shown our roses at the state fair."

"Yes! Mona. My sister is married to her nephew." I wondered what Edith would make of that.

She didn't seem shocked. "She gave me a cutting years ago, of a beautiful old-fashioned yellow rose she got from one of her aunts. Couple years later I showed it at the fair and won first place. She came in second with one of her pinks. She said that was the last time she'd give me anything!" Edith laughed out loud. "Of course, it wasn't."

"I guess I better get back," I said. "Thank you, Mrs. Ramsey."

She looked me up and down. "Edith. You're in the family way, aren't you, Mrs. Martinez? You shouldn't be traipsing along the road like that."

"I know. My mother would kill me. She doesn't even want me walking in Arboria Park."

"I should think the exercise and fresh air are good for the baby. Just not along the highway."

"I don't know why I did. I was looking at the foundation of the old cider house and . . ." I stopped, not sure whether Edith still mourned the cider mill after more than thirty-five years.

She nodded. "On a beautiful day like this, it's natural to keep moving and satisfy one's curiosity. Part of our animal instincts. Well, would you like to see more of the farm, now that you're here?"

"Yes! I mean, as long as I'm not bothering you—"

"Contrary to my reputation, my dear, I'm not a hermit or a recluse. A bit of company now and then is much appreciated. Come along, and I'll show you more."

She showed me the roses, behind the azalea grove, and then another patch next to the house. "Irises, daisies, coneflower, bee balm," she said. "I learned over the years to stagger things so there's always something blooming, right up to frost with the chrysanthemums."

We walked around the back of the house. "I used to have quite a vegetable garden back here. Not much now. A few tomato plants, some squash and beans. That's all."

"My dad used to plant tomatoes every year, in the backyard. He's on oxygen now, though. Emphysema."

"Sorry to hear that," Edith said. "I know other folks in that predicament. I was lucky. I never smoked or drank, and I've always kept busy with honest physical labor. I tried to keep this farm going myself after Kermit passed, but I ran into too much opposition with the menfolk. Everyone I hired tried to tell me what to do instead of vice versa. And the bank wouldn't deal with me at all. Finally I gave up and rented out the land, and they can do what they like, and I keep my mouth shut. My only rule is they can't overdo it with the pesticides. If it's poison for the bugs, how good could it be for you?" She stepped up onto the back porch, where I'd seen her a quarter century before. "Let's have some tea."

I followed her inside, and she bustled around her old-fashioned kitchen, putting on a kettle of water and getting out a china teapot and cups. "Do you take sugar with your tea?" She pulled open a foil-wrapped loaf. "Mrs. Conway, the woman who takes me grocery shopping and to my appointments, brought me this banana bread yesterday. I was going to freeze it until I had company. So I'm glad you're here to share it."

Since the day she'd chased me off her land, I'd always thought Edith Ramsey was, if not a witch, at least anti-social. Dad had always said she was "a prickly sort." I couldn't get over how friendly she was acting.

She poured our tea and sat down. "So, Stacy—may I call you that? When is the little one due?"

I nodded. "September 20th, more or less. I just found out it's a girl."

"Amazing, how they can do all that now." Edith looked wistful. "I never had a child. Don't know if the problem was with me or Kermit. Nowadays I suppose they can do all sorts of things. I always thought if I'd had a child, maybe Kermit would have tried harder to hold on to the farm and the orchard. His family had owned this land since Adam. But he knew he had no one to leave

it to, except his nieces and nephews, who never cared about it."
She sighed. "None of them want it, except for the money they'll
make selling it for a shopping center or a bunch of houses."

I felt apologetic about living in Arboria Park. "I know it
sounds hypocritical considering where I've lived all my life, but I
think it should stay a farm too."

"I'd like to make my will out that way," Edith said. "I'm in
good health—doc says I may make a hundred at this rate—but
I'm not getting any younger. I wish there was a way to preserve
this place. I hear things about how you can set up some kind of
land trust or something to keep it a farm. I need to find out more
about that."

"Maybe I can help. My husband, Greg, works for the state
environmental department. I'm sure he could find out about farm
preservation programs and what you have to do."

"I would certainly appreciate it," Edith said. "I've asked at
the senior center—I go there now and then—but nobody there
knows."

We ate half the loaf of banana bread and drank so much tea
I needed to use the bathroom.

"What to expect when you're expecting!" Edith joked, and
directed me to a small powder room off the kitchen.

"I really should go," I said when I emerged. "Gosh, it's almost
one. I've kept you from your lunch."

"Looks like today's lunch was banana bread." She smiled.
"Worth it for the company. I'll get a big meal later. Mrs. Conway
is taking me for our weekly supper at the Shady Branch."

She walked down the drive with me and fretted about me
walking home. "I'd like for you to come back and see me, but you
must find a safer way."

"Maybe I'll have my brother build me a bridge across the
creek," I teased her, then stopped myself before explaining how
Matt had become so good at carpentry—renovating a house for
his boyfriend to make it handicap-friendly.

....

Eventually, as my visits to Edith's became more frequent, I fessed up about Matt, along with a lot of other stuff. She was surprisingly nonjudgmental about such things; a slight frown might furrow her surprisingly unlined face, then she'd seem to shake it off as part of life as we sat over tea or I helped her weed her little vegetable patch. "Now, don't lean over so far or you'll never get back up!" she'd admonish me. "Sit down on that step. You've done enough for today."

When I told Greg about how Edith wanted to preserve the farm, he gathered all the information he could about the state's new farm preservation program and Edith and I went through all the papers together—at least what we could understand. By the time spring turned to summer, I was going to see her a couple of times a week. But Edith always insisted I drive there.

"We'll walk around on the farm for your exercise," she said one morning as we sat in her kitchen.

"It's getting too hot for much walking anyway, except first thing in the morning," I said. "And I'm getting bigger."

She eyed me up. "And it's still going well?"

"Everything's normal. I actually feel pretty good. Just— awkward. I'm always bumping into things."

"Are you cool enough, sitting here? We can go out on the porch." An old-fashioned fan purred on a shelf.

"I'm fine. I can't get over how cool your house is, actually."

"It's the design," Edith said. "There are windows on three sides in every room. Makes for excellent cross-ventilation. A few well-placed window fans, and who needs air conditioning?"

She told me all about how things were done in the old days—her childhood on another farm, meeting Kermit Ramsey at a grange dance, and helping him take over the farm after his father's accident with a corn cutter meant he could no longer work. "Below Cobbs Road, this was all rural," she said. "We raised all sorts of things. I enjoyed the orchard the most. After the peach blight, nobody made any money off that—did you know some of those grand old farmhouses downstate were called peach mansions during their heyday? But we did all right with the apples. I tried so hard to convince Kermit we needed to expand. The Thompsons over there west of Foster, they hung in and now they make a fortune off pick-your-own, hayrides, and overpriced jams. We could have tried that."

I sipped the lemonade she'd made to go with the blondies I'd baked. "I'm sorry too. I suppose my dad would have found another house somehow, somewhere, if Arboria Park hadn't been built."

"And the sad part was, Kermit didn't benefit from the money he made from selling the orchard." Edith looked down at the table. "It was a brain tumor. They cut him open, but they couldn't do much. Another one of those things they could probably fix nowadays. He wasn't in the ground a week before his relatives were after me to sell the rest to them. But I dug my heels in. They weren't going to push me off, no sir. So, I won. But I also failed."

"Oh, Edith. You didn't fail. You kept your farm."

She gave me a sad smile. "Yes, it's a farm, but I'm not really a farmer. And I wanted to be. But because I'm a woman, it's like everyone wanted me to fail."

"I understand—kind of," I said. "I guess I'm a failure too, but I never even figured out what I wanted to fail at. I gave up social work because it started to drive me crazy. I felt like I wasn't really helping anyone. Then I got a job with a business printing company. The customers wanted forms, thousands of them, converted over to computerized, typeset versions. So I did that. It paid better than social work, actually, which was great when we bought the house. It was boring, but I kind of liked it. No life or death decisions. If I made a mistake, I just redid it. Nobody died, or threatened to sue me or the state. It felt—comfortable. But I got laid off, finally, when they'd converted everything. And then I found out I was pregnant. So Greg said we'd be okay if I didn't work for a while, and to take some time to think about what I really wanted. I know he was disappointed when I took that other job. He wants me to do great things, only I can't think of any."

Edith smiled again. "It's nice that you have that chance, at least."

"I know. But once the baby's a little older, I'll need to go back to work. And I don't know what to do."

"Life is full of regrets," Edith said. "I've told you mine. You have yours. But we have to carry on. Life is to be lived, no matter what our mistakes."

....

On a rainy day in August, as I lumbered out of my car, Edith came out of the house to greet me. "I talked to that lawyer in town your husband recommended," she said. "And it looks like we may qualify for historical preservation. All those things we read, you know, about needing historical documentation, he thinks we can do it. I've been searching through the attic and found all sorts of papers about this farm and what's happened on it for over two hundred years."

"That's wonderful, Edith."

"The lawyer—Mr. Cox—thinks the house and some outbuildings might even be eligible for the National Historic Register."

As we sat in her parlor, she showed me old photographs she'd found in her foray through the attic. "That's Kermit's parents, on their wedding day. There's him as a boy with his sister, Josie. It's her children and grandchildren who are going to hate me, if they find out what I'm doing. Well, I'll be dead by then!"

....

By mid-September, I was having trouble sleeping, my feet were swollen, and I just wanted the baby to come. When I talked to her now, I called her Sophie, the name Greg and I had decided on.

"I wish Edith had a prettier name," I told my rounded belly one day. "I don't think you want to be Sophie Edith. How about

Sophie Apple?" The baby kicked violently. "Okay, maybe not. Your papi likes Sophie Lorraine, so maybe we'll go with that."

The next day, I told Edith what we were planning to name the baby. She looked startled.

"Oh, my. Lorraine was my sister's name. The one who died of influenza as a child."

"Oh, Edith, I'm sorry. I won't use the name if . . ."

"Don't be silly. I'd love for your little one to have Lorraine's name as part of hers."

As I walked back out to my car, I bent over in pain. I'd had a few false contractions already.

"Come back in and sit for a minute," Edith urged. "Don't try to drive yet."

A few minutes later, I felt another, and a third. And then a wetness. "Oh, God, Edith, I think my water just broke. On your kitchen chair!"

"Never mind that," she said. "I should telephone somebody. You can't drive to the hospital yourself. Maybe I should call the ambulance—"

"No, Edith, I'll call my brother. He might be the one driving the ambulance anyway."

She handed me her old rotary dial phone, the one my dad had installed.

Matt was home. "Jesus, Stacy. I'll come get you because I can get there before emergency services can, but you should have called them."

"I'll be okay. It's a first baby. They take longer."

Edith fussed at me until Matt arrived, and she continued to fuss as he helped me into his car. I was surprised she didn't insist on coming along.

On the way, I said, "The contractions have stopped already. See? Just a false alarm."

Matt shook his head. "Your water broke, Stacy. For God's sake, this is not a drill."

It wasn't a false alarm. I was in labor, but the doctor said it might still take a while. Matt called Greg, who came over right away. "I don't want anyone here except you and Mary," I told Greg. "Matt has to go on duty."

I lay for hours enduring each contraction and listening to the doctor and nurse note everything and tell me all was well.

Mary came over after work.

I broke down after Greg had left the room to get something to eat. "How did you stand this?" I asked. "THREE TIMES."

"You really do forget." Mary squeezed my hand. "It'll be worth it, I promise. Everyone is so excited for you. JC's gone over to get your car from Edith's, and Ruby wants to be the one to call everybody when Sophie arrives." She tried to distract me with tales about Ruby and Jason's latest adventures, Autumn's New York internship making music videos, and JC applying to be vice principal of our old junior high. When Greg returned, she massaged my shoulders and gave me ice chips while he held my hands and helped me breathe.

Sophie finally arrived at eleven that night. She was healthy. And perfect.

Greg held her. "She's just a baby. They all look alike, really. But she's . . . beautiful. She looks like you."

"She looks like *you*. Her eyes dance, like yours."

"She's a bit cross-eyed, you mean." He handed her back to me and knelt next to the bed. "She looks like *us*."

•••••••••••••••••••••••••

Sophie came home to the yellow and lavender nursery. I showed her the leaves changing color outside the window and spun the bird mobile over her head, telling her that soon she'd be able to go outside and see real ones. Through sleepless nights and some dark fall and winter days, we got to know each other. I made sure Dad saw her as often as possible, biting back the pain of knowing he'd never be able to do the things with her that he'd done with Autumn and Ruby and Jason. Mom held Sophie and gave me good advice on teething and colic, but mostly she was preoccupied with caring for Dad. And any time I mentioned Matt her face would change and I would know it was time to go before Sophie sensed the chill and began to squall.

I called Edith a few times over the winter, making sure she was okay. She and Mr. Cox were working on the land trust project, and she was eager to see Sophie when the time was right.

The first balmy day in March, I dressed Sophie carefully, strapped her into the car seat, and drove to Edith's. We had tea and cookies in the kitchen, and Edith marveled at Sophie. "Look at the way she tracks us with her eyes," she said. "When I speak she looks at me, then back at you when you answer. That's a sign of intelligence."

That night, as Greg and I cuddled on the couch with Sophie, I told him, "I feel bad saying this, in a way. But it was almost like Edith was my mother, or grandmother, through the pregnancy and birth. And Mona too, sometimes. I just haven't been able to feel close to Mom."

"Because of the way she's treating Matt and Jeff." Greg rocked Sophie up and down on his knee. "I know. She blames you. And you wanted to be close to her. For Sophie."

"I wish my family was together. I wish Dad wasn't sick, and Mom had the time to enjoy a new grandchild . . . I'm glad your parents are visiting again this summer, anyway."

Sophie gurgled and waved her hands around.

"I think it will be good for her to grow up near a farm," I said. "It was good for me. And I'll make sure she knows all of Edith's stories about the old days, and the history of this place."

Greg gave my arm a squeeze. "I know you will."

·····················

The next warm day, I brought Sophie into the backyard.

"The trees are budding," I told her. "Soon those dogwoods will be all pink and white, and there will be tulips and hyacinths.

We'll smell them and pick a few, and we'll go see Mona's flowers, and Edith's, and your Grandmom's too. And someday, when you're bigger, Daddy will get his telescope out and we'll look at the stars here, or over at the playground. Or at Edith's. She said we could." I lifted her up. "I want you to learn all kinds of things. About plants and flowers, and the Earth and stars, and architecture and history and art and science. You can be anything. A scientist, like your dad. A farmer, like Edith. Or a teacher and an artist or musician, like your Aunt Mary and Uncle JC. Or a filmmaker, like your cousin Autumn, or a gymnast, like Ruby, or someone who builds things and figures out how they work, like Jason. You could act on stage like Uncle Tommy, or take pictures like Aunt Megan, or save lives like Uncle Matt and Uncle Alex, or be a writer like Uncle Jeff and Aunt Lisa. You can learn to cook wonderful food like Grandmom Evelyn. Just don't listen to what she says about life." Sophie gazed at me. "And be smart about things, like Pop-Pop Tom. And Grandpa Javier and Grandma Delia want to take you to Puerto Rico someday so you can learn all about it."

Sophie smiled and shrieked at a plane flying overhead.

"Maybe you'll fly a plane someday. Or skydive from one." I pulled her close. "You can do anything you want, Sophie. Anything."

12—RUBY, 1993

••••••••••••••••••••••

I shuffled into the kitchen yawning, still in my pj's at 9:30 A.M. I'd been out late at a Friday basement show at Syrup Space, the punk house over on Maple Street. It was a beautiful spring day, and I wanted to get some coffee and breakfast in me so I could go out and enjoy it.

"How was the show?" Mom was sitting at the table, going over invoices from her gallery. She and some friends had rented a house downtown for local artists to show and sell their work. She volunteered there on Saturdays.

"Pretty good. A touring band headlined. Little too grungy for my taste." I poured some coffee. "That old man came by again. You know, from over on Cobbs? He didn't yell at us this time. Chris and Ty and Gina are kind of cultivating him." I took a sip and imagined the caffeine shooting into my extremities. "He's coming again tonight, because it's a punkabilly band, and he says he was a famous rock 'n' roll and rockabilly musician back in the '50s and '60s. I thought that might be bogus, but Chris was at his house and saw some pictures and records and stuff. His name is Duke Santoro. Ever heard of him?"

"Can't say I have." Mom put down her pen. "Maybe he was a

bit before my time? I didn't really get into music until high school. Ask Stacy; I think she was hearing music in the womb. Or your father may know. He and Jason are out jogging."

I put my bagel in the toaster oven and watched Mom bundle her papers into a manila envelope. Jason and I called her an old hippie, but she didn't look like one. Her hair was cut in a stylish bob, with blond highlights. She'd recently started wearing her glasses all the time, not just for reading.

"Try not to be too late tonight," Mom cautioned me. "We're having Jeff's birthday brunch here tomorrow. Matt's taking him skydiving today."

"Jeff can skydive?" I poked around in the fridge to see if Jason had eaten all the cream cheese.

Mom laughed. "Apparently, yes."

No cream cheese, but I found some strawberry jam. I had just fished it off the bottom shelf when the back door opened. I got out of the way so Jason would have a clear shot at the refrigerator. He was eating a lot these days, but he was still slender, like me. We were both tall, too, and athletic. Jase looked a lot like Pops, while I had the same dark, wavy hair as my half-sister, Autumn, though with deep olive skin instead of her porcelain with freckles. But I leaned toward music, more like Pops, while Jason was very mathematical but still artistic, like Mom. He wanted to be an architect.

Jason started to drink orange juice out of the carton but saw me glaring at him and poured it into a glass. Pops leaned over and kissed Mom.

"I'm at the gallery until two," she said. "What's your day like?"

"Soon as I get cleaned up, I'm going over to school to meet with kids who've been identified for summer school," he answered. "Get them to outline their goals, set up rewards, sign their contracts. Should be home when you are."

My Pops was an assistant principal who headed a program for kids with academic and discipline issues. Back when he used to be a high school band director, he tried to find ways to channel problem kids into positive directions like music and individual sports and art. One of his conditions for taking his current job was starting a real program. He was finishing up his fifth year at it, and the program was about to go district-wide.

Jason found some frozen waffles. "How are the dirty punks?"

"How are the gangsta rappers?" I shot back. We both loved all kinds of music, but I gravitated toward the punk-house scene, like our aunt Stacy and Autumn, whereas Jase veered between hip-hop and classical. That kind of summed him up, actually. He'd wear unlaced sneakers and baggy jeans with a sweater vest, and write a profane rap version of Shakespeare for his AP English project.

"Your mother and I watched Richie Havens on PBS last night," Pops said, laughing. He knew we'd both roll our eyes at that.

"Have you ever heard of an old rockabilly musician named Duke Santoro?" I asked him. "He's that old man who was making the noise complaints about Syrup Space, but now he's interested in seeing some of the bands. Says he toured the country thirty-five or forty years ago, played with Carl Perkins and Waylon Jennings, even Elvis Presley."

"Name sounds vaguely familiar," Pops said. "Have a look at my rock 'n' roll history books. He may be in there somewhere."

....

When I walked back over to Maple in the evening, I was armed with a little information. I had met my friend Amber for a tennis game over at the high school courts, and when I got home I'd helped straighten the house and prepare treats for the birthday brunch, so I hadn't had much time. But a quick look through some of Pops's books had rewarded me with a mention of Duke Santoro in a list of hot-shot rockabilly guitar players ("Duke Santoro, of the Texas Strangers and the V8 Vigilantes"). Another book said he'd played on records by Brenda Lee, whom I'd heard of, and Janis Martin, whom I hadn't.

Duke wasn't at the house as the first two bands, local punks, played their sets. But he made his stiff way down the steps as the second band finished. We usually stood around during sets, or moshed a little if the band was hardcore, but Chris Dimos, a college sophomore who lived at the house and booked most of the shows, found a chair for Duke.

I didn't approach him at first, just listened as he chatted with Chris and with the Holy Terrors, the band setting up to play next. They were a four-piece from the DC area, influenced by psychobilly acts like the Nekromantix. They unpacked a huge upright bass from a coffin-shaped case that had a caricature of Jayne Mansfield and the words "Leave a Good-Looking Corpse" painted on it. Duke looked at it and shook his head.

The spooky-sounding bass, the loud drums, and the staccato guitar set the mood. *Pretty good for a bunch of kids,* I thought. Their hairdos covered a range—a Mohawk, a ducktail, a crewcut, and a Jerry Only devilock—and they dressed self-consciously in bowling shirts and two-toned shoes, but with a punk swagger. I watched Duke watch them. Sometimes he leaned forward, tapping on his knee; other times he sat back, frowning or smirking.

When they finished, he said, "I could do without all those songs about zombies dyin' and such, but you play mighty well."

The Mohawked lead singer stuck out his hand. "Thank you, sir." He actually blushed as Duke shook it. "Coming from you, that means a lot."

Duke nodded toward the guitar player (the one with the devilock), who was hanging back. "*Every* song doesn't have to be at breakneck speed, son. But you seem to know when it's good to leave a gap now and then, and that's not easily learned."

The Terrors crowded around Duke and asked him a million questions, until Chris finally suggested, "Let's go upstairs, where it's comfortable."

I trailed them into the living room and watched Duke hold court. He made suggestions and demonstrated a few licks on Dale Terror's Telecaster. Tony Terror tapped his drumsticks on the coffee table, and Randy Terror fumbled to get the big bass back out of its coffin.

"You know this one?" Duke asked, switching gears. He started to play and sing Carl Perkins's "Put Your Cat Clothes On," and nodded to Bucky Terror. "You take it. I never was much of a singer." He laughed. "Just a slinger."

They raced through a few more songs, and Chris and I and the other kids who were hanging around sang along to the recognizable ones. After a while, Duke looked at me. "You have a nice voice, young lady. Reminds me of Janis Martin. What's your name?"

"Ruby Harris."

He smiled. "'Rock and Roll Ruby.' Who knows that one?"

"Johnny Cash?" Bucky asked, and then they sang it to me.

"Your turn," Duke told me. "Let's hear you cut loose."

I panicked. "I'm not sure what to sing." But then inspiration struck. "How about 'Viva Las Vegas'? It's an Elvis song *and* a punk classic."

Instruments got passed around, people took turns singing, and Duke kept playing. Chris brought out his acoustic guitar, and at one point I dared to strum out a bit of rhythm on it and do backing vocals on George Jones's "The Race Is On."

Duke nodded approvingly. "You play too?"

"A little guitar and piano, some bass. My Pops is a multi-instrumentalist, and I guess I am too. I've never played upright though."

Randy tilted the bass toward me. "Give it a shot. My fingers need a rest."

The bass felt heavy in my arms, but I did my best through a couple of songs. Somebody suggested a slap-bass number, and I handed it back to Randy. When he couldn't get the hang of it, Duke showed us how. We both tried it, and I did better than Randy.

"Get rid of those fingernails of yours, and you'll be all right," Duke said.

I laughed. "No problem. They're fakes."

Finally one of the Terrors said, "Hey, we better hit it," and I looked at my watch and jumped up. "Me too. I've got a long walk, and I'm blowing curfew here."

"You need a ride, young Ruby?" Duke asks. "You shouldn't be walking alone."

I wasn't sure whether walking home alone at 1:00 A.M. or accepting a ride from a near-stranger was dumber (at least in the eyes of my parents), but Duke seemed all right. I accepted his offer, and followed him across the backyard to his house on Cobbs.

He motioned toward a sedan in the driveway. "Let me tell my wife I'll be back in a few minutes." He leaned inside the front door and spoke to someone, then came back to the car and opened the door for me as I told him my address.

"I read about you in one of my father's books," I said as he backed out of the driveway. "You're from Texas. How'd you end up here?"

"That lovely lady inside the house there. My wife, Marcella. She's from the Eastern Shore of Maryland. Met her in the late '60s, playing a dance just over the state line. Never thought I'd settle down, but she roped me in good. For many a year, half the time we lived wherever I was playing the most, and half of it we traveled all over the world. It was a good life. I've got arthritis now, and I finally got tired of the road. I didn't make a fortune off my career, but I saved what I could. Didn't need to spend it chasing women after I met Marcella! We decided to find a little ranch house we could afford, near her family, some other retired folks around, and this neighborhood fit the bill. And then right behind my house are these kids playing loud, crazy music every weekend!"

"I think they—we—are all glad you joined in."

"Never been sure about that psychobilly business, but it was more fun than I expected. Your dad's a musician?"

"Yes. He used to be a high school band director, now he's vice principal at Hawthorne Middle. My sister Autumn's a punk drummer and my aunt plays guitar. Gosh, they'll all want to meet you when I tell them about you."

"You never know. Tonight showed me I need to keep a toe in, now and then."

I pointed out my house, and he pulled up in the driveway. "Good night, Miss Rock and Roll Ruby. You showed those boys a thing or two." He walked around to open my door again, and tipped his cowboy hat at me as I got out of the car.

························

I could see the skepticism on Pops's face when I told him about my ride. But he seemed to soften up the next morning at Jeff's birthday brunch as I described my evening to everyone. As I had anticipated, my Aunt Stacy was the most interested. After brunch I called Autumn in California. She reminded me that she had seen The Cramps when she was only fourteen, and said she'd look for Duke's records in second-hand stores in L.A.

After that weekend, Chris and I haunted Duke's house regularly. Marcella, who was a good bit younger than Duke—probably my mom's age—was gracious and welcoming. She was in the process of organizing all of Duke's stuff.

"We've hauled all this junk from place to place for years," she said. "I couldn't wait until I had time and space to sort it out. All these old show posters, and programs, and the autographs— heavens, we've even got a personal note from Elvis and Priscilla."

"And the records," Duke interjected. He had hundreds, if not thousands. Old 45 singles from the '50s rock era, 78s from further back—country, swing, jump-blues, even bluegrass. I pressed him for details about his career and the music.

"I was born near Dallas, grew up part of the time in San Antone, and had family down near the Mexican border," he told us. "So I got to hear a wide range of Texas music. And border radio—good Lord. Started playing country and some western swing when I was fifteen. Then I got out of Texas, on the road, and heard even more."

Duke was happy to tell us his stories. He and Marcella played records for me and answered all my pesky questions. I was most interested in the early women rock 'n' roll and rockabilly singers: Wanda Jackson, Sparkle Moore, Lorrie Collins, even Brenda Lee, who'd been a little '50s rocker before she went more sedate later. And Janis Martin, the female Elvis.

I listened to the guys, too, and to more recent revivalists like Brian Setzer, Rosie Flores, and Reverend Horton Heat. I bought used records at the farmers' auction, and Duke let me tape anything I wanted.

We played together, too. Duke said I had a great voice for rockabilly. "Pretty, but not too pretty. You can sound like you mean business," he explained one summer afternoon when Chris and I were jamming around with him.

"Tough but tender," Marcella added.

I tried to learn some guitar from Duke, but even Chris, who was a more advanced and accomplished player than me, found him too intimidating to copy. Duke said copying people was bullshit anyway; you had to find your style.

Duke could play bass and drums too. "In my band, we used to switch off instruments," he said. "Wowed the crowd every time. Right in the middle of a song, Jack Farlow would take over on my guitar and hand off the bass to Bad Bill Hartnett, and Bill would throw his drumsticks at me. Then we'd switch again. Took us months of practice before we tried it live."

I found myself enjoying the stand-up bass the most. Pops asked around until he found me one, and I forsook my fake nails to conquer it. Duke was delighted. He told me how Jack Farlow would stand on his bass, play it upside down, anything to get the crowd going. Marcella showed us a few crude home movies of their performances, and Chris and I came up with some moves to show Duke. I lifted the bass over my head, lay on the floor with it on top of me, and even experimented with hanging upside down.

After weeks of this, I talked Mom into having Duke and Marcella over for Sunday dinner. I invited Stacy and my Uncle

Greg and my little cousin, Sophie, too. I babysat her sometimes, and she was already messing around on her mom's Stratocaster. I figured we'd have a hell of an all-girl family band someday.

I ran outside to meet Duke and Marcella when they arrived.

"I made sure Greg forced Stacy to bring her guitar, and Pops and I have ours set up too," I told them before they'd even made it out of their car. I couldn't wait for my family to hear Duke play live, since they'd heard him on record plenty of times at that point.

Mom greeted them at the door. "Hi, I'm Mary, Ruby's mom. She's told us so much about you two."

"Thank you for having us, ma'am," Duke said, and took off his hat. Marcella handed Mom a homemade pie, and I ushered them into the living room where everyone was waiting, including my eager sidekick, Chris.

Pops stood up and held out his hand. "Mr. Santoro. It's an honor. I'm Ruby's father, JC Harris."

I could see the shock on Duke's face. More than shock; it was horror. How had it never occurred to me to mention my father was black? How had it never occurred to me it might matter to Duke?

Marcella took control and shook Pops's hand. "We're so pleased to meet Ruby's family. She's such a charming young lady, and so talented. She's become Duke's protégé."

"Really?" Pops said. He was eying Duke, who in turn was staring at the floor. "Well, we're a musical family here."

"Let's all sit down," Mom said nervously. Stacy looked at me and then at Duke. "Mr. Santoro, I'm Stacy Martinez, and I am so delighted to meet you. Ruby says you have interesting stories to tell, and have played with so many legendary people. I hope we can prevail upon you to play a little."

Duke finally looked up. "Thanks. I'd like to."

Pops handed him his own guitar. "This isn't a hollow body, like you're used to."

"Thank you," Duke said. "It'll work."

He started with an old song of his band's called "Get the Jump on That." Sophie leapt up to dance.

I looked at Pops and saw the concern in his eyes. Mom, too. She'd gone over to sit next to him, her arm in his. Jason stood by the entrance to the dining room, his face stony.

Stacy joined Sophie, dancing to the song, and everyone clapped when he finished.

"Ruby tells me you play," Duke said to Stacy. "I'd sure like to hear."

Stacy blushed, the way she always did when someone asked her to play. "I'm not that good. I mean, I don't know if I can keep up . . ."

Duke gave her some variation on his line about everyone having their own style and pace, and Stacy finally pulled out her guitar. She played along hesitantly at first, but then I could see she was losing herself in the music and having a blast. Sophie insisted I dance with her. Mom danced too. She looked a bit more relaxed, but my heart felt heavy. I didn't sing along, or fetch my bass where it was lying in the hallway. I cursed myself: Duke was from a different generation. From Texas. And while it was wrong to stereotype people, he might have been brought up in a time or place where racism was casual. I knew, too, what Jase always pointedly teased me about: I didn't look black. I looked "exotic," to be sure—I got mistaken for Italian or Greek or Hispanic sometimes. My actual background usually came out on its own, if it had to, and in all my talks with Duke I simply hadn't thought about it.

Stacy kept Duke busy telling his stories during dinner. Jason got up and went to his room before dessert. I couldn't really blame him.

After everyone left, I put my arms around Pops. "I'm sorry, Popsy. I guess I just didn't get around to telling him a few things."

"It's all right," Pops said. "I think he was just surprised, that's all."

"Or a racist redneck cowboy who never ate dinner with black people before," Jason said, coming back into the room.

"Jason, let's not make assumptions before we have the facts," Mom said. "I hope he will still be Ruby's friend and mentor. If not, it's our job to make her feel better, not worse."

"Thank God for Stacy and Sophie," I said. "I want to talk to Stacy tomorrow, get her take on it."

"That's a good idea," Mom said. "You know, she wouldn't have stepped in and been so polite to Duke if she thought he really was racist. She sizes people up very well. She must have thought he was all right, or she would have lit into him."

"I hope so."

·····················

I couldn't bring myself to go over to Duke's the next day, or the one after that. Chris called and asked if I wanted him to intervene in any way.

"No thanks, Chris. I'll talk to Duke when I'm ready."

"For what it's worth, all he said to me was that he got caught by surprise, and he hoped your father didn't think he was some sort of dirty old man or something."

"That's *never* been an issue."

"No, but it may be his way of working it through. The way he talks about you, he really thought he'd help you become the new Wanda Jackson and start a rockabilly revival. Now he's wrapping his head around why a black girl would love this music so much." He paused. "And maybe thinking a little about where this music comes from."

After I hung up with Chris, I found Pops in his basement studio. "I can't decide what to do," I told him. "I've always loved punk rock. And now rockabilly. You taught us to love everything. But maybe I'm a traitor to my half my heritage."

"Rock 'n' roll is a fusion of white and black music," Pops said. "Rockabilly and R&B. You could definitely argue that it was also a cooptation of black music and musicians. It didn't take long for it to split apart, with both sides going their separate ways. But I'm a black man, and sometimes I listen to Bob Dylan and play Sousa marches. And is it wrong for white people to love Otis Redding or Billie Holiday? For a biracial young man like your brother to sample Gene Krupa and Tchaikovsky on his hip-hop mixtapes? If we can't reach across the divide with music, how can we do it?"

"There had to be some black rockabilly artists. I mean, Chuck Berry and Little Richard and Bo Diddley are on the rock 'n' roll side. We have to look."

Pops took my hand. "Then I guess we will."

We scoured the college library and traveled to some old record stores in Baltimore on our quest. I dug deeper into Texas and Bakersfield country, western swing, Tex-Mex, and rhythm and blues, too, to see how it all fit together. In the meantime, I attended a few shows at Syrup Space—harder stuff like Avail and Chisel, so I knew Duke wouldn't show up. If he did, I was prepared to be polite, but I hoped I wouldn't see him until I worked out a few things.

....

My seventeenth birthday was on July 17th. That's one reason I was named Ruby; it's my birthstone. Mom and Pops gave me a beautiful ring, and we were all going out for dinner to my favorite restaurant. We'd already had a big extended family get-together for my parents' nineteenth wedding anniversary the past weekend. Black and white folks, listening to each other's music and getting along.

Early in the afternoon, I walked over to Cobbs Road. It was a hot summer day, and kids—of various races—were playing games in the street, leaping in backyard pools, chasing the ice cream truck. Arboria Park was very well integrated. That's one reason my parents had stayed in the neighborhood. It was comfortable. Duke and Marcella had chosen this neighborhood too. They must have seen it for what it was.

Marcella answered the door. She seemed surprised, and then she hugged me.

"Haven't seen you for a few weeks, Ruby. We missed you. Duke missed you."

"Thanks, Marcella. I've been busy with a project. I wanted to show Duke part of it."

"He's helping me sort through a box of photos from the '50s." She led me through the living room, to the spare room they used as a workspace for Duke's archives.

Duke looked up from labeling pictures. He wasn't wearing his cowboy hat, and for the first time in a while he seemed old to me.

"Let's show Ruby some of these photos," Marcella suggested. "Then she has something she wants to show you."

The pictures were amazing: A very young Duke and some other musicians, with their instruments, in front of an old wood-paneled station wagon. Duke backstage somewhere, pretending to strangle Jerry Lee Lewis. Another group photo that included Elvis, still just a kid.

"This era fascinates me," I told them. "To be present at the birth of rock 'n' roll as a cultural phenomenon. My mom can remember before it existed. My Aunt Stacy loves that she was kind of born along with it. I would've loved to have been part of it, but I've always known something." I opened the bag I was carrying. "There weren't many biracial girls hanging around that scene. Or black ones. They wouldn't have been welcome. But there were other scenes where they might have been. Black music—R&B, the blues, gospel, what they called race music then—are part of rock 'n' roll along with country and western. Somehow all they merged together to create something amazing. Bad things happened too, of course—people exploiting each other, or excluding each other. Or worst, ignoring each other." I pulled out a homemade tape. "There were black singers and musicians playing something like rockabilly. Borrowing the country swing from whites, while the whites borrowed R&B from them."

I handed the tape to Marcella, who placed it in the player. Roy Brown's "Hip Shaking Baby" filled the room. It was followed by Ray Sharpe's "Linda Lu."

"Those could be rockabilly," I said. "But the artists were black. Similar sound."

Then came Big Joe Turner, Big Mama Thornton, and Ruth Brown. "Here's what the white artists were influenced by," I said. "So much great music, whether it's from the hills of Texas or the churches of Memphis, intersected and came into public conscious-ness during an era we're made to think of as stale and sedate."

Duke stared at his photos as the music played. I saw his hand move toward one of him and Jack Farlow in front of a nightclub called the Georgia Peach.

"There's much more," I said. "And I know I'm not playing you anything you haven't heard before. I guess before I saw you again, I had to confirm for myself that I had a place in this music. What I found is I have more than one. My parents have always taught us that we belong anywhere we want to be. We were raised to be confident in who we are. Maybe that led to a little bit of denial. I'm sorry I didn't make things clearer to you about my background, but I'll never apologize for what it is."

"You're right," Duke said, leaning forward. "I have heard that music before. It was a glorious time. Could've been a chance to resolve some things that got fought out later, in other ways. Yes, I played for segregated audiences. And sometimes me and my bandmates, we sought out black players we could learn from, heard things that filled our heads with wonder. We'd play a dance full of white teenagers, some small town somewhere, and right down the street there'd be another dance, all black folks, and if the two bands had gotten together we'd have blown the roof off. But it never happened. Wanda Jackson had a black piano player for a while, but it was tough on both of them."

"That's good to know," I said. "That someone tried."

"Well, that was a long time ago," Duke said. "Time to change.

I'd like to start by apologizing to your father, for reacting the way I did. I have a feeling he's someone I'd enjoy talking with. I want to help you any way I can. And I'd love to play with that aunt of yours again."

I laughed. "And you haven't met my sister yet. She's coming back to visit, later this summer."

Duke shook his head. "That's one amazing family you have."

"Now that I've delved into this, I think I owe it to myself to explore the other side too," I said. "My mom's side. There's some ethnic music, like Irish, that's buried back there somewhere. I want to find that too."

"You will." Duke smiled. "Rock and Roll Ruby, you will find it all."

The doorbell rang, and Marcella went to answer it. It was Chris; he'd come to tell Duke that the Holy Terrors had a day off between shows in Baltimore and Philadelphia in a few weeks, and they wanted to come back to Syrup Space. "But only if you promise to come see them, and maybe play with them," Chris said.

"Hell yes," Duke said. "If you and Miss Ruby will agree to join me to open for them."

"We'll need a drummer. Gina might be up for it," Chris suggested. "Guess we better start rehearsing."

"I'll come by your house tomorrow," Duke agreed. "I promised Marcella we'd finish this box of pictures today."

Chris pulled up a chair. "Can I help?"

· ·

Chris walked me home later. "I'm glad you sorted things out," he said when we left Duke's. "This has been weighing on me."

"It's complicated," I agreed. "Duke's a product of his time and place. But he knows it. And I guess I should give him credit for being willing to learn."

Chris accompanied me down to Mimosa, then said he had

to go to the shopping center to buy cat food. He kissed me on the cheek before he headed off. He'd never done that before.

At home, Jase was waiting with a birthday mixtape. We listened to it before getting ready for dinner. It was crazy: loops of all kinds of music we had in the house, all linking together somehow, bass line to bass line or beat to beat. Jason played around with sounds in 3-D, just like he did with images.

I told him I wanted him to come see us perform when we opened for the Holy Terrors. He looked freaked out but said yes. I invited Mom and Dad, too, and of course I'd make sure Stacy and Greg were there, and Sophie if they'd let her stay up. I figured with any luck, Autumn might be around too.

13—STACY, 1999

"She's a tough nut to crack," Bettina admitted. Her comment wasn't intended as literal, but it could have been. "She's opened up a little with the ladies who've taken her under their wing at mealtime. She'll come and sit sometimes when someone plays the piano. But that's it."

"I'll talk to her again," I said as I got up. Every conversation in Bettina's office went this way. "To encourage her to keep going in the right direction."

Bettina walked me to the door. "Don't worry so much, Stacy." She dropped her usually crisp and professional manner to hug me. "They usually come around."

I passed through the sunny atrium, where several residents were sitting and chatting, and walked down the west hallway. Greenhaven was the best assisted living facility around, everyone had assured me, and we were lucky to get Mom in there, and in a private room at that. Unlike most of the other facilities we'd toured, it was neither grubby and depressing nor antiseptic and artificial. The décor was more like a nice hotel; the residents ran many of the activities themselves, like the lending library, the card games, and the book club. Bettina, the facility's administrator, and the activity director, Kimiko, went out of their way to give

Mom opportunities. She still got around well enough to ride the Greenhaven van to the mall or the public library every week if she wanted, or go to church. But she was having none of it, and so every visit Mary or I made to Greenhaven involved the same conversation with Bettina.

I stopped at the corner window before making the turn to Mom's room. The sun shone; tulips were blooming in the residents' garden. The raised beds and containers were cared for by folks who still wanted to garden; less mobile residents watered the houseplants in the atrium or the lounges. We kept encouraging Mom to participate, but so far she hadn't.

Though she had agreed to move into assisted living, Mom had taken one look at Bettina four months earlier and made up her mind about Greenhaven. She'd been aloof but polite while Mary, Matt, and Tommy had toured the home with us. But as soon as they left, the gates had opened.

"You're putting me in some cheap black nursing home!" she had raged at me.

I had tried to hold my temper. "Mom, that is not true. You won't live with any of us because you don't approve of our lives. And this isn't a nursing home, and the staff and residents are white and black and everything else. Like the neighborhood."

"So from one ghetto to another."

It's manipulation, I said to myself. *Don't fall for it.*

"You're in a great neighborhood now. West of town, where you always wanted to be. Fox Catch is only a mile away, and Olga volunteers here sometimes."

She couldn't argue with that, but she had waved her hand dismissively.

I turned away from the window and took a deep breath as I headed for her door. It was closed, though most of the people on her corridor left theirs open during the day if they were in. A few were in their rooms, reading or dozing, but most were elsewhere, doing things.

I tapped on the door. "Mom?"

She was sitting in front of the TV, as usual. Her room should have been bright this time of day, since it had a southern exposure, but the drapes were closed. A screen divided her bed from the rest of the room; she had a kitchenette with a microwave and tiny fridge. We'd furnished the room with a few good pieces from the house—a rocking chair, some end tables—and a brand-new sofa and wing chair. It was cozy and attractive.

"How was lunch today?" I asked as I sat down. She shrugged.

"Bettina says they're having book club this afternoon. Some of the ladies were making treats to serve."

"Kimiko's already been by to tell me. I don't want to go."

"Mom, it would be good for you to get out of this room. They've really cut you some slack letting you be alone this much, but it has to stop. You need some social stimulation. You're still mobile, and mentally alert, and if you want to stay that way, you should be more active."

"So they say." It was another dismissal. "Are you going over to the house?"

"Yes. I'll finish painting the living room this afternoon, and put some more boxes in the car for tomorrow."

"Selling my things to *strangers* at that dirty farmers' auction. What you're not throwing away. This is how you treat me."

"Mom, we are not going down this road again. We've taken what we want and can use. We have to get the rest out of there so we can finish painting and fixing things up. The realtor was adamant about it, if you want to get a good price."

"What difference does it make? Nobody *decent* will want that house anyway. We should have moved when we had the chance, to a nice neighborhood. Then I wouldn't be here."

I tried not to take the bait, but I couldn't help myself. "You would be here no matter where you lived, if you had insisted on hoarding and not looking after yourself the way you have the past few years."

She ignored me in favor of Oprah. At least she couldn't hoard here. She got three good meals a day and had people to monitor her health. But it was still hard going. She disliked George, the nurse practitioner, insisting he must be gay (on no evidence other than that he was a nurse and not a doctor). She'd been evaluated by a psychiatrist but was not cooperating with the nice social worker who came in to talk to the residents with "problems." Kimiko was knocking herself out trying to come up with activities Mom might enjoy.

I left after a dreary half hour and headed for Arbor Circle. Five months of cleaning and clearing out the house so far. I was bearing the brunt of it, because everyone else was working and I, once again, wasn't. Mary and Matt helped when they could, but Matt had a new job, coordinating emergency services for the county. Jeff had tired of rewriting press releases and moved to the other side of the desk, doing PR for the college. They had moved out of Arboria Park and into a lovely ranch house on the lake. One of us finally had made it into a posh neighborhood, but because it was Matt and Jeff, Mom never visited.

I had one wall left to paint in the empty living room before picking up Sophie from softball practice after school. Having one room almost finished felt good.

Mom's descent had been slow and subtle, at first. Dad had been gone for over eight years. At first she'd said she might want to move, maybe to a nice apartment, but wanted some time to think before she decided. That had sounded reasonable. And then there had been some small battles, like her balking at hiring a cleaning service (she was angry to learn that, unlike in the 1950s, it wasn't easy to find an "Amish girl" to scrub floors or iron for a pittance). And there was her continuing hostility toward Matt and Jeff, for whose existence, of course, she blamed me.

I thought of Ruby as I concentrated on covering the dingy wall with smooth strokes of antique white paint. She was the one who had helped stave off more problems initially. When she got interested in rockabilly and the '50s, she had spent a lot of time with Mom, getting her to tell stories and plowing through the basement in search of artifacts. She'd found a few old dresses and hats to wear onstage, and Mom had given her some vintage jewelry to go with them. But when Ruby went off to the state university to major in music education, she hadn't been around to help out her grandmother as often. Jason had mowed the lawn, and Sophie and I had kept up the garden, because we knew that was important to Mom. It was normal for her to do less around the house, we'd reassured ourselves and each other. She was getting older. And at least she seemed to have a social life, going out in the car almost daily. Except for the cold war over Matt and Jeff, we had managed to convince ourselves that everything was as all right as it was going to be.

But Ruby had sounded the alarm when she came home for spring break her senior year. She'd gone into the back room of Mom's basement, where Dad had kept his tools and where Christmas decorations and "special occasion" dishes had sat for years in neatly labeled boxes on shelves—and she'd found the room packed to the gills with clothes and household items haphazardly thrown in boxes or just piled on the floor. There had been shopping bags, too, full of new things that Mom had never used. Further investigation found the bedroom closets similarly stuffed, and more things piled on the beds in our old rooms. Mom always kept those doors shut—to keep the dust down she said.

After these discoveries, I went through Mom's bank records and her checkbook. Everything was balanced to the decimal point, but she was spending hundreds of dollars a month on clothes and food and household items she never used. Her time out of the house was spent not with friends, lingering over lunch, but shopping alone.

Nearly two years of battling later, she'd moved to Greenhaven. What was left of her savings would pay for a few months, but we needed to sell the house to secure her future.

I finished the wall and cleaned up, then carried the boxes I'd packed over the weekend out to the car. They filled the trunk and backseat.

I went straight from there to pick Sophie up from softball practice. She frowned as she got into the car. "There's no place for my stuff."

"You can hold your things until we get home."

"How many more boxes are there?" she asked.

I shrugged. "I've been selling for five weeks now. I'm guessing two, maybe three weeks more. How was practice?"

"My fielding's so much better since Uncle Matt helped me. He's gonna try to come to my game on Friday. Will you be there, or do you have to paint that stupid house again?"

"Of course I will. Dad, too, if he can leave work early. I'm sorry I'm spending so much time at the house, but there's a lot to do, and we have to get it on the market as soon as possible so Grandmom won't have to worry."

As I slowed for a traffic light, Sophie unbuckled her seatbelt and turned around to paw at the contents of a box. "Why does Grandmom have all this junk, anyway?"

"Sophie, sit back down and buckle your seatbelt. You know better than that." She complied, and I added, "Some of it is just a result of living in the same place for almost fifty years, and as she got older she had problems thinking through what she really needed."

"My other grandparents aren't like that," Sophie observed. "Or Ms. Mona. And Mrs. Ramsey was *really* old, and she wasn't like that. She had some stuff, but it was interesting stuff."

I felt a lump in my throat. Edith had been gone almost two years, and I still missed her. She'd left her farm to the state to turn into a park and historic site, but her relatives were still fighting it in court, wanting more than just the field behind the Pines that she'd left them.

"Maybe Grandmom will be happier when you finish the house," Sophie said. "Will she come to look at it then?"

"If she wants, but I doubt it."

As we turned off Cobbs onto Oak, Sophie said, "I don't want to ride my bike up here anymore, 'cause the people are creepy. See that house over there? Jessica says it's a *crack house*. You know, like people go there and do drugs."

"Some people don't know how to behave," I said, quoting my dad from nearly forty years before. "This section's gotten kind of rough. I hope it turns around. The realtor thinks it will. That's why she wants us to fix up Grandmom's place. So someone will want to live in it, not just rent it out and turn a blind eye to the tenants' behavior."

"Our street is okay," Sophie said as we neared home. "But maybe we should move if it gets icky."

"Your grandfather used to say that's *why* the neighborhood would seem to go bad now and then. Too many people moving out, not being committed to it." I turned into our driveway. The spring flowers were blooming, but I hadn't had time to weed. I pulled the car into the garage so the boxes wouldn't be a temptation for someone to break in. When had I had to start worrying about things like that?

························

I was at the auction house by six forty-five the next morning, unpacking the boxes. On Tuesdays and Fridays, long rows of rough wooden tables were set up outside the building, where people sold everything from farm produce to car parts. Some were permanent; other sellers were like me, just renting space for a few days or weeks. Don had helped me decide what to do. Larger items, like furniture, went into the auction. Some things, he said, were just junk and could go for a buck or two a box. A sizeable amount of what Mom had been buying, though, could fetch more if I had the patience to sell it separately, he told me. So all spring I had rented space on Tuesdays and sat there from opening at seven thirty until two or three, depending on when things wound down and how much I'd sold.

Don and Nancy, who was now his wife, had a permanent stall inside the auction house itself, trading beautiful antique furniture. I loved to browse there, and sometimes I'd stop by after I'd packed up before heading home. Nancy also had a consignment clothing stall.

Mona Harris was already setting up her church sale table next to mine when I got there. It was nice when she volunteered there; it gave me someone to chat with when things got slow. I handed her a cup of coffee I'd picked up on the way. "Good morning, Mona. What have you got this week?"

She laughed. "Pretty good haul. One of our deacons and his wife are retiring and moving south, and they donated a lot of nice things." She sighed. "Our church folk are aging. Moving on. There's some good young ones coming up too, of course, but they're too busy for this sort of thing."

As we set up our tables, we greeted some of the other regulars: junk dealers and farmers' wives, Amish families and Filipinas. Organic produce, handmade crafts, flowers and plants, clothing and shoes that had clearly "fallen off a truck" or were illegal designer knockoffs—you could find it all. Many tables were like mine, selling old glassware and dishes and small household items. Mona knew everybody, and she'd taught me how things worked early on. The first customers to arrive were always the Amish and other farmers, along with earlybirds who wanted their pick of the freshest produce and the best junk. I'd had to learn to haggle and joke around and put up with the looky-loos. Mona would keep an eye on my table while I went inside to get us freshly made pretzels or apple fritters to snack on at midday. After I'd packed up in the afternoon I'd go in again and buy something to take home for dinner: Amish-butchered meats and ready-made salads; baked goods and cheeses; hand-dipped ice cream and bulk candy. An old black man sold fresh fish and clams out of a couple of large coolers; Mennonite girls in bonnets counted change by hand; a new stand sold tacos and burritos and played mariachi music. I loved it all.

I sold some mismatched glasses to a woman whose daughter was moving into her first apartment, and a set of mixing bowls to someone else. Then I helped Mona hold up a lovely hand-crocheted bedspread from her table so someone could look it over.

"I hate to say it, but Clarence and I may be next to move on," she confided after she'd made the sale. "House is too big, too many stairs for us now. And the cold winter weather. We may head south, like the birds."

"I'll miss you if you do," I said.

A women who was making her way down the aisle stopped at Mona's table to browse, then picked up some Tupperware containers at mine. "I'll take these. I never know where all my lids go!"

"That's the truth," I said. "Do you want a bag?"

She opened a large tote that already contained some fresh asparagus and a pie. "Just put them here." She looked around. "I'm a little disappointed. I bought this pie inside, but it's from an Amish bakery in Lancaster County. I thought the local Amish would be selling here."

"Some do," I said. "Mostly vegetables and meat, and some of the men sell hand-made furniture."

"I live in Farm View," she said. It was a newish development west of town. "I thought it would be quaint, all the buggies and farms around. But the Amish aren't what I expected. I asked one of them if they'd give my kids a buggy ride, and they said they were too busy. They leave horse poop on the road. And our development wanted to put in a pool and a clubhouse, and the zoning people said it was too close to that Mennonite church."

"They're being swallowed by development," I said. "A lot of them have sold out and moved to the Midwest. That whole area was rural not that many years ago, and now it's just housing developments from the railroad tracks to the state line. Named for whatever was destroyed to build them. Farm View, West Woods, Fieldcrest . . ." I stopped myself as I saw her face tighten.

"Well, good day," she said and hurried away.

Mona chuckled. "Guess she didn't want to hear that the Amish folk aren't here for her amusement."

"I need to learn to smile and shut up," I said.

She laughed again. "No, you just keep telling it like it is. Someone has to."

Once I'd sold most of my things, I packed up the few straggler items and then went inside the auction house to visit Nancy Kozicki and see if she'd sold any more of Mom's clothing.

"Got some cash for you," she said as I came in, before I could even ask. "I can't believe how many of your items still had price tags. They'll hand you twenty dollars in a New York minute when there's a Macy's tag saying it was originally seventy-five."

"I'm glad they're good for something," I said as she handed me the wad of bills.

"Take a look around, if you want. You're a size ten, aren't you? Just got a bunch of new things in. Even a ball gown." She pointed.

I looked at the spangly dress and laughed. "Well, if I'm invited to a coronation or something, I'll know where to shop."

"Looks like your mother was prepared for one," she said, giggling, then looked stricken. "I'm sorry, that was rude of me."

"No, you're right. I don't know why she had all those things she was never going to wear. Some of them weren't even her size."

Nancy smiled. "Do you remember those little booklets of Barbie clothes we had, growing up? Did you have those? Everything from ski clothes to tutus. Your consignment was kind of like that."

"Senior Citizen Barbie," I agreed, and had to laugh.

....

I drove back home with my cooler full of goodies for dinner. As I drove up, Greg was coming out of the house with Sophie. Her eyes were swollen, like she had been crying.

"I was about to call your cell," Greg said. "Sophie got bit by a dog, and I'm running her over to the emergency room to get checked out."

"Sophie, what happened?" I swept her up in a hug.

"When I was walking home from Asha's after school, a pit bull ran out of a yard on Elm, and he bit my leg before I even knew what happened." She pulled away. "It hurts."

On the way to the hospital she explained further. "I didn't touch him or try to pet him or anything, honest. He came out of nowhere." She trembled. "A man came out of a house with a stick and chased him away. He said he didn't recognize the dog. There are lots of pit bulls in the Park now."

"What was the man's name?" I asked.

"I can't remember. Something with a J. He was nice. He held a rag on it until it stopped bleeding, and he wanted to call you. I just wanted to go home."

At the hospital, the doctor cleaned the wound and gave Sophie a couple of stitches. "She'll be all right. She needs antibiotics and something for pain. Stay off it as much as you can tonight, but you should be able to walk around—gently—tomorrow."

"Can I go to softball practice?" Sophie asked.

"Better wait a few days, until the stitches come out. You won't be able to run too fast for a bit anyway."

Sophie slumped and put her face in her hands, and I put my arms around her.

"Any way to find out if the dog's been vaccinated for rabies?" the doctor asked. "Otherwise, we may want to give her a shot to be safe."

Greg and I looked at each other. "It was loose, probably a stray," Greg said. "Sweetheart, can you remember if he had a collar, with tags?"

"No," Sophie sobbed. "He didn't."

The doctor shrugged. "If she were my daughter . . ."

It killed me to watch Sophie trying to be stoic for the painful shot. On the way home, Greg drove slowly down Elm. "Show me where it happened, and where the man came out of the house."

Sophie pointed out the house.

"I'm taking off work tomorrow, and I think you should stay home from school," Greg said. "We'll talk to the man who helped you, and maybe find the dog too. So you won't have to have more shots."

....

Mona came over with her little poodle, Trixie, the next day, and Greg and I walked up Elm to find the man who'd helped Sophie. Trixie's inclusion was deliberate; I didn't want Sophie to develop a fear of all dogs. To my relief, she greeted Trixie with her usual enthusiasm when Mona arrived.

We knocked on the door of the house on Elm. A middle-aged black man answered, and we explained who we were.

"How is that little girl?" he asked. "I wanted to call you, maybe take her to the ER myself. But she took off, said she just wanted to go home." He motioned us inside. "Please come in. I'm Lloyd Jennings. My wife and I have lived here six years or so. I'm retired Air Force."

"Me too," Greg said. "Sophie's going to be okay. Thank you for helping her. She said you hit the dog with a stick, and he ran off?"

"I'd never hit a dog normally. I have one of my own. He's in the backyard, where a dog belongs. Not running around loose. I was over on the side of the house, raking my wife's flowerbed when I heard your daughter scream, and I hit that dog with the handle of my rake, didn't even think. Thank the good Lord he let go and ran. Some of those things, what I hear, they don't even care if they're shot. He ran up north, where I figure he's from. I drove around a little looking last evening, but I didn't see him." He shook his head. "I don't know what's happened on Oak and Holly, they're just no-good drug addicts and criminals. Black, white, Spanish, Chinese, what have you, all no good. Cars parked in the yard, people driving up day and night, and they all have those nasty dogs, either chained up snarling or running loose. I think it's the same couple of landlords who own all those places. Getting as bad as the Pines, isn't it?"

"I'd like to know who those landlords are," I said. "I'm getting ready to sell a house on the Circle, and I want to avoid selling to those kinds."

"Well, good luck. My wife and I would like to bring your daughter a little get-well gift, if that's okay."

"If Mona can stay a few more minutes, let's get the car and have a look," Greg suggested as we walked outside after talking with Mr. Jennings for a while. "Maybe the dog is loose again."

Mona assured us that she was happy to stay longer, and we set off in the car. On Holly, near Greg's old house, we spotted a pit bull running. It headed west, and we drove after it.

"Dogs always ran loose when I was a kid," I told Greg. "I knew every dog in the neighborhood. If they weren't friendly, they weren't running around. Bad ones were fenced in."

"Times have changed. Seems to be the opposite now."

A huge bearded shirtless man, covered in biker tattoos, stood on the corner at Oak. "You seen a dog?" he hollered as we pulled up to the stop sign.

I leaned out the window. "I was going to ask you the same thing. Does your dog happen to be a fucking pit bull? The one who bit my daughter yesterday?"

"My dog's a Rottweiler, bitch. And he never bit nobody didn't deserve it."

We saw the dog again on Elm, but when I got a good look at it I said, "I don't think that's the one. Sophie and Mr. Jennings both said he was brown and white, and this one's gray. How many loose dogs are there around here, anyway?"

Greg called the police when we arrived home. They'd already gotten a report from Mr. Jennings. Greg sighed when he hung up. "Don't know how much of a priority this will be. If we lived in town, with city police and animal control, it might be, but the state cops have too much to do to worry about us. That's why the drugs and crime are getting out of control here. Everyone knows we're under-policed."

"I know. That's the reason we've had the punk houses here for twenty years. Lax law enforcement."

Greg urged me to finish my work at Mom's. "I'll look after Sophie, and write a report for work."

I dragged myself to the Circle and got to work. I was knee deep in the stuff piled in my old bedroom when Greg called my cell a couple hours later.

"Would you believe the police tracked down the dog?" he said, his tone bright. "Apparently rabies gets their attention. The owner did have a vaccine certificate, but he's getting fined for letting the dog loose, and it'll be confiscated and put down if it gets out again. And they'll have county animal control pay more attention to the area, or so they say."

My heart ached anyway. For Sophie; for my neighborhood; even for the dog.

·······················

Sophie improved enough to get back to softball. She seemed okay, if a bit subdued, but she didn't get off the bus early at Asha's house anymore.

Just after we put Mom's house on the market, the realtor called. "Did you see the morning paper? This may be a problem for us."

The problem was a major drug bust on north Oak. People from three houses were involved, all owned by the same absentee landlord. Within days, a half dozen other houses on Oak and Holly were abandoned by their tenants.

The realtor kept her ear to the ground. The landlord was selling all his properties in the Park. There were over a dozen.

"It could go either way," Greg said. "Some may be bought at a bargain by people who want to fix them. Or another investor may snap them up and rent them indiscriminately again."

"Either way, it's still going to make our sale tougher."

Greg put his arms around me. "Maybe not. Elm still looks nice, and so does the Circle."

. . . .

Bettina ran toward me in the atrium as I entered Greenhaven. "Good news!"

"Yes?" I said, too skeptical to let myself feel excited.

"Some ladies needed a fourth for bridge on Monday, and they talked your mother into it," she said. "She had a nice time. And one of them, Mrs. Metzger, had her over to her room for tea yesterday! I knew it would just take some time."

"Thank you, Bettina," I said. "I needed some good news."

Mom was alone in her room, but she seemed a bit brighter than she had since her move. I updated her on the latest house showing, then said, "Bettina says you had tea with a Mrs. Metzger?"

She glowed. "Yes. She's *Doctor* Metzger's widow, Dorothy. They had a beautiful home on the Avenue. You remember that stone house, near the hospital? Such a lovely person. She had cookies delivered from the bakery. She showed me pictures of her grandchildren, and she said she used to garden before she got arthritis. We must have talked for two hours!"

"Mom, I'm so happy to see you've made a friend. Now you must ask her over. You have that beautiful tea set we found in the basement." I went over to her kitchenette and pulled it out of the cabinet. "See? Let me know when she's coming, and Sophie and I will make something to serve. Muffins or cookies?"

Her expression turned to something like panic. "I could never do that. Someone like her—"

"Why on earth not?"

Mom's hands fluttered. "She's a doctor's wife, Stacy. From a wealthy neighborhood, not Arboria Park."

"So what? I had a thirteen-year-old client once who getting was beaten by a doctor's wife in a nice neighborhood. They're no better than anyone else, for God's sake. Obviously she likes you. You both live in the same place now. And your room is lovely, one of the nicest ones in this wing. You have nothing to be ashamed of."

She bit her lip, and her eyes moved toward the wall above the TV. The photo wall.

Mary had designed it. She'd covered the wall with framed pictures, starting with our parents' wedding photo and then all the baby and school photos of us kids and the grandkids, along with milestones like weddings and graduations. Young Autumn learning to ride a two-wheeler, with Dad holding on to the back, and adult Autumn with her boyfriend and filmmaking partner, Drew, at a cinema festival. Little Ruby on the balance beam; big Ruby performing onstage wearing her mom's old prom dress. Six-year-old Jason in a superhero Halloween costume; teenage Jason running at a track meet. Toddler Sophie reaching to touch my guitar; eleven-year-old Sophie strumming her own. Tommy's acting head shot; Matt receiving a certificate from the mayor after saving a kid and his dog from drowning in Walker's Pond. No photos of Matt and Jeff together, but Jeff did appear in a family shot Megan had taken at Mary and JC's twentieth anniversary party. A beautiful, concise history of our family, designed to spark interest and answer questions. Questions Mom didn't want raised, interest she wanted to avoid. The reason her door was always closed.

The pictures all ran together as I willed myself to hang on, the way I had when I saw Sophie's wound, or when I was told of Dad's death, and Edith's. I put down the teapot so I wouldn't drop it in the crevasse that seemed to open in the floor; an irrevocable moment was pulling away the ground below me, along with my past and future.

"Mom?" I heard my choked voice, pleading one last time to take that moment back. "It's us you're ashamed of, isn't it?"

She looked away from me, down at her fingers, which were twisting in her lap. "I tried so hard with you kids, to give you the best we could. And starting with Mary—"

"Starting with Mary, what?" I took a step toward her. "We all went to hell? Never mind that she put *herself* through college while working and raising a kid, achieved her dream career, and married a good and successful man. That Tommy's beat the odds and made a living doing what he loves. That Matt's a hero, with a house by the goddamn *lake*, and that Jeff is the nicest man alive and hasn't let a disability stop him. That your granddaughter conceived out of wedlock is an awarding-winning filmmaker, and your biracial granddaughter is a talented musician, and her brother just graduated from college with honors. And my Sophie—maybe it even bothers you that she's half Puerto Rican? That we're all kind of bilingual and anti-racist and not homophobic? And I know I'm a failure, but the others aren't, and most families would be proud of any *one* of them, let alone the lot."

She still didn't look at me. "Stacy, the world views it differently—"

"What world? *Your* world? We all have friends, and fulfilling lives. We left behind anybody who wasn't on our side. Except you."

She finally looked up, and there was anger in her face. "You left me behind years ago. None of you ever cared about my feelings, or your father's. You're all selfish. And you—what have you ever done, except cause trouble and egg the others on to turn their backs on what they could have been?"

The earthquake stopped at that moment. Her anger had sucked out all of mine, and now I felt calm as I moved toward the door. "All I *did* was clean and fix up the home Dad provided—the one we kids loved but you never appreciated—and sell the junk you bought to fill the hole in your heart. The hole you put there yourself."

I walked down the hall, through the atrium, out the front door of Greenhaven, and all the way to my car. There, though, I fell apart, weeping until I'd used every tissue in my purse and was blowing my nose on a paper towel from the roll under the seat. Then I sat for another ten minutes, staring out at the cars on busy Route 8, heading downtown or away toward Fox Catch and every other swanky shithole where Mom had ever wanted to live. Where Mary never would have slept with Don or met JC, and Tommy would have gone to college, and Matt would have liked girls or at least made himself live a respectable lie. Where even if I hadn't decided what I wanted to be it wouldn't have mattered as long as I married a doctor or lawyer, and we only learned enough Spanish to order drinks in Acapulco. Dad could have moved us to Oakley Estates if he'd really wanted to, but he knew, all along, that it would never be enough.

I drove straight to Mary's. It was summer vacation; maybe she'd be home.

I told her the story as best I could when I got there, then broke down again. She hugged me the way she had when I was a little girl who skinned my knee, when she'd comforted me with a Band-Aid and some big-sister gesture like letting me play with her lipstick.

"Do you remember that book Ruby loved when she was little?" she asked when I calmed down. "The African folk tales? There was one about a farmer and his cow. The farmer was so proud of his cow—his wealth—that he put all his energy into caring for it and protecting it, and ignored his own sons. He gave them nothing, and eventually he lost them all. That's Mom. Her vision of life was more important than forgiving or supporting us when we screwed up, like I did, or letting us be ourselves. The person she's hurt most is herself. That's what I try to remember, and that's why we've all tried to do right by her. Even Matt. He'd have every right to cut her off. He's learned to walk away, though, if she goes too far, and so have I. And now you have to. The house is on the market, and it's time for you to take your life back. Go over every week or two like I do, if you must, and if the visit isn't going anywhere, just leave. That's all you can do."

Mary was right. She was still a good big sister.

"I was going to call you tonight," she said. "JC's accepted an offer to be principal at Central Shore. We've always wanted to move to the beach. The kids are gone, and this house is too big now. I thought about Mom, but I can still come up every week to see her, and her needs are being met."

"What about your job?" I held on as the earth shifted a little again.

"I'll miss it, but it's time for a change. I'm going to work in a gallery. I want to run one someday. And really work at my own art, try to sell more paintings."

"I'm happy for you," I said, and meant it. "You guys deserve this."

"It's going to be weird, leaving the Park." She glanced around her sunny kitchen. "End of an era."

I told Greg and Sophie about Mary's news over dinner, then waited for Sophie to be picked up by Jessica's mom to go to a sleepover. Sophie fretted over the brownies she'd baked from scratch to take. "I think I left them in too long. They're not as gooey as the ones I made for Grandmom."

"This is a cakelike recipe, not a fudgy one," I assured her. "But everyone will love them. Just like the cookies you made for your own sleepover."

"Grandmom says you have to put nuts in, but Petra and Asha hate nuts," Sophie said. "So I put chocolate chips in instead."

"Good choice," I said.

A horn honked outside the house, and Sophie ran out to the car.

"I have something else to tell you now," I said to Greg, and I related the day's events. I shed a tear or two, but mostly I was cried out.

He listened, then said, "Mary's right. Time to withdraw a little. Maybe your mother will have to make some kind of life for herself, and to appreciate you, if you're not at her beck and call."

"Maybe," I said. "I want Sophie to keep knowing the world won't end if she doesn't put in the nuts. I worry about her, because she's kind of a perfectionist, and I don't want that to take over. Like it did for Mom."

"And you," Greg said. "In your own way." He moved back slightly and let go of my hand. "Might as well get all the bombshells over in one day. I've been approached about a job—in Philadelphia. And I'd like to consider it. We'd have to move. But maybe it's a good time, with Mary leaving."

"Abandon Arboria Park?" I said.

"Interesting you'd use that word. Are Mary and JC abandoning it, or just moving on for exciting new opportunities? Did Matt and Jeff abandon it, or seize a chance to have their dream house? This is a great opportunity for me, but that alone wouldn't be enough. It's a chance for you—and for Sophie, too. We don't have to live in the city itself if that's too much of an adjustment at once. Just close enough so you and Sophie could have a lot of cultural opportunities—and multicultural ones. It could give you a real chance to find yourself, and discover what you love. Things you don't have access to here, like the music scene. You could go to shows, and even take Sophie to some. She loves music as much as you do, and we need to encourage her." He moved back over and put his arm around me. "There's a difference between running away and walking away. Walking away can be an act of bravery, especially if you're heading toward something."

I shook my head. "I don't know what to think. Everything's so confusing now—"

"No decisions tonight, or even tomorrow," he said. "Let's think a little, and consider the possibilities. We don't even have to sell the house right away. We could rent it out, find some good people. Do our part to keep the neighborhood working."

"I guess I'm just overwhelmed. First Mona, then Mary. Half the Park will be up for sale."

Greg smiled. "Anyway, we'll sleep on it, and talk some more."

....

Toward the end of summer, Mary and JC had a big good-bye bash at their house. Autumn, Ruby, Tommy, and Megan all came in for the occasion. Jason, who was packing up to go to grad school in architecture, showed off the skills he used in his side job as a professional

DJ, filling the house and yard with the sounds we'd all grown up with or learned about over the years. The afternoon was an open house, so friends came and went, and then in the evening we held a family barbecue in the backyard. This, of course, included Don and Nancy, Mona and Clarence (about to leave for Florida), and Olga's family.

Mom sat in a lawn chair. Subdued but not hostile, she seemed lost—as usual—as everyone reminisced and talked about their plans for the future.

Autumn and Drew's were the biggest surprise. Autumn hung over the back of Mom's chair. "Hey Grandmom, guess what? Mom's moving, but Drew and I may be coming back. We've applied for jobs at the college."

"Now you tell us," JC said. "After we've had an offer on the house."

Autumn laughed. "Sorry, we can't afford to buy yet. We've been living like vagabonds. All our money's gone into promoting and distributing our films. The clock's ticking, and if we want to have a baby eventually, we need something a little steadier for a while. They're starting this project making educational films, and I've applied to head that up. And Drew's applied to teach media arts."

Mary sighed. "Anybody else got a surprise? Moving in or out?"

"Don't look at me," Ruby said. "My home's the road, for the moment. I wish we could all afford to buy this place together. Just to have parties in once a year, even."

"The ultimate punk house," Autumn agreed. "Well, first Grandmom's got sold before we made it the next Gilman, and now ours."

"A nice young Indian family, the Pradeeps, are buying it," JC said. "Funny thing, with all these houses suddenly for sale in the neighborhood, there's interest in fixing them up. Real estate's gotten so crazy high, this is a good entry point for young folks again."

"I'm glad," I said. "I don't feel as much like I'm abandoning ship. The Dominican lady who bought Mom's house loves the garden and wants to keep it up."

"Maybe we'll rent your place, Stacy," Autumn said. "That can be our new punk house! Are there any at the moment?"

"There was one on Cedar. But the kids graduated this spring."

"I miss Syrup Space," Ruby said. "I'm glad Duke and Marcella stopped by today."

"We're going to live in New Jersey," Sophie announced. "There's a lake and a park, but then you get on the highway and it's like there's a bridge, and the city."

"Hey, Drew!" Autumn yelled over to where he was talking to Don. "Wanna live in the Crescent? Gotta keep some punks in the Park, and some Hallorans."

Megan came out of the house with her camera. "Let's do a group shot now, before we lose the light."

"Come on, everyone," Mary called. "Mom, stay in your chair, and we'll all gather round."

Megan set the timer on her camera. "Okay, everybody ready?"

I smiled. "I know I am."

14—2007

....

Subject: BAD NEWS!!!!!!

Mom
The highway people decided to go with some version of
the Arboria plan. Links below from the Weekly & the
News Call. Jeff is finding out more from his contacts
& Rosie's told Autumn a little but she has to be careful
so she doesn't get fired. Mr. Jennings is having a
neighborhood assoc meeting on Thurs & asked me to
talk to student renters & get them & their landlords
to come. Highway dept meeting is next week. Will text
later if I find out more.
❤ Sophie

My stomach lurched as I read Sophie's e-mail and clicked on the news links. I was sitting on the enclosed back porch at our house in New Jersey. The frame house, in an old-fashioned neighborhood with a delightful hodge-podge of architectural styles, had come to feel like home. I'd planted bulbs and bushes in the small yard, and slowly gotten the house just the way we wanted it. Yet I still thought of Arboria Park as my origin, my roots, my base.

And now the State Department of Highways and Transportation was either going to slice the Park in half or destroy it altogether.

For years, even before we moved away, there had been talk of a new road. The excessive development west of town was cut off from the main highway and the beach bypass by the railroad tracks and the downtown. The old country roads, including Foster, were at or over capacity, with traffic jams during rush hours. Relations with the remaining Amish were tense; even the college (now a university that was taking over most of the old downtown) was fighting with the city over blocking off streets so the students walking to class wouldn't be killed by the traffic pouring across town. It had been clear for a long time that a road was needed from what was now called the "West Side"; and various plans had been floated, all of which had some neighborhood or subset of people up in arms.

I read the *News Call* piece intently. "A spokesperson from the Transportation department said that all engineering, environmental, and historical studies on the Arboria options were complete," it said. "Relevant portions will be available for public perusal at next week's planning meeting and online. The full studies should be online soon."

My e-mail program was pinging away with notifications. Autumn, still employed at the university. Jason, at the Philly architecture firm where he worked. Ruby, about to board a plane in Boston, saying she'd be in touch later. Mary and JC at the beach, Matt from his office. Jeff with some press scuttlebutt, Tommy from upstate New York where he and Megan were sorting out her mother's estate.

The messages swam together. I called Greg at work.

"I have to get myself together enough to go see Sophie," I said. "I work tomorrow, and I can't wait two days."

"Just make sure she's around, not in class," he cautioned me.

"She has one right now. She'll be home by the time I get down, but I'll text her." I knew my daughter's schedule like my own.

Sophie had thrived in New Jersey. She'd made new friends, played softball, and volunteered at the local animal shelter, fearlessly walking pit bulls and talking us into adopting our beloved mixed-up mutt, Rollins. And she'd played in a few short-lived bands with high school pals: punk, hardcore, even metal.

I had thrived too, in my own way. There was so much to see and explore, both in our new neighborhood and in the city. And I had found a wonderful part-time job: library assistant at one of the historical organizations in Philly. I mostly just shelved books, carried boxes of documents around, and directed volunteers, but I loved it. The cool, hushed halls, lined with shelves; the polished floors; the long tables where scholars and genealogists sat under old-fashioned, green-shaded lamps to pore over research; the curving marble staircases; the chandeliers in the lobby; even the computer terminals, where we were gradually getting more material online—all of it gave me a feeling of calm and contentment. During slow times I peeked at books that drew my attention, re-igniting my passion for history. I was drawn to what I learned was called "material culture": the study of objects and architecture. It prickled at me the way learning about sociology had when I was thirteen.

I'd share my findings with Greg, and he'd urge me to go further: go back to school for a master's in history, library science, or museum studies. But I was content with learning what I wanted at my own pace. Hundreds of years of architecture and history awaited me in the city and the suburbs. I didn't need the pressure of *having* to learn about it in a certain way; I just wanted to explore. And to have the time to follow my other passion: music.

Like Greg had promised, Philadelphia offered a banquet of possibilities for me and Sophie. We sampled all kinds of music and venues, but still favored the DIY punk scene. We went to shows together and became known as an unusual duo: I was always the oldest, and at first she was among the youngest. We were always up front or in the pit, sweating and shouting in the basement of the First Unitarian Church or a punk house in a dodgy part of West Philly or Fishtown.

Aside from music, Sophie's passion was cooking. She was living in our Willow Drive house in the Crescent, now a junior in the university's nutrition and culinary arts program. Autumn and Drew and their little girl, Berry, had snatched up a spacious Victorian near the campus, when the university offered some homes it had bought up at a bargain rate for faculty housing, and they kept an eye on Sophie, who lived with her childhood pal Asha and their friend Sean. Many students—those who didn't like the sterile campus dorms, the rowdy fraternity row, or the student ghetto squeezed between the manicured Avenue residences on one side and the drug-and-crime-ridden Clancy Street on the other—lived in Arboria Park. There were still a couple of punk houses there, too, and Sophie and her friends sometimes hosted acoustic shows in our former den and basement.

During the real estate boom, a lot of families had moved in to the Park because it was still the ground floor for home ownership, just as JC had predicted. New developments had gone up endlessly over the past ten years, either monstrous McMansions priced beyond what an average Air Force, Fine Foods, or state government employee could afford, or shoddily constructed townhouses that soon deteriorated into the same absentee landlord ownership that had always plagued parts of the Park. Driving down any Park street you might see a house that looked nearly abandoned next to one that had been completely remodeled. So it remained both shabby and vibrant, and the declining economy provided both pockets of problems and possibilities for renewal.

I drove past our old house on the Circle (recently remodeled and looking neat as a pin), and over to the Pines (Olga's Spruce Court duplex had burned down a few years before and been rebuilt into an almost unrecognizable single-family home). The familiar pastel shingles were all gone; the duplexes were all white or beige vinyl now. I passed Mary's Mimosa place, and the

Oliva and Gardner residences. The Olivas' former house was getting a new roof and porch; the Gardners' place was falling apart.

The Crescent as a whole had held up well. Mona's old place still looked nice. And Sophie and her friends kept ours looking as good as college students were capable.

"Mom." Sophie embraced me as I went inside. "Are you staying down for dinner? Asha's making chana masala—that's chickpea curry—tonight."

"Maybe. I have to work tomorrow, so I don't want to be too late." I hid a smile as I looked at the posters and fliers tacked on the walls, the two cats and a dog milling at my feet, the coffee cups all over the living room. Upstairs, I knew from previous visits, Asha had painted our old spare bedroom a bright purple, and Sean slept in a hammock. The house was a riot of discarded sneakers, laptop chargers, and piles of books.

Sophie spread out some papers on the kitchen table. "Rosie gave Autumn these highway department maps. She'd be in a lot of trouble if her boss knew. They're more detailed than the ones in the paper." She pointed to one. "This plan would take out the Pines and Cedar, run through the middle of the Park, and curve over to take out Birch and tie up with the highway. So Willow would be cut off, and everything north of Mimosa. But the latest, and this is a secret Jeff found out, is they're in negotiation to possibly get the shopping center too. Then they'd put a big overpass junction across the entire neighborhood and tie it not just to the highway but to the beach bypass out by the base."

I felt sick again. "You said you talked to Lloyd Jennings?"

"Yeah, he wants everybody at the meeting. Even former residents. Maybe you can help with that."

Lloyd was the perfect person to head the sometimes-dormant neighborhood association. He was black, so the sizable minority population in the Park trusted him. He was a homeowner who had started out as a renter—ex-Air Force, now a double retiree who could represent the many older neighbors, as well as those who had settled back in the neighborhood after finishing their duty. And his Korean wife was a school counselor who knew everybody whose kids had attended Hawthorne Middle for the past few years.

"Your grandfather was head of the association for a couple of years, back in the '50s," I told Sophie. "And Mary was for a while in the '80s."

"Mom, I know how much this means to you." Sophie took my hand. "More than the rest of us combined, probably. Maybe we should go talk to Lloyd, and when Asha and Sean come home later we can start contacting people."

·······················

As I drove the two hours home that evening, Asha's delicious curry sat like a hard lump in my chest. The kids were determined to involve everyone; they were talking to professors of history, engineering, sociology, and urban planning, and hoping to get the university to put its weight behind some yet-to-be-identified alternative. And Lloyd and some of his neighbors still hoped some pushback might work. "Those folks from the Brooklawn Heights area," Lloyd said, "they got together with the merchants and stood up on their hind legs and the state backed off that Polk Street plan right quick."

But I knew that a half dozen or so other possible routes had already been studied and discarded. Going through town would disrupt too many businesses, and too many people with clout. Skirting the edge through a disorganized, less economically privileged neighborhood was politically safer.

"They got the guns, we got the numbers," Mary said when I called her the following evening. "Has Lloyd talked to the people in Oakley Estates? They can't be happy about this."

"He has. They're being bought off. The plan will annex them to the city, which satisfies most of them. They've gotten a little rough around the edges over the years, and their property values will shoot right back up, even with a highway nearby, if they get city services."

"There has to be something," Mary said. "They think they can push around a shabby neighborhood, but what if everyone pushed back?"

I repeated what Lloyd and the kids and I had agreed on that day. "All we can do is try."

·····················

"Listen to this," I said to Greg a couple of weeks later. The studies were up online. Greg had read the environmental one, the gist of which was that there were no major wetlands in the way. Jason was taking a crack at deciphering the engineering one; I was looking over the one that had determined the area's prospects for historical preservation.

"It says that Edith's farm is the only historically significant thing in the area." I scrolled further down the screen. "Since it's now a park and historical site, they can't touch it. But the field behind the Pines is fair game."

"Well, it's just a field," Greg said. "The farmstead itself is what's historical."

"Oh, Edith." I sighed. "She felt bad about not leaving her nieces and nephews something, so she gave them that field. And now it's the key to tearing up the Park. Edith's revenge for the orchard."

Greg leaned over my shoulder. "What does it say about the historical significance of the Park itself?"

"There's a bunch of criteria we definitely don't meet," I said, reading on. "'Neighborhood is directly associated with the life and career of an individual who made important contributions to history.' Well, nobody famous ever grew up there that I know of."

"I'd argue that," Greg said. "Look at your family alone. Broadway and TV actor, film director, rockabilly musician . . ."

I laughed. "Yes, but Tommy isn't Tommy Tune, Autumn isn't Michael Moore, and Ruby's not a world-famous diva."

Greg read another piece of the criteria out loud: "'Should be associated with a group of individuals, including merchants, industrialists, educators, and community leaders, important in the history and development of a locality.' I'd still argue your family qualifies." He kissed my neck. "Including you. You helped get the punk house movement off the ground there."

"I hardly think they'd consider that historically significant. Next requirement: 'The architecture has to be an important example of a distinctive period or notable architect.' And we flunk that one, too, because they say the houses in Orchard Acres and other subdivisions were similar, and the houses in Arboria Park are 'not high style' and don't 'feature distinctive design details.' They're not special enough in design to be pure examples of their era, according to this."

Greg shook his head. "Who could meet all these requirements?"

"There's one more criterion. We would have to 'yield important information about vernacular house types, yard design, gardening practices, and patterns of domestic life.' And it says 'oral history and ethnography would be the most useful methods for determining the significance for this criterion.'"

"That's it! Fight it on those grounds, that they need to look into this some more."

"But they're saying it's not unique enough because there were so many neighborhoods like it."

"But who's kept track of the history of those places?" Greg asked. "Mostly, no one. But you know the history here better than anyone."

"Well, they've already done their 'historic overview.' They say we mirror local and national trends in terms of architecture, population, and reason for being. We're not special."

Greg sighed. "I still think it's something to go on."

....

Sophie and her friends, armed with the reports, talked to various academics at the university and did their own research. She e-mailed me some studies, which I shared with Greg.

"Here's a master's thesis called 'All Made of Ticky Tacky: The Postwar American Suburb of Arboria Park.' By—oh, my God—Archibald Kennersley III. *Arch.* The hippie my sister had a fling with in 1968."

"Well, what does he say?" Greg asked.

"Not much we don't already know, in terms of the history and the houses. A bit of snide '60s commentary about the banality and *surrealness* of it all." I sighed. "Talk about surreal. First we help Edith set up a legal trust that helped pave the way for this road. Then, in the only actual academic study of the neighborhood, Arch shits all over it."

························

Lloyd Jennings and many of Arboria Park's other residents doggedly attended meetings, wrote letters to the editor and newspaper commentaries, and kept a constant pressure on the Transportation Department and local officials over the following months—but they met with limited success.

"Listen to this." Mary read aloud from the Sunday newspaper's editorial page. "'Though it is impossible not to feel for the residents of Arboria Park in the probable loss of their homes, there is a much larger picture to consider. These same residents are among those complaining of an inability to access Cobbs and Foster Roads during peak hours, or to cross the highway without waiting through multiple signal cycles. No one in this part of the county is unaffected by the growth in traffic due to the shift in city and county growth patterns, the expansion of a potentially first-class university, and the city's position as a gateway to the beach resorts. Arboria Park is an unfortunate relic of a time when development was haphazard and random. We have an opportunity to correct this accident of history and plan a sensible solution that will benefit the entire local area, the city, and the university. And to ensure that we remain a viable location for job growth and economic expansion, and that the quality of life of our residents on the West Side is worthy of the investments they made in their homes."'

"So now we're an accident of history," I fumed. We were all sitting around in the Willow Drive house after a sumptuous Sunday dinner prepared by Sophie and Asha. Mary and JC had driven up from the beach and joined us, along with Autumn, Drew, Berry, Matt, and Jeff. "And the investments of the people on the West Side are more important than the people here. Money talks."

"It gets worse," Mary said. "The letters to the editor responding to Lloyd and Hua-Shin's op-ed last week: 'Arboria Park is a slum, and deserves to be torn down whether a road is built or not.'" Mary threw the paper down in disgust, and JC picked it up and continued reading.

"'This drug-infested sinkhole should not stand in the way of economic progress.' 'This is an opportunity to rid the area of a criminal element.' 'A so-called neighborhood of unemployed single mothers, drug addicts, possibly illegal immigrants, and irresponsible college students deserves to be wiped off the map.' Well, isn't that lovely?" JC peered over the top of the paper. "They wipe Arboria Park off the map, and by some miracle everything else they dislike goes with it. Nice to see our neighbors to the north and west are so supportive."

"Rosie thinks they'll announce this week that they're going with the plan to take out the whole development," Autumn said. "The way that editorial talks about economic development, I'll bet they know, or think, that's how it will go."

"From a purely practical point of view, it makes the most sense," Jeff agreed. "The last thing they want is to leave two small, isolated groups of houses under a bunch of overpasses."

"Buying out five hundred houses, though," Matt mused. "That's a lot of money."

The newspaper addressed that very subject later in the week, after Rosie's prediction proved correct. I read the latest editorial online at home. "Though it will be an expensive proposition to buy and bulldoze an entire large neighborhood, doing so will cost less in the long run than attempting to serve the needs of an impoverished and newly isolated enclave in an undesirable location. The decision also means the area will not be faced with additional needs in a few years to upgrade the link between highways. This proposal guarantees a straight shot to the airbase, the beach resorts to the south, and additional development to the north, such as the new box store complex being built near the racetrack. One-and-done, as opposed to a piecemeal response."

I was spending many of my days off running back and forth to Arboria Park or keeping track of everybody's various projects on its behalf. Lloyd and Sophie were getting more people involved, but it didn't seem to help.

"Everybody feels sympathy for the folks on the West Side," I said to Lloyd one day. "Well, their developments weren't exactly 'well planned' either. The county let developers run wild in the '80s and '90s, and the city annexed it all, and then all the new medical buildings and shopping centers went up. Even the new high school. The town's entire center of gravity shifted west without a thought of what that meant. And yet *we're* the accident of history and the textbook example of poor planning."

"The university recommendations are for better public transit in town, and buses and maybe a train to the beach. They make sense, but nobody listens to them," Sophie said. "Everyone still wants their own car to go everywhere."

"So they're ignoring the past, and they *think* they're planning for the future, but they're missing the point." I paced around Lloyd's living room. "Some lives and futures count more than others. We're too black, too Asian, too Hispanic. Too many old people, too many college kids."

"That's what's missing from our arguments," Lloyd said. "That sense of passion beyond the immediate need for traffic relief for the West Side and a quick trip to the beach or the mall. *People* are being affected. How can we emphasize that without being reduced to stereotypes about working-class neighborhoods?"

....

I arrived at Sophie's one rainy afternoon, planning to take the kids somewhere for dinner. They'd worked so hard, around their own classes and college activities, to come up with ideas and canvass the Park with Lloyd. I thought we all needed some cheering up.

I tapped at the front door and went inside. Music blared from our old den.

Sean was playing *Guitar Hero*. "Hey," he said. "Wanna play? I just got the new version. Sophie's on her way back, but she's running late."

"I've never been able to figure that game out. Maybe because I play a *real* guitar." I knew Sean and Sophie ribbed each other all the time about his addiction to the game. "I just can't get how it works."

"This one's got some great songs on it," Sean said. "Check this out."

He played along with Living Colour's "Cult of Personality." When he was done, he looked over, grinning. "Awesome, right?"

I nodded. "They had a lot of great songs. My favorite was always 'Open Letter to a Landlord.'"

"I don't know that one," Sean said. He continued messing with the game.

I wandered down to the basement. I found Sophie's guitar, and after plugging it in and turning on the amp, I began to play and sing to myself. "Open Letter," a song about tearing apart run-down buildings without realizing their true value, about memories. About neighborhoods and racism and economic destruction. About fighting for what's yours. I realized Sean's noise from upstairs had ceased, and he was on the steps. I stopped playing.

He gestured at the guitar. "Play some more."

"I can't, Sean. I didn't realize you were listening."

"Come on." He sat down on the staircase.

I repeated the beginning, then improvised some chords and started the verse.

This is my neighborhood.
This is where I come from.
I call this place my home.
You call this place a slum.
You want to run the people out.
This is what you're all about...

By the time I hit the chorus, Sophie had clattered down the steps with Asha and was harmonizing with me. When I hit the last chord, we all stood in silence for a minute. The explosive sense of purpose and zeal I felt inside me was mirrored in the faces of the kids.

"Sing *that* to those highway people," Sean said. "And the rich ones who want the road."

"I'm calling Lloyd." Sophie pulled out her phone.

I took off the guitar and turned off the amp. "Whatever for?"

"Because I just thought of something. We need to have a rally, with music and speeches and stuff. We can play that song."

"Honey, slow down. You sound like your Aunt Mary, wanting to bring back the '60s. We've talked about a rally, but a few people carrying signs isn't going to get enough attention."

"*Something* has to help." Sophie sat down on the steps. "I'm so tired. The Jenningses are ready to look at houses somewhere else. Everybody's giving up." She put her head down and dissolved in tears.

It tore at my heart. I sat down next to her and then I started to cry too, the brief elation I'd felt moments before giving way to despair. Asha put her arms around us, and Sean stared at the floor, hands in his pockets.

"I don't want this to be the last time we play music together in this basement," Sophie sobbed into my shoulder. "It's so not fair."

"I know." I stroked her hair. "But we need more than just music and speeches, and it has to be more than just us here in this basement, and Lloyd and Hua-Shin. We need something for everyone to get behind, a way for everyone to say what's in their hearts." I let Sophie go and took her face in my hands. "But if you're not ready to give up, then I'm not either. Let's figure something out."

······················

"I'm taking a leave of absence from work," I announced to Greg the next evening at dinner. "We've come up with an idea, and I need some time. So I'm going to take three months."

He looked surprised. "I know you've been putting every waking minute into Arboria Park, but is this really going to—"

"We have an idea. One last, big idea. It was yours, actually. I talked to the kids, and Lloyd, and Mary and Matt and Autumn. It will take a lot of work. The first step is to really research the history of the Park, from the orchard on. Come up with some kind of, of *living exhibit* of the last fifty years that will show that we really are unique and at the same time an example—a live example—of a typical neighborhood. We need to find all the old-timers who are left, and reach out to each household individually, not wait for people to come to us. We'll take pictures, and Autumn and Drew will film, and we'll collect photos and artifacts from every current and former resident we can find. We'll cover the history of the base and the personnel who lived in Arboria Park, the Fine Foods people, and the punk houses. We'll show how the houses and streets have changed, warts and all, but also how it's never stopped being a place for young families to buy their first house. We'll have a rally, maybe at the shopping center because that parking lot is huge and mostly unused, where everyone will tell their stories, and share their photos and their talents. We have the resources, we just haven't been utilizing them properly." I jumped up from the table. "It's a chance to show that Arboria Park has value beyond a bunch of crummy ranch houses and lower class minorities. It has a past and a present, and it could have a future." I took a breath. "And if it doesn't work, it will be the best sendoff and funeral a neighborhood ever had. It deserves that much."

Greg got up and put his arms around me. "I'm so proud of you."

"It means I'll be around even *less* than I have the past few weeks."

He nodded. "This is important. I put in a lot of hours going to school, and later at my jobs, to accomplish what I wanted. Now it's your turn, and I'll help however I can. This will be the biggest DIY punk project the Park has ever seen."

15—2008

The first Saturday in May: rally day. My three-month sabbatical proved to be only the beginning; it took us way longer than that to get to this point. It had become more than a full-time job for me, but everyone had worked long hours around their other lives to make things happen.

The highway project, meanwhile, had continued along its own parallel track. We'd still been showing up for public meetings, with as many people as we could gather, to follow its progress. Studies had to be signed off by this person or that department. Estimates were requested for construction and demolition costs, real estate experts were consulted. Delays piled up, but not all were in our favor; there were whispers that some were deliberate, that, with the housing market skidding to a halt, it was in the state's interest to let property values drop more before it made offers to the residents. The argument played out in the local media, and I'd found myself, along with Lloyd, appearing on radio talk shows and giving quotes to the papers.

Despite these distractions, we'd forged ahead. More residents and former residents had come on board to help. And now we were all at the shopping center parking lot just after dawn, setting up for a rally.

We'd passed the hat for money to do things as first-class as we could, and Autumn had gathered university students with event experience to help set up a big stage, with a screen behind it, at the Birch Street end of the parking lot. Drew was in charge of audio/visual. His students would show slides behind the various speakers and film the entire event. They also had filmed interviews with residents and organized photos into various displays, using the university's media facilities. The graphic displays set up in the parking lot featured various aspects of Park history (the orchard, construction, the original owners, its 1950s heyday, the changes over time, its ties to the base). One was a tribute to the Park's military veterans, including those who had died in Vietnam or Iraq or Afghanistan. And there was a display about the punk houses, of course, and a photographic history of the Park's kids and teenagers. We were lucky to find a couple of houses whose extreme transformations over the years had been documented, providing a visual history of how a house had evolved from a small '50s-style ranch into an expanded, up-to-date version that could easily fit in a newer, more upscale neighborhood.

Jason had dusted off his DJ hat to provide music between the speakers and performers throughout the day. Mary had designed T-shirts printed with "Save Arboria Park," and provided Sharpies for people to write their current or former addresses on them. She'd ordered five hundred—ever the optimist. I watched her set up the table, a grandmother now, still trim and stylish at age sixty-two. Even seven-year-old Berry had a role, helping her grandma. They had piles of cardboard and markers for people to make signs.

Lloyd had his own army of foot soldiers from the neighborhood helping out. And perhaps best of all, Ruby had arrived with her band to be our headlining musical act. Ruby and Her Romeos, featuring Chris Dimos on guitar, would play a set, and Duke Santoro, though increasingly immobilized by his arthritis, would sit in with them.

What was giving me more butterflies than anything else:

Ruby, Autumn, Sophie, and I were playing a set together. Sophie was hell-bent on the idea, and the rest of the family had backed her up. I was terrified.

The familiar scent of Fine Foods chocolate was in the air. I walked over to what Tommy called the Original Gangsters display: a list with photos, generated from painstaking research, of the first owners of each house. I traced over my parents' names. "Thomas Halloran, Sr. and Evelyn Halloran, 3 Arbor Circle, April 1952." Their names appeared on another list elsewhere, of deaths. I'd seen Autumn over there earlier, touching Kip Vanderwende's name and shaking her head.

Greg came over to me. "You okay?"

"A wreck. I'm so afraid nobody will come."

He laughed. "It's a beautiful, sunny day. Everyone who's speaking or performing will have families and friends come to see them. Sophie's friends have invited all their buds. And it'll be like a street fair. People will bring their kids."

I hoped he was right. We were providing a few other activities, like face painting for the children. Matt had arranged for a fire truck and police car to display, and food was being donated by a couple of the remaining businesses in the shopping center.

The handwriting was on the wall there, as well. We had the parking lot to use for free, with the parking spaces close to the stores blocked off for patrons to use. But most of the businesses were leaving as their leases ended, knowing the probable fate of the shopping center.

"The local press is interested, too," Greg pointed out. "They'll show up, out of curiosity."

"That's why I'm afraid," I said. "This parking lot looks huge all of a sudden. Like it did when I was a kid, and they'd have carnivals here, or car shows—or young people would race cars around it. It always seemed enormous then."

"Well, good," Greg said. "It will need to be big, to accommodate the crowd that's going to show up."

························

A smattering of people did arrive at the rally's scheduled start time, ten A.M.—mostly parents of the children from the shopping center's dance school and mixed martial arts studio, who were among the first performing groups. But by the time Tommy went on to talk about the history of the shopping center, his modest fame (some people recognized him from TV commercials) had drawn a larger audience. He led off by saying, "I don't own this shopping center— but I played the owner in a movie!" as his cameo from Autumn's teenage horror film showed on the screen behind him. He spoke about the early days of the shopping center—the old-fashioned hardware store, Strommer's Deli, the five-and-dime where kids went for toys and soda-fountain treats—and how eventually those stores were put out of business as malls were built. Slides showed the original center, with its full parking lot, in the 1960s; the deserted horror-movie set of the 1970s, the 1980s chain stores, and the drab pawnshops and payday loans that had characterized it in recent years.

"But it has come back again," he said, pointing to the actual stores. "No supermarket anymore, but Indian and Mexican grocery stores. Thai and Jamaican takeout. Owned, once again, by local folks serving the community, not corporate chains. Like back when it was built."

In between the speakers and entertainers, Jason kept the crowd pumped up with all kinds of music—rap, reggaeton, Motown, everything he could think of to reach across generations. He encouraged people to dance, and they did.

By twelve thirty, even more people were milling around. We had given Ruby the prime early afternoon spot and leaked word of her appearance, and as she and her band set up, a group of kids in full rockabilly regalia gathered at the foot of the stage. Megan asked them to pose in front of the shopping center. "You're dressed like some of the original shoppers here!" she told them, and the kids eagerly leaned against poles and lounged on an old car.

Jason introduced the band. "I'm proud to announce our next musical act, conceived right here in the Park. My sister Ruby discovered rockabilly when she was sixteen and never looked back. Ladies and gents of the Park, straight from a European tour, Ruby and Her Romeos!"

Ruby wore a vintage polka-dot dress with some of Mom's old jewelry. Looking every bit the glamorous entertainer, she smiled at the now sizable crowd. "Good afternoon, everyone. What a lovely day. Sorry we had to meet under these circumstances. I'm Ruby Jean Harris, formerly of 162 Mimosa." She spun her custom-made bass around to show the address painted on the back of it, and her drummer did a rim shot. "If you don't know me, I play music based on what was popular when this neighborhood was young. When rock 'n' roll still scared the grownups. What the cool kids heard on the radio." She smiled impishly. "Those cool kids are now senior citizens! This first song is for everyone who was ever a teenager in this neighborhood. Black or white or anything else, any era." She nodded over to the drummer. "Hit it!"

It was her rockabilly arrangement of Meat Loaf's "All Revved Up with No Place to Go," with some lyrics she'd rewritten herself. "When we played our guitars we made this whole Park rock!" she sang, winking over at Chris. You could see their wordless onstage communication, born of fifteen years of work together.

I was glad to see that more than just the rockabilly kids were dancing. As Ruby sang, a man ran onstage with a saxophone and wailed. It was JC, and the crowd whooped when he was done.

"Thank you!" Ruby shouted over the applause at the end of the song. "And for that sax solo, thank you to my father, the one, the only, Doctor Josiah Clark Shut-That-Door-I'm-Not-Air-Conditioning-This-Whole-Block Harris!"

The band shifted into a screwball version of "Twenty Flight Rock" that Ruby called "Twenty Block Rock," with the numbers replaced by names of our streets. After even more applause, she announced, "This next song is dedicated to one particular generation, the kids of the '50s and '60s. Some of them may remember this song. It was originally written and sung by Janis Martin, a teen herself who was known as the Female Elvis back in 1955. And our special guest coming onstage now *played* with Janis Martin, and Elvis, and a heap of other folks. And now he lives on Cobbs Road. The legendary Duke Santoro!"

Duke, who had undergone both a hip and knee replacement in the past few years—he joked that he was a "bionic rocker" now—made it onstage to a chair, wearing his trademark hat. Once he was settled in, the band started into "Drugstore Rockin." Chris and Duke traded licks in the middle, then Chris gave way to Duke. Arthritis now affected his fingers too, and he couldn't play quite like he used to. But even at three-quarter power, Duke was still impressive. I heard someone nearby murmur, "He played with Elvis, and lives on Cobbs? Who knew?"

Mary, next to me, was glowing. "Aren't they wonderful? And this crowd!"

"I know, I can't believe it!" I crowed. "Are we low on T-shirts?"

She laughed. "Oh, we ran out almost two hours ago."

For the band's last song, the Stray Cats' "Rock This Town," Duke stayed onstage to play another solo, joined by JC. By the end, the audience seemed to have doubled in size and was yelling for more.

"Thanks, everyone," Ruby said to them. "But we have to go. There's a lot more to come, so stick around. And I'll be back a bit later, to play with another band. See you then!" She waved and blew kisses.

Mary sighed. "My kids are really something. Or am I just one of *those* moms?"

....

The Parkers were all in their forties now. Rosie was a traffic ana-lyst at the highway department, Benny Aquino an orthodontist, and Billy Persinger a graphic designer. Still, they ripped through their Ramones cover set, and Sophie's generation of punk kids danced along with the fortysomethings—Patty Melt and Sylvie among them—and the in-betweeners like Ruby and Chris. Jeff did guest vocals on "I Don't Wanna Walk Around with You," and the Parkers finished with "In the Park."

Then it was time for Patty, Autumn, Chris, and Sophie to describe the history of the punk houses, with more slides and film clips, followed by a thoroughly rousing performance by the Cedar Crew, a local teenage hip-hop group. When they finished their set, we handed the mic over to anybody who wanted to speak briefly.

"My name is Keisha Moore, and I live at 34 Maple. I like having a yard for my kids to play, and a place where they can ride their scooters on the sidewalk. It's safe, and we have a real house we can afford to rent. Our landlord will get money, but what about us? I don't want to end up on Clancy Street, dodging bullets."

"Mike Olivetti, 126 Elm. Two years ago we put an addition on our house with a new roof and siding. Who's gonna reimburse me for all that? No way I'll get out of this house what I put in. It's not fair. I care about my property as much as anybody from the West Side."

"I am Ibrahim Hassan from Holly Street. I came here from Pakistan. I did not know in America they can take a man's house away."

"Dawn Krieger, 19 Mimosa. I was one of those Park drug addicts they talk about in the paper. But I've been clean two years, and I found the Lord and got a job, and my mom gave me a second chance. We made mistakes, but we don't deserve to get kicked out."

"Olga Prendes Butler, formerly 6 and 10 Spruce. I came here as a young woman who married an American. When we ended the marriage, I did not want to go back to Spain because of the politics, and I had no family left there. I met new family here. I live on the West Side, but my heart is in this place."

I stared out at the audience, clutching my notes. It was four P.M. now—time to deliver my "History of the Park" speech—and the crowd had increased even more, somehow. It seemed like everyone who'd ever lived in the Park was there.

"Good afternoon," I said into the microphone. I tried to stare over the crowd, not into it, toward the Avenue entrance into the shopping center. But there were people all the way back now, some holding signs they'd created at Mary's table or gone home to make when she ran out of cardboard. The local TV news van, which had left earlier in the day after interviewing a few people, was back. And there were bigger news trucks too, from as far away as Philly.

"I'm Stacy. I grew up at 3 Arbor Circle, I lived on Birch for a few years, and my husband, Greg, and I own 18 Willow, where we lived for fourteen years. Our daughter lives there now. We've already heard a lot today about the history of the Park and its people. But I'd like to go all the way back, to 1950 when this neighborhood was an apple orchard . . ."

Once I got started, the words rolled out effortlessly. I told the crowd before me about the Ramseys, and what happened to their farm. I talked about Arboria Park's beginnings—how the builders, like many of the time, concentrated on houses that were easy to duplicate and quick to construct, and imagined the Park as an ideal place for families, with big yards for children to play in, located close to the base and town.

"It sounds like the classic, all-American neighborhood, doesn't it?" I said. "But not special enough, according to the criteria used to evaluate its historical significance. Not like Edith Ramsey's farm. Just one of many developments slapped together, with identical ranch houses marching up identical-looking streets."

I was on a roll now. I talked about the problems that cropped up in subsequent years—how the base and Fine Foods added a sort of transience, people moving in and out. How when developments with larger houses sprang up in the 1960s, they were marketed as a way to escape newer, "different" neighbors. (While cleaning out Mom's house I'd found the old Oakley Estates newspaper article, which flashed behind me as I spoke.) And how over the next forty years, it became an endless cycle. "Developers grabbed up any piece of land they could, within city limits or outside. Very little thought was given to how each neighborhood related to others. Housing and services are not driven by people's needs and practicality of long-term cost, but rather on developers obtaining land and squeezing the maximum amount they can get out of it. City and county are bought off by the promise of adding to tax rolls. That's why all the houses went up on the West Side in the first place. The land was there, and demand could be *created* by convincing people they were unhappy where they were, or it wasn't good enough."

I could have gone on forever, but I knew it was time to wrap it up. "We know we may be fighting a losing battle today," I said, "but it deserves to be fought. The forces that want to build this highway may be victorious, but it will be an expensive victory, and not just in dollars. After this rally, reports of the history we've uncovered over the past months, the photos and interviews many of you have provided, all of it will go to the Department of Highways and Transportation. Part of their report said that no oral history research was necessary. Today we proved that they did not do their due diligence, but we have. They want to believe they are simply tearing down some outdated houses and perhaps even putting the residents out of their misery"—a wave of bitter laughter rose from the audience at that—"but I hope we have showed them today that they've forgotten to add a few important things to their calculations. And maybe once the people of this city and county and state know the true cost, they will be less ready to sign the check. Thank you."

I dashed off the stage during the applause and shouting,

straight into Greg's arms. "I'm so proud of you, Stacy." He kissed my forehead. "You are still the most amazing girl I've ever known."

"I know I forgot things. I rambled too much . . ."

"No way. You tore it up."

I looked at him—hair now going silver, lines around those laughing eyes. He was still the most amazing boy I'd ever met, too. "I couldn't have done this without you, and my family."

"Well, one down, one to go," he said, laughing.

I put my hands over my face. "Don't remind me. Now we've got to play."

"Nonsense. You've been waiting your whole life for this."

Ruby had changed into a sundress, with one of Mary's T-shirts over it, and flip-flops. She took Autumn's and Sophie's hands, and they formed a ring around me.

"Listen up, girls." Ruby spoke with the same no-nonsense manner that had forced all of us to snap to attention since she was a toddler. "We will close out this day with something people can take with them, to keep going tonight and tomorrow and next week." She let go of the others' hands and embraced me. "You're a tough act to follow, Stacy. You always were."

....

Jason played another DJ set while we set up. It was like a block party or festival now for sure; people were dancing and having fun, but also signing the petition and waving their signs at passing cars on the highway. Children were busy making a crayon mural on a piece of drywall someone brought, drawing their houses and other things they thought symbolized the neighborhood.

Mary went on stage to introduce us. "My name is Mary Catherine Halloran Kozicki Harris," she said, as cool and collected as always in front of the massive crowd. "I grew up on 3 Arbor Circle and lived in the Park for forty-seven years, at 6 Spruce and 162 Mimosa. This next band is special to me, because I'm related to them. You've met them all at different times today:

my darling daughters, Autumn Kozicki Lansdale and Ruby Jean Harris; my charming niece Sophie Martinez; and my beloved little sister, Stacy Halloran Martinez, who just riled you up a few minutes ago and is about to do it again. Hard as it is to believe, this is their first public appearance together. Please welcome The Halloran Spitfires!"

I walked onstage and stood uncomfortably at the center mic, glancing to the side of the stage at Greg and my family, who had been joined by Duke, Rosie, Chris, and Patty. Mary blew me a kiss and placed her hand on her heart.

We started with the Smithereens' "House We Used to Live In," with Sophie on lead vocals. Her voice was the highest of all of us, and the most girlish; she gave the song pathos but with a glint of steel underneath.

I looked around as everyone applauded. At least one of the TV trucks was filming; the boys who had been skateboarding all afternoon near the Avenue entrance stood at the back of the crowd now, boards under their arms. And how long had those cars been stopped along the shoulder of the highway, windows down, occupants sitting on hoods or on the grass embankment?

Ruby stepped away from her mic and cleared her throat, and I snapped back to play the slow guitar intro as she sang it.

I had fought with the girls over this song, insisting that Ruby sing it, or Sophie. But to a woman, they'd stood against me. "You have to sing it, Mom," Sophie had insisted. "No one but you."

But we had agreed to let Ruby start, buying me a few moments to lose myself in the song. Then we launched in with everything we had, jolting the crowd. I stepped up to my mic.

"This is my neighborhood . . ."

People immediately started roaring out the lyrics themselves, and it made me feel less exposed. Ruby and I harmonized the chorus together when it came back around, with Sophie and Autumn adding oohs and aahs in the background. We had rewritten the second verse a little, to personalize it:

*We need a shortcut to the beach, our western
neighbors cry,*

You say sorry to our families, but your sympathy's a lie,

*You say it's for the common good, that you must
destroy our neighborhood...*

By the time we hit the chorus again, everyone was jumping up and down, an undulating mass. Sophie teetered at the edge of the stage in her Chucks during her solo, leaning down over the outraised hands. She spurred me to reach down and pour all the passion and pain, frustration and aggression of the past months into my guitar. As I did, the skateboard kids crowd-surfed their way up front, and parents held their children and signs up in the air. Duke stood up from his chair next to the stage and waved his hat as Jason held on to his shoulder and fist-pumped. The Cedar Crew kids led the crowd to roar, "Go, go, go!"

I couldn't even hear myself, or Ruby or the others, on the next chorus. By the time the song urged everyone to fight for their neighborhood, all I could see were fists of all colors. The crowd moved as one, up and down in unison. Without any sort of open communication, the girls and I all just knew to stretch that section out beyond what we'd rehearsed, for a full thirty seconds that slowed down to seem like forever. Later, Drew's footage would confirm the power of the moment. We hit the final chord over and over, and cars stopped on the highway, horns honked, people cheered. For some reason the only individual scream I could make out was Mary's, as she stood with her arms raised, Berry next to her, at the side of the stage.

Then it was all a blur. Lloyd wept onstage as he thanked everyone. Even though we all knew the rally was officially over, nobody went home. People lingered until after dark, and the restaurants and grocery stores brought out more food. As the moon rose, the lights came on, and our volunteers dismantled the stage and equipment. Yet people stayed in the parking lot, embracing one another, laughing and crying, and adding to the mural.

When things finally broke up, a full twelve hours after the official start of the rally, we adjourned to Sophie's house with our instruments, the piles of signed petitions, and the displays. We drank beer and toasted and sang again, for ourselves and our family and friends, and the friends who were family. And all over the Park, similar celebrations went on, into the wee hours, and no one called the police.

16—2011

··························

In the end, we lost. Lawyers we consulted said nothing more could be done.

The next best thing to winning a fight is leaving your opponent so bloodied that the victory is a hollow one. At least, that's what my Irish side believes. And the rally did re-ignite controversy. We didn't go down easy. We even presented a plan, developed by university professors and a retired consultant, for two smaller-level measures to corral some traffic around the city, widening existing roads including Cobbs.

Then, rather suddenly, all debate was cut off. We could either negotiate the best possible deals for ourselves, or face eminent domain. Offers were somewhat more generous than the pathetic initial numbers that had been floated, and we believed the noise we'd made had made a difference.

We came away from the rally with boxes of photos people had brought to add to our collection, and more poured in to each of us by text and e-mail. Thanks to social media, news spread far and wide. A guy even came up to Ruby after her show in San Francisco to hand her an envelope full of pictures of his grandparents' house on Maple, circa 1975. Sophie and her friends sorted all the photos, and I categorized them by street and era. Almost every house was represented in some way, though some couldn't be identified for sure. Backyard barbecues and Christmas decorations; kids in Halloween costumes or prom attire posing for the camera; people showing off new cars and renovations. Gardens and pets; drug busts and basement shows; even somebody being carried out on a stretcher to an ambulance.

It took about eight months to buy up and settle on all the properties, and almost another year to tear them all down. Ahead of the wrecking ball, we took pictures of every house as people packed up and moved out. Strangers let us in to photograph their homes and give us souvenirs, stuff they'd ripped out of the house whether they had owned it or not. Some grieved over the renovations and improvements they'd made over the years, now destined to be bulldozed, while others gleefully indulged in large-scale acts of vandalism. The last of the punk houses, Heart of Oak, held an "Assured Destruction" night where we all took axes and hammers to every empty room after the last note sounded. I was the only one weeping as we bashed in the drywall.

When Sophie moved out, we were comforted that Hallorans had lived in the Park from its founding to its demise, and that its basement punk shows had continued to the very end.

Autumn, Drew, and a handful of their students filmed the demolitions. I couldn't be with them the day the Circle house was torn down, or Mary's on Mimosa. Even seeing the destruction of the Olivas' old house was too much.

"Get me out of here," I sobbed to Greg. "I can't watch them destroy the Gardners."

He put his arm around me and guided me to the car. "It's okay," he reassured me. "You don't have to witness everything."

I knew I couldn't even be on the East Coast when they reached our house on Willow, so Greg took me to San Diego for a week. For once I gave up the window seat on the plane; I didn't want to look out and see any grids of 1950s houses on the landscape below.

A few months ago, Greg and I rented out our New Jersey home for a year and sublet a condo in Philadelphia. For a change of pace, to enjoy what the city had to offer, to clear my head a little. We get around on foot or by cab, and try to figure out the trolleys. It's fun, but I miss my house and yard in Jersey. We're speculating about where to retire someday. We're all getting older. Mary and JC, though officially retired, are still busy, with Mary running her gallery and selling paintings and JC working as an educational consultant. Matt's planning to retire next year, since Jeff's having some health problems.

Sophie, meanwhile, has graduated, and she's living in an apartment in South Philly. "G-Ho, Mom," she keeps reminding me. "You've got to know and identify your neighborhoods correctly!" She works at a vegetarian café, and in her free time she helps with a community garden that donates surplus food.

We're going to shows together again, and even playing a few. When we saw a pale, skinny English boy named Frank Turner blow up a South Philly living room, we had to swallow the urge to call someone at Heart of Oak so they could book him. I have moments like that often, thinking there's still an Arboria Park.

I have recurring dreams, some variation on rows of houses in Easter-egg colors. Vacant and vandalized, burned or crumbling apart like the rowhouses in some of Philly's most blighted neighborhoods. I have dreams of Mary lying in front of the bulldozers, too, while the girls and I sing and begin a human chain around the entire development.

Duke and Marcella moved to an apartment in Maryland, near Marcella's sister. They had to put some of Duke's stuff back in storage. Ruby's helping them look for a museum or someplace that might want some of it. Marcella hasn't given up hope of finding a little house somewhere, though it will have to be a rental.

It's been a painful and traumatic few years. Yet I feel I finally have a purpose. We started an Arboria Park Facebook page and a history website with all the photos and information we collected.

And I'm turning them into a book. I work on it now on my days off. It will be the story of the life and death of a twentieth-century subdivision, but so much more.

The story is plain in my favorite photo from the rally. We have hundreds of pictures from that day too—ones we took ourselves, those shared by neighbors, and even some from the extensive news coverage. But this one, taken by Megan just after the Spitfires played, is one I can't stop looking at: Mary with her fight-the-power fist in the air; me with my guitar held over my head; Autumn between us, her drumsticks crossed at her chest; Berry standing in front of Autumn with her "Save Our Park" sign; Sophie lunging toward the camera, brandishing her guitar like a weapon; and Ruby leaning into Mary on the other side, clutching her bass. We all look fierce as hell. There are other photos of us that day with the men in our lives, but this all-woman picture says something about our family, and Arboria Park, and about the times we lived through, that I haven't quite been able to put into words yet.

Rosie still feeds us intelligence. There's a proposal for a small townhouse development squeezed in at the Avenue where the old sample houses once marched up Cobbs. And the city has committed to creating a park to pacify the residents of Oakley Estates (who got considerably less sanguine about the road project once the bulldozers showed up on the edge of their neighborhood and they temporarily had only one route out of it, onto Foster). It's a triangular section that starts where the road exits onto the highway, runs along the former Crescent and the creek, past the playground, and into the field. So I may yet be able to walk again in what used to be my backyard, and Mona's, to the place where Greg and I stargazed so many times.

"I can take my grandchild to the playground there someday," I told Sophie. "Like I took you, and Autumn, and Ruby and Jason . . ."

"Mom!" Sophie frowned. "It's going to be a *long time* before you have a grandchild. Believe me."

I grinned. "I'll wait."

On the planning maps Rosie shared, the park is called "South Side Park." But we've launched a petition, and this one has a pretty good chance of succeeding. Because of course, there can be only one name:

Arboria Park.

"This too will soon slip out of reach, this too will soon come to an end."

—Against Me!

ACKNOWLEDGMENTS

·····················

This book would not exist without the following people: excellent editor Krissa Lagos and the wonderful folks at She Writes Press: project manager Cait Levin, art director Julie Metz, and publisher Brooke Warner.

My partner in life, love, and most recently suburban environmentalism, Roland Wall; and my brother and fellow explorer of twentieth-century suburban architecture, music, and culture, Mark Eugene Tyler.

My friends Noël Ioli and Denise Wood, who have stuck around the longest; my "road dog," Sharon Concannon; Kathy Miller Edger and the other music-minded ladies of the queue, front row, and social media. (Also the late Sandy List, Lucinda Nored, and Susan Reinhardt.) My one-man transatlantic mental-health support group, Andy Waterfield; writers extraordinaire Kerry Dunn, Stephanie Kuehnert, and Sarah McCarry; super ex-bosses Joan Irwin, Janet Binkley, and Roderick McDonald.

For soundtrack, Josh T. Landow and everyone at Y-Not Radio and Noise Complaint, and former Philly radio god Jim McGuinn.

Too many musicians to name, but I would be remiss not to mention my Victory Boys, Buddy Yarnall, Toodle Casey, and

DIY-or-die Paul Lemley, for getting me into house shows (literally and figuratively); my good-luck charm, Dave Hause; Social Distortion; Laura Jane Grace and Against Me!; Brendan Kelly; The Holy Mess; Chuck Ragan; and the Philly and Delaware punk scenes. And of course Frank Turner, whose inspirational anthems have kicked my ass and kept me going through the past seven years and counting.

ABOUT THE AUTHOR

Kate Tyler Wall is managing editor of an early American history journal in Philadelphia. She grew up in a 1950s-era housing development in Dover, Delaware, which inspired lifelong interests in music, history, exploring, and the power of place. She has a degree in political science and journalism (American history minor) from the University of Delaware. She now lives in another 1950s tract house in Newark, Delaware, with "suburban ecologist" husband Roland Wall and beagle-basset buddy Pilot. At age fifty she started writing fiction and becoming a "famed punk rock attendee" (Punknews, 2014). When not roaming the East Coast seeing around 180 bands a year, she likes walking, reading, the beach, and fighting the power.

Author photo © Ginger Wall

SELECTED TITLES FROM SHE WRITES PRESS

She Writes Press is an independent publishing company
founded to serve women writers everywhere.
Visit us at www.shewritespress.com.

How to Grow an Addict by J.A. Wright. $16.95, 978-1-63152-991-7. Raised by an abusive father, a detached mother, and a loving aunt and uncle, Randall Grange is built for addiction. By twenty-three, she knows that together, pills and booze have the power to cure just about any problem she could possibly have . . . right?

Start With the Backbeat by Garinè B. Isassi. $16.95, 978-1-63152-041-9. When post-punk rocker Jill Dodge finally gets the promotion she's been waiting for in the spring of 1989, she finds herself in the middle of a race to find a gritty urban rapper for her New York record label.

The Rooms Are Filled by Jessica Null Vealitzek. $16.95, 978-1-938314-58-2. The coming-of-age story of two outcasts—a nine-year-old boy who just lost his father, and a closeted young woman—brought together by circumstance.

The Belief in Angels by J. Dylan Yates. $16.95, 978-1-938314-64-3. From the Majdonek death camp to a volatile hippie household on the East Coast, this narrative of tragedy, survival, and hope spans more than fifty years, from the 1920s to the 1970s.

Pieces by Maria Kostaki. $16.95, 978-1-63152-966-5. After five years of living with her grandparents in Cold War-era Moscow, Sasha finds herself suddenly living in Athens, Greece—caught between her psychologically abusive mother and violent stepfather.

The Sweetness by Sande Boritz Berger. $16.95, 978-1-63152-907-8. A compelling and powerful story of two girls—cousins living on separate continents—whose strikingly different lives are forever changed when the Nazis invade Vilna, Lithuania.